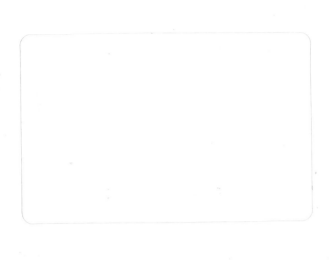

THE GONE AWAY PLACE

CHRISTOPHER BARZAK

The Gone Away Place

Alfred A. Knopf
NEW YORK

THIS IS A BORZOI BOOK PUBLISHED BY ALFRED A. KNOPF

Knopf, Borzoi Books, and the colophon are registered trademarks of Penguin Random House LLC.

Visit us on the Web! GetUnderlined.com

Educators and librarians, for a variety of teaching tools, visit us at RHTeachersLibrarians.com

Library of Congress Cataloging-in-Publication Data
Names: Barzak, Christopher, author.
Title: The gone away place / Christopher Barzak.
Description: First edition. | New York : Alfred A. Knopf, [2018] |
Summary: After tornadoes demolish Newfoundland, Ohio, Ellie, seventeen, is haunted by ghosts of the dead, as well as survivors struggling to cope, but a chance encounter shows her how to free the lingering spirits.
Identifiers: LCCN 2017044047 (print) | LCCN 2017057858 (ebook) |
ISBN 978-0-399-55609-8 (trade) | ISBN 978-0-399-55610-4 (lib. bdg.) |
ISBN 978-0-399-55611-1 (ebook)
Subjects: | CYAC: Tornadoes—Fiction. | Dead—Fiction. | Dating (Social customs)—Fiction. | Friendship—Fiction. | Memory—Fiction. | Family life—Ohio—Fiction. | Ohio—Fiction.
Classification: LCC PZ7.1.B3735 (ebook) | LCC PZ7.1.B3735 Gon 2018 (print) |
DDC [Fic]—dc23

Printed in the United States of America
May 2018
10 9 8 7 6 5 4 3 2

First Edition

For Matthew J. Lattanzi,
whose absence lingers in so many hearts

1

The Last Will and Testament of Ellie Frame

This is the hardest story I've ever had to tell. Not because I don't have anything to say, though. And not because I don't have anything of value to leave behind. It's the hardest story I've ever had to tell because *I'm* the one who's been left behind. And there's no one my last words will find. There's no one to read my testament and say, *Ellie was my best friend*. Or *She helped me push my car out of a snowdrift down the road from her house that year we had a freak snowstorm in the middle of April*. Or *Ellie was my girlfriend, and whenever she saw me, she always kissed me first on the cheek, then on the lips, and in private, when no one else was looking, on the space between my neck and shoulder. That was Ellie Frame. Remember her? She always had a smile ready, even for people who seemed to perpetually scowl at the world*.

Her.

The girl with the camera.

I think she was the editor of our yearbook.

Everyone I ever loved is gone now. Dead. Dead as dead can be.

Dead as dead can be. An expression that, only a few weeks after "the outbreak," as my mom calls the storms that took so many lives, is open to interpretation. It turns out that *dead as dead can be* is different for everyone. For you. For me. For the dead. Because some of them remain very much . . . alive, even now, after they've lost everything: heartbeats, brain waves. The last breaths they held in their chests as they knelt in the hallways of our high school, right before the roof and the walls began to fly apart, whirling up into the sky, higher and higher. The last thoughts they held in their minds. The last words they held in their mouths, right before the world turned to fire around them.

Some people, dead or alive, simply can't leave. They have their reasons. And no matter how much grief their presence may cause, they sit across the table from us anyway, pretending to sip at a mug of coffee. Or they stand just over there, in a dark corner, waiting for something even they don't know they need. Some are angry, some are frustrated, some are confused, and some are sad—so, so sad. Some of them are all of these things, and nothing any one of us can say or do will put them at ease.

And this is the hardest story I've ever had to tell for reasons that go beyond not having anyone left to hear it. It's hard because already I've made a mistake in trying to tell it. I said, *Everyone I ever loved is gone now,* but that isn't completely true.

2

My mom and dad are still with me. It's my friends who are gone. Becca, Adrienne, Rose.

And him—Noah. The one who, whenever I saw him, I would kiss first on his bristly cheek, then on his lips, where the scent of cinnamon gum still lingered, and, when no one else was looking, on the space between his neck and shoulder, that soft and private place where no one, he said, had ever kissed him before I did.

All of them are gone now. And Newfoundland itself is barely recognizable, unless you squint at the wreckage of the place in just the right way, at just the right time of day, when the shadows of evening move closer, in order to see the ghost of what it once was.

My parents, on the other hand, are all too present. They hover with worry. I hear their concerned whispers coming from their bedroom at night, when they think I've fallen asleep, when they don't realize I'm awake and holding my breath, trying not to scream, trying to figure out how to tell this story, if to no one else, then to myself. I love them, I do love them. I love them more than anything, really. So when I say that *everyone* I ever loved is gone now, that's not the truth.

It just feels like it.

⌒

The last day I didn't feel alone in the world was in the middle of May, when I could see the end of high school opening up on the horizon. The summer I envisioned would be beautiful, like a dream you'd never want to wake from. A dream of three perfect months made up of laughing with friends. And three perfect months of seemingly endless days spent in my backyard, swinging in a hammock under the trees, with Noah's arms around me as we planned a future where he'd be driving from Ohio State to Pittsburgh every weekend to visit me for the next four years. His cheek would be pressed close to mine, close enough for him to turn and kiss me awake whenever I'd start to drift off. "No sleeping," he'd whisper, then kiss the corner of my mouth so that I'd turn toward him, smiling, to kiss him back. "We have to stay awake to enjoy all of this before we go away."

But life has a way of changing quickly. Something you could have never imagined just . . . happens. And when it's over, everything you knew and loved—your friends, your neighbors, the place you call home—is taken from you.

Noah and I were standing between our cars in the school parking lot on the day that changed things forever. We were continuing an argument that had started the night before, a stupid argument, the most stupid argument in the world. But I didn't realize it right then because we were busy arguing about Ingrid Mueller, the girl who lived across the road from Noah in a farmhouse so old, it looked like something out of *Little House on the Prairie*. The surrounding farmland hadn't been used for nearly a decade, after Ingrid's father was killed in a hunting accident when she was eight. Shot through the heart by Charles Johnson, the feed mill owner, who mistook Mr. Mueller for a deer breaking through the brush below his tree stand. Ingrid's father hadn't been wearing any orange safety clothing mandated by law, even though he was hunting, so Mr. Johnson wasn't charged in his death. And for the same reason, my mom once explained to me, the insurance company wouldn't pay out the full amount of Mr. Mueller's policy, which meant Ingrid's mother had to get help from the state. The people in Newfoundland pitched in, too, of course. It's what we do for each other. Neighbors and parents of Ingrid's school friends brought food in the days and weeks after her dad died. Sometimes, a check or a card with some money in it. "A little something to help her keep the lights on," my dad once said. But since then Mrs. Mueller had pretty much vanished from the public eye. And if you did see her, it was when she stepped out into the daylight to collect her mail.

Ingrid was in my grade, but after her father died, it was like she became a ghost, in the innocent way we all thought about ghosts back then. She rarely spoke unless called on, seemingly able to blend into the walls if you weren't looking at her, only to reappear in different places, right when you thought you were alone. She didn't make eye contact, looked away from people most of the time, down at the tips of her worn-out shoes, her eyes always sliding off to one side to peer at a blank wall or a corner. Her clothes were always three years behind the trends, and she cut her own hair—badly. If she'd been a popular girl with the money to buy what everyone else was wearing, the uneven hair could have been a fashion statement, but on Ingrid it came off as just another sad detail.

Noah was her friend, maybe her *only* friend. That isn't to say I wasn't nice to her; I was always nice to Ingrid. But Noah was a real friend to her and knew her in ways that nobody else did. He helped her and her mom on a regular basis, neighborly things. Mowed their lawn in summer. Fixed broken things, if he knew how to fix them. Wobbly table legs. A light switch that had stopped working. One time, he climbed a ladder up to their old slate roof to reaffix several pieces that had come loose and slid off after the winter ice had melted.

He did other things for Ingrid, too. Things that never bothered me until he and I had been together for a while. On Sweetest Day, when everyone bought carnations and had them delivered to their crushes during homeroom, Noah always sent one to Ingrid, even if he had a girlfriend at the time. Two years ago, when he wasn't dating anyone, he ditched homecoming to take Ingrid out to dinner at one of the restaurants where everyone ate before the dance. These displays of attention let Ingrid know someone cared about her. And though a lot of girls would have thought it meant something more, Ingrid never seemed to push Noah for anything other than the friendship they'd shared since childhood.

But after Noah and I had been dating for about six months—the longest either of us had dated anyone—Ingrid started acting strange. In the hallways between classes, she'd be drearily drifting toward her locker with her head down, watching her feet, and suddenly she'd look up to meet my eyes. She'd never smile. She'd never say hello. Not even when I said hello first, trying to spark at least some sense of friendliness between us. And during lunch, I'd sometimes look up from whatever I was eating and find her staring at me across the long expanse of the cafeteria. I never once saw Ingrid eat anything but an apple during lunch, and even as she lifted a half-bitten core to her mouth to sink her teeth into the remaining flesh, her eyes would never leave me.

"She's weirding me out," I told Noah after enduring several weeks of Ingrid's newfound creepiness. We were sitting together on the couch at his house. "I think she's mad that we're still together."

"Ingrid isn't mad," Noah said. "You're just imagining things, Ellie."

"No, I'm not," I said. "I mean it. I think she's mad we're still together. I think she has a time limit in her head for your relationships with other girls, and ours has expired. This is the longest you've ever been with anyone. I think she's trying to scare me off you."

Noah snorted, hearing that, trying to make me feel silly, telling me I was overreacting. He slipped one arm around the small of my back to pull me closer, to kiss me, leaving the taste of his cinnamon gum on my lips. Then he pulled away again, holding me at arm's length to say, "Ellie, I hope you don't scare that easily."

"I'm not *afraid* of her," I said, then pursed my lips, still worried, still frustrated by his nonchalant response. "But I do feel bad, if that's what this is about, her not wanting us to be together."

"I'm telling you, Ellie," Noah said, bringing one finger up to my temple to tap at it. "It's all in your head. Ingrid isn't like that. Ingrid's just . . . you know . . . Ingrid. She's quiet. And a little socially awkward."

I brushed his tapping finger away from my face and scowled. "Why won't you believe me?" I asked.

Noah just pretended like I hadn't asked the question. He tried to pull me close again, to kiss away the anger in my voice. So I backed away, flailing my hands in the air to emphasize every word I said next. "I'm not making this up. I'm trying to tell you something. You're not supposed to act like I'm a delusional idiot."

"Look at you," he said, laughing lightly again, smirking in a way that made me only madder. "When you go to Pitt this fall," he said, "I bet you're going to major in psychology, aren't you?"

If I could breathe fire, I would have opened my mouth right then and watched him melt into a puddle in front of me. But instead, I took a deep breath and folded my arms across my chest, then looked away from him, exhausted from going around in circles. I didn't like where this was heading. I'd never seen this side of him before—Noah didn't blow off my feelings, *ever*. He wasn't like some of the guys at school who treated their girlfriends like objects. It was one of the things I liked about him. We had things in common. Things that meant something. Things we took the time to talk about.

We'd gotten together in the fall when we both used our elective periods to work on the senior yearbook. And we'd talk for hours about things no one else was all that interested in: possible repeating imagery for design, the layout, the stuff other yearbooks always did that we thought was outdated. We'd talk about our vision for the yearbook, and how we were going to make a digital edition for it. We planned out a website with audio and visual content, in addition to a printed book. Something that people wouldn't just toss into a drawer. We wanted to make something that would still speak to us after the print yearbooks had been forgotten, and we were all old and gray and could log on to the yearbook website and see ourselves and our friends as we were when we were young and fresh, just starting out.

Initially, I'd assumed Noah was nothing but the kind of guy who traveled the hallways in a pack of soccer players, the ones who take up all the space and laugh too loudly, as if they own the place. But when he took yearbook as an elective that fall, and in the first week nominated me as head editor, telling the others in class that I took the best photos for the school's online news and always wrote interesting editorials, I had to rethink my idea of him.

I hadn't known he'd ever even noticed me before, let alone noticed something I'd done—something I'd put my heart into, like my photography and writing. And soon I found myself starting to pay more attention to him, too. Smiling at him in the hallway. Waving at him from across the soccer field behind the school, where he and his teammates were practicing, pretending I was just taking a shortcut to the library. Asking him for his opinion on photos I'd started to take for the yearbook. We discovered we both geeked out on talking photography, the way a really good photo could reveal the essence of a person, and eventually it got to be that I couldn't wait for my free period to see him. I knew he was feeling the same way, because he was always in the yearbook classroom before I even got there, waiting for me.

Then, one day in October, as we were poring over a bunch of sample pages, we bumped foreheads. When we looked up, the tips of our noses touched, just barely, enough to make us laugh briefly. And when neither of us pulled back afterward, we just leaned in further, without thinking.

The months that followed felt so natural and easy. So when he showed me this other side of him during our argument about Ingrid—this dismissive side I couldn't stand in guys, this side he might as well have topped off with something like "Come on, baby," it was so sexist—I just got up from the couch and left, ignoring his calls from behind for me to stop, to wait.

I refused to answer his texts later that night, even though they buzzed at regular fifteen-minute intervals, my phone lighting up with pleading notes for me to talk to him, until finally my phone stopped buzzing around midnight.

The next morning, we continued the argument in the school parking lot. It was a replay from the day before, except worse. More heated. Because, overnight, Noah had gone from feeling guilty to feeling angry, and he was trying to turn the argument into one about my flaws and faults, rather than solving the problem that had set us fighting.

He said, "You're so heartless, Ellie."

I scoffed and shook my head. "What are you even talking about?" I said.

"This," he said. "You. Right here. How you're acting right now. Like you're . . ."

He hesitated, but I could tell whatever he wanted to say was on the tip of his tongue, so I pushed him to say it. "Like I'm what?" I said, feeling all the muscles in my face tense up as I waited for whatever he was holding back.

"Like you're so above everyone," he said. "Like you can't do anything wrong. Like you've got to have everything exactly the way you want it. Your way or the highway. I can't stand it."

I stood there, mouth gaping, thinking, *Who is this guy?* And when I realized that we weren't going to resolve anything—when I felt like, *This is it, we're probably breaking up*—I said, "Whatever, Noah. Call me when you're able to see me for who I really am."

I got into my car, slammed the door, and took off without any particular destination in mind. I just wanted out of there. I wanted to cool off. But for the next hour, as I drove around side streets and back roads, chewing my bottom lip, I grew angrier as each minute passed without a text from Noah. The message could have been anything. It could have been simple. It could have been *I'm sorry. I didn't mean those things. I just blew up because I don't want you to be mad at me. I love you.*

When nothing like that came through, though, I decided I couldn't go back to school like I'd planned to. Not without Noah giving me some reason to turn back in his direction.

Instead, I drove to the outskirts of town, taking the winding dirt road that led up to the Newfoundland Lighthouse.

The Newfoundland Lighthouse isn't a true lighthouse. It's really just an old tower that looks like one. It's a replica of a lighthouse that the founder of Newfoundland, Ephraim Key, had built back in the mid-1800s, before moving his new wife to this patch of earth he'd claimed. She'd been the daughter of a shipping merchant in Boston, and was used to standing by a lighthouse near her childhood home, watching her father's

11

ships come into shore. Ephraim Key had the lighthouse built as a wedding gift, so that, when she arrived, she'd have something in this oceanless place to remind her of home.

It was a story I'd loved ever since my mom first told it to me when I was a little girl and had asked her how I'd know if someone really loved me. "That's how you'll know, Ellie," she'd said when she'd finished the tale, pointing to the lighthouse on the hill in the distance. "You'll know by the great lengths they go to for you to feel like, wherever you are, as long as you're with them, you're home."

Noah and I used to go up to the lighthouse, usually after a date when neither of us wanted to go home, but neither of us had a place where we could be alone together, either. A lot of people used the lighthouse for the same reason, but no one ever disrespected the place. It was always left clean and undamaged by anyone who used it. The only time I ever saw the place cluttered with anything, it was in autumn, when brown, papery leaves would float in through the open windows and collect in piles on the lantern-room floor.

After I arrived at the top of the hill, I got out and walked up to the door of the lighthouse. I squeezed its old-fashioned handle, and it opened on squealing hinges. Ahead of me, a stairway of worn-down stones spiraled up, and I followed its pathway until I came to the circular lantern room at the top. A large, old oil-based lantern stood on a pillar in the center of the room. It was empty now, but the town lit it once a year, on Newfoundland's Founder's Day, when you could look up to the lighthouse and see its orange beams reaching into the night. I went to the lantern and stroked a line of dust off its glass, then sat down with my back against the pillar and watched the sky through the windows around me.

It was a hot, humid day. It was a day that felt more like the middle of August than May, really. I didn't think about any of that right then, though, because I was still so furious, and nothing else could take up even a sliver of my attention. I was that focused on being angry. If I could have, I might have noticed how the mild morning I'd woken up to had quickly disappeared over the past couple of hours, and how my shirt had begun to stick to my back as the temperature rose and the air turned thick with humidity, almost rippling with particles of water. If I could have stopped being angry for even a moment, I might not have given in to my burned-out feelings and fallen asleep at the base of that lantern in the Newfoundland Lighthouse while a storm began to brew around me.

Sleep is what I fell into, though. And when I woke an hour or two later, it was to the sound of metal scraping and sirens blaring; it was to the sound of something like a train roaring; it was to the bits of dirt and twigs and young leaves that flew in through the open windows to strike my face before they were taken up again by the wind and blown out another window.

I rubbed my eyes and pulled myself up from the floor, looked around for my phone. The screen was filled with texts—from my mom, my dad, from my friends, from Noah. *Where are you? Are you safe?* I tried texting Mom back first, but the text didn't go through. It was frozen in time, suspended between my phone and hers.

The scraping sound that filled my ears continued to grate, though, and I crawled to one of the windows to see what I could make of it. And once I stood at that window, what I could make of the noise—what I began to comprehend very slowly—was this:

The end of the world had started while I lay sleeping.

From high on my hill in the lighthouse, Newfoundland drifted in a dark haze below me. The sky was the color of a fresh bruise, and when lightning flashed across it, the town hall and the school and the grocery store and the public library stood brightly lit against the horizon, all where they were supposed to be, at first making it seem like this was just another ordinary storm. It wasn't ordinary, though; it was nothing near ordinary. It was a storm that grew larger and larger as I watched. It was a storm that stirred the wind faster and faster, until suddenly and, finally, on the far side of town, the source of the roaring and metal-screeching noise appeared.

What looked like a twisting spire of smoke suddenly came into view on the horizon. *A tornado,* I realized. Only one, I first thought, as I watched it move across the fields, bending every now and then like the flame of a candle. Then a second spire appeared, seeming to pull away from the first, as if it were some kind of nightmarish, self-replicating creature. And when a third came into view, erupting out of the blackness in the distance, I realized I had started to cry. I stood there and felt the tears, hot on my cheeks, rolling down and down as I watched the three funnels circle one another. Slowly at first, then gathering speed, like a carousel, and pulling closer to each other, until they merged into one enormous monster, tearing through

14

the woods and chewing up trees as they moved toward New-foundland's downtown.

Meteorologists later said it took no more than fifteen minutes for the tornadoes to destroy the town, but it felt like an hour. And I saw it happen. I saw it all. I watched as transformers blew up on the grid of the lampposts, one after the other, lighting the posts on fire afterward, making them look like strange torches in the dark of the storm. I watched as bricks were plucked from their mortar in the town hall, then the library. I watched as the roof of the high school's gymnasium was peeled back like the lid of a can, and what looked like sports equipment was sucked out, with the bricks and tree limbs, whirling in the air. I watched as parked cars were pulled down the street, tumbling end over end like dry leaves in the wind. I watched and watched and watched, unable to tear myself away from the act of watching, as if I had to be a witness, as if the storm needed me to see it.

And I continued to watch even as the wall of black came closer to the lighthouse, roaring louder in my ears, until I clamped my hands over them and fell on my knees, defeated, but still watching.

In the last seconds of what I thought would be the end of my life, the tornadoes became distinct to me. They hadn't formed into one funnel, as it had at first seemed. They were circling around one another, in unison, but still separate entities. Then one broke away and turned toward downtown again, while the other two hovered below me, as if they were trying to make a decision. They would take me with them, I thought. They would rip me out of the lighthouse like they'd ripped bricks and scaffolding into the air, and they would destroy me.

But instead, they turned away like the first one had, as if rejecting me. One girl in a lighthouse wasn't worth their time, I supposed, not when so many others waited, cowering before them.

It was then, as the two spires turned toward the center of town, that something large and round, like the top half of a silo, went flying out of the whirlwinds, hurtling into the west wing of the high school, where it seemed to explode like a missile. There was a blinding flash of light. Even from as far away as the lighthouse, I could feel the aftershocks. They were so forceful, I was knocked backward onto the stone floor and hit my head. And then I was out, like the proverbial light, until hours later, when I rose and saw that the sky was an impossibly perfect blue again and, below me, Newfoundland was gone.

2

Patty Frame—All Strikes

I was on the phone with a client when I heard what sounded like pebbles striking the windows of my house. Then, from overhead, a thudding on the roof. For a moment, I stopped listening to the man who had hired me to sell his deceased parents' house here in Newfoundland. He was in the process of cleaning out the family home. "I'm sorry," I said, interrupting him, "but do you hear anything funny over where you are right now?"

"I do, Patty," he said. "What is that?"

I got up from my desk and walked to the window, pulled back the curtain, and found small balls of ice sitting on the outside sill. More plunked against the window as I stood watching. "Weird," I said. "It's hail, I think."

My client said, "Hail? This time of year?"

"Like I said, weird."

I asked if we could talk a bit later. I wanted to batten down the hatches if we were in for a freak storm. He agreed, and I went to check all the windows, finding on the southwest side of the house a mass of dark, heavy clouds roiling in the distant sky, just past downtown.

Downtown Newfoundland isn't much of a downtown. It's more of a village green, where the town hall, school, and library sit next to faded family-owned stores, which have tried to hang on over the years. These days, most Newfoundlanders don't mind driving thirty minutes away to buy everything they need from one of the superstores that bookend a dreary shopping mall that seems to have more vacancies in it with each passing year. The clouds rolled like boiling water above those low-slung rooftops. Lightning began to streak through the sky, which seemed to turn darker with each passing second, and my phone squelched with a weather alert in the seconds before a *boom* made me lift my head again. It was just in time to watch what looked like dark threads unspooling from the heavy, layered clouds: thick at the top, narrowing toward the bottom as they reached for the horizon. "A tornado," I whispered, as if I had to say the word to understand what I was watching.

I should have headed straight for the basement, but it was as if I still needed convincing that what I'd seen was real. So I snatched up the remote from the coffee table and quickly scrolled until I came to a weather channel, hoping what I saw might be something else altogether. I hadn't seen a tornado in years, maybe not since I was a little girl, and even then it never came close enough to where I lived to do much damage. The station was broadcasting an emergency warning, telling people to seek shelter, that there were violent storms in our region, multiple tornadoes, the radar flashing with garish reds and purples—storm cells, I realized.

I remember sinking to the couch, suddenly out of breath, and that's when the lights began to flicker. Then the power snapped off and the TV was black, leaving a lingering image of the anchorman for a few seconds before he was gone, too, and I sat alone in the dimness of my living room.

My first thought was *Ellie*. Then *Dan*. My daughter and my husband. Ellie was at school, and I tried to calm myself, because the high school doubled as a community shelter, where anyone could go if they didn't have a basement. She'd be safe there, I thought. It was my husband I was most worried about then. He worked for the power company. He could have been out on a call, sitting in a bucket at the top of a power line, vulnerable to the storms that were raging toward Newfoundland.

Violent, I kept thinking. The word the anchorman had used for the storms. Hail still beat against the house. *But tornadoes are made of wind,* I tried to tell myself. *They're not alive. They can't think. They can't be* violent, *for God's sake.*

A piece of hail hit a window to my right just then, and a crack streaked through the glass to match the lightning outside.

I took out my phone and texted Dan.

Are you okay? I asked.

Then to Ellie:

Are you safe, honey?

I then watched as both of the texts failed to send, trailing red dots next to the messages, asking if I'd like to try again. A second later, the hail suddenly stopped, and I could hear the wail of Newfoundland's tornado sirens in the distance.

I finally ran down into the basement. It's cold, unfinished, housing only a washer and dryer, some clotheslines I'd strung across the ceiling, and a Ping-Pong table that hardly got used after Ellie started joining her high school clubs and activities. There was an old couch down there, too, which I sat on for a few seconds, throwing the beam of my flashlight around in the dark and at the narrow basement windows that occasionally lit up from the lightning.

I couldn't sit for long, though. Helpless is the feeling I hate most in life. So I ran back upstairs and pulled out an old emergency scanner my husband and I kept in the kitchen. We hadn't used it for years, not since we'd bought our first smartphones. But my phone wasn't working, so the scanner seemed like the thing to try.

I took it, a box of crackers, and a pack of water bottles, and hustled back down to the basement. I turned the scanner on, hoping it was still charged enough to work. It crackled and fizzed, and I started to spin through its channels until I found one that worked.

News came to me in broken patches, mostly from the frantic voices of emergency service workers about downed lines and trees, a house fire, cars piled up in an intersection. I could hear fear in their voices, and with each squelch from the scanner, with each boom from outside that set the house rattling around me, my own fear grew, filling the basement like a fog.

More reports of funnels and wind speeds came a little later, while the wind still shook the house foundations. I sat curled up under the dusty Ping-Pong table, wrapped in an afghan my mother had made for Ellie when she was a newborn. Eventually the reports on the storm, and the tornadoes it continued to spawn, trailed off, and I felt tears prick my eyes as the forecasters began to sum up what they knew so far: three, maybe four tornadoes had touched down in Newfoundland itself, more in the region around us, and reports coming in of mass destruction. Downed power lines, trees falling into houses. But also news of whole neighborhoods being leveled. The roof of the roller rink, where I met my husband when I was sixteen, collapsing.

And all of that had apparently happened in the space of no more than an hour.

I grew up knowing we lived on the far edge of that part of the Midwest known as Tornado Alley, but the last time anything like this had happened was in 1985, when I was still small enough to have no real memory of it. When I was little, the name reminded me of a bowling alley. It was only when I grew older that I thought about that name differently, when I understood that the bowling pins were human lives.

The tornadoes that tore through Newfoundland that day? They were all strikes.

I raced upstairs. And that's where I was when the scanner began to say something about an explosion downtown, a fire raging at the high school, emergency responders trying to bring it under control.

Nothing made any sense right then or for a while after. I wish I could have remained calmer. I wish I could have been more rational. But I felt a scream push its way up through my

21

chest, then my throat, until I opened my mouth and my daughter's name came rushing out in a wail. And when I flung open the front door, at first all I could see was a bruise-colored sky, and all I could hear was the word *violence,* swirling and swirling, until what looked like a rift in the sky opened up, and light poured through, shining down on Newfoundland for a moment.

And I swear that, as I stood there, I could see shadows flitting in the sky. Shadows that looked like people. They flew higher and higher, and as I watched, I imagined they were the spirits of Newfoundland's dead flying away—so many of them—passing through that brief gateway of light before, once again, it closed and left us in darkness.

3

The Last Will and Testament of Ellie Frame, cont.

Amid the sirens sounding throughout Newfoundland, I drove slowly, stopping every so often when I came to trees that had fallen across roads during the storm. In those places, I'd go around if I could or head back in the direction I'd come from if the tree was impassable, hoping to find another way home, hoping I wouldn't come across something even more danger-ous, like the downed power lines I found on Elswick Road, jumping and snapping across the pavement, throwing sparks. And when I finally did pull into our driveway, which was all littered with the torn leaves and bark and white flesh of broken branches, my mom flung the front door open and came run-ning down the porch steps, her face red from crying. She was still crying even as she yanked open my door and leaned in to hug me so hard I thought I'd stop breathing.

"Oh my God, Ellie, you're here, you're safe," she said, her

voice ragged. "I was so worried you were there with the rest of them." I could smell cigarette smoke on her, thick and pungent, and that was enough to tell me how worried she must have been, since she'd quit three years ago. She must have hidden a pack somewhere secret, in preparation for some horrible event she couldn't foresee but knew would come one day. That was how my mom thought. Always the planner.

I hugged her back and kissed her wet cheek, saying, "I'm here. It's okay. I'm safe."

My mom isn't usually the crying sort, and to see her like that cracked my eyes open a little, allowing some of my own tears to surface. The floodgates wouldn't open until a few moments later, though, after I'd assured her that I was a real, live person and able to get out of the car on my own to stand in front of her. The floodgates didn't open until she started to calm down, and I asked what she'd meant when she'd said *the rest of them*.

Mom looked shocked by that, and for a long moment afterward, she searched my face, as if trying to find something.

Eventually, she said, "Your father. I have to let him know you're okay."

Mom took hold of my hand then and pulled me behind her onto the porch and into the house, as if I were a five-year-old she refused to lose in a crowded mall, leaving the car door open behind us. She wasn't thinking straight. Or, actually, she was thinking with extreme focus. And because of that, ordinary things like leaving car doors open, the alarm dinging behind us, were outside of her concern.

In the kitchen, she took our old landline phone and started

24

punching in numbers, then turned to look at me over her shoulder to say, "I'm so glad we kept this phone. Cell service isn't working." A few rings later, her face lit up and she said, "Yes, Gus, this is Patty Frame." Gus manned the emergency lines at the power company my dad worked for. "Can you get in touch with Dan for me? I mean, right now? Tell him I have her. Tell him Ellie's here with me. She's safe, Gus. She's home now."

While they were talking, I heard the sound of a basketball smacking against a floor or a wall, and looked out our kitchen window toward the Barlows' house next door, where their son, Timothy, stood on their back deck, dribbling his basketball as if nothing very big in the world had changed around him. He was fifteen, a sophomore at my school. *So he's safe, too,* I thought, and I was glad for him and his family that he'd stayed home from school for some reason.

"Thank you," Mom said again as she wrapped up her call with Gus. Then she hung up the phone and turned to me, sighing with relief, her whole body seeming to sag a little, like she was deflating. "Gus will be able to get your dad on the radio," she said. "Your father is an absolute wreck. Where were you, Ellie?" she asked. "Why weren't you at school?"

This was a question I'd started to think about, but just barely. The clock on that thought had started at the lighthouse, when I'd begun to realize that what I had seen might be even worse than I could imagine. And then Mom had said—

"What did you mean when you said you worried I was with 'the rest of them'?" I asked again.

"Ellie, honey," Mom said slowly, looking just past my head in the direction of downtown, "it's about your school."

I stood there, blinking, feeling my lips begin to tremble as she continued to talk.

"Something happened there during the storm. Some kind of . . . explosion. There are reports that half of downtown was destroyed. Your father is there right now. He went to look for you, to find out more." She paused for a moment then, and I thought again about what I'd seen from the lighthouse earlier. The flash of bright light in the distance, coming from the direction of downtown.

I blinked some more, lifting my face to meet her red-rimmed eyes, after which I immediately broke down sobbing. I couldn't look at my mom and not do that. We looked alike, people always said, and I could see it. We had the same high cheekbones, the same ash-blond hair, the same blue eyes. So, sometimes, when I looked at her, I imagined I was looking into a mirror, only the person on the other side of the silver didn't know exactly how I was feeling. It was me but not me at the same time.

Mom pulled me to her and rocked me slowly while I tried to tell her through my tears what had happened. It was hard to put into words, though. "A fight," I said, forcing my tongue and lips to shape the words. "A stupid fight," I told her, wiping my cheeks and eyes as I began to explain how I'd left school that morning and gone to the lighthouse. Began to explain how I'd seen it all happen from there, or at least what happened to the downtown. Began to explain how I'd seen something that looked like the top half of a silo fly at the school, and then the flash of bright light, the aftershocks that followed. I'd almost forgotten all of it after I'd hit my head on the stone floor, only to come to later, hoping that it had all been a nightmare.

"What happened?" I asked her.

"A gas tanker." She said the words soft, whisper-thin, in my ear as she held me, rocking us back and forth together in the kitchen. "I think it was a gas tanker you saw hit the school. I'm not sure. The news on the scanner is so scattered."

I couldn't hold any of it in my mind. Everything she said was like sand falling through the sieve of my fingers. And the thing I wanted to know most, the question still lodged inside me, I couldn't ask. Because if I did, I might not be able to handle the answer.

When I eventually pulled away, my mom kept hold of my forearms, like I might disappear at any moment in a puff of smoke, like I was no more than a ghost that had wandered back to see her one last time before exiting the world forever, and she was going to do whatever she could to keep me here on earth with her. And right then, feeling the weight of her, was when I found the strength—or maybe the stupidity—to ask what I wanted to know.

"What about—" I said.

I stopped then, looked down at my shoulder, biting my bottom lip, unable to finish the question after all.

"Noah?" Mom finished for me.

I turned back to her, still biting my lip, and nodded.

"I don't know, honey," she said, frowning, shaking her head. "I haven't heard anything. I'm sorry, but I don't know."

My dad came home half an hour later. It would have been sooner, but he had to navigate the blocked roads as well, making what should have been a ten-minute drive three times longer. Mom was in the kitchen, trying to call people from the landline, hoping to reach anyone, hoping to find out something, but each call went unanswered. I was sitting on the couch in the living room, trying to make my phone browser tell me something beyond the fact that there wasn't any service, when Dad came through the front door. I looked up from my phone and, without saying anything, he walked over to the couch with his arms held out, motioning for me to come hug him.

I stood to let him pull me into his chest, where his arms tightened around my shoulders. He was wearing an Ohio Edison polo shirt and khakis as if he were at work, which he would have been if he hadn't gone off in search of me. The company had let him go down to the school to find out what he could. Now here he was, his big arms holding me, him kissing the top of my head like I was still a little girl.

"Where were you, Ellie?" he said after he was finally assured I was real. His eyes were glassy from holding back tears. "Why weren't you at school with everyone else?"

There it was. Not the same words my mom used, but close. *Everyone else.* Why? Why wasn't I there like I was supposed to be? Each time they asked, I couldn't help but feel guilty, like I'd done something wrong. I'd cut classes. I'd run off because I was jealous of my boyfriend being nice to a lonely, awkward girl who just needed a friend.

"The lighthouse," Mom answered for me, after she saw my lips squirming to form words.

"What were you doing *there*?" Dad asked, wincing in disbelief.

Mom met his eyes and shook her head in that *not right now* way, though, and said we should probably just wait to talk about all of that later.

Dad took her cue and danced away from the subject, kissing the top of my head once more instead. "It doesn't matter," he said. "None of that matters. Whatever the reason, I'm glad for it. I'm glad you weren't at school today, sweetheart. The place is an absolute disaster."

I choked up then, put my hand to my mouth, trying to hold in a sob. So the vague things Mom had heard on the scanner and the flash of light I'd seen from the lighthouse really did mean the downtown—and the school—had been destroyed.

"Dan," Mom said.

But I didn't hold his saying that against him. Mom had already gone through all of this with me, so she understood where the landmines I wanted to avoid were planted. Coming over to take me out of his arms and into hers, she sat me back on the couch beside her and ran her fingers through my hair, saying, "Shh, baby. It's going to be okay. Everything's going to be okay now."

But everything wasn't okay. Not even close. In the evening hours, after my dad left us to go back to work, numbers began to trickle in. They screeched across the scanner my mom held to her chest like a baby while we sat next to each other on the couch, fidgeting, clasping our sweaty hands together every now and then, listening to the news of things I didn't quite want to understand. News of life and death. How many of us were gone. How many of us were missing. How many were injured, but still with us. We listened to the squelching scanner for what seemed like unending hours, taking breaks to boil water after an alert over the scanner advised it, and the numbers of the dead just kept growing.

Twenty-three confirmed in the first twenty-four hours, though no names were announced. Those wouldn't come until days later, after families were notified, identities confirmed. And there were more tornadoes than they originally thought, not just the three I'd seen overtake downtown. Twisters had touched down in other places, too, burning trails of destruction through large parts of the tricounty area. During the second day after the outbreak, when the electricity was restored, we watched footage of the wreckage on the TV in our living room: streets where all of the houses had been obliterated beneath the gales, twisted lampposts, a roller rink that was now a hole in the ground, a cemetery where headstones and statues had been sucked out of the earth and spit back again, some landing more than a mile away, the wings of stone angels shattered. And no matter what reporters said throughout the footage, no matter how many survivors were interviewed, declaring their survival to be a miracle, I couldn't help but think, *What about Noah? What about my friends? Where are they? Where is their miracle?*

Because if I could have known that any one of them was still alive, I might have been able to breathe easier. If just one of them could have returned the texts I'd tried to send after I got home safely, I might have given belief in miracles a shot.

Instead, my phone remained silent, a dead thing I kept looking at, hoping it would suddenly spring to life.

And instead of relief, the numbers of the dead just kept rising.

Day two after the outbreak: sixty-five. Plus confirmation of the gas tanker having been the source of the school explosion.

Day three after the outbreak: ninety.

I kept thinking of how there were only two thousand people in all of Newfoundland.

And still no texts were coming. Cell phone towers were down, and what capacity had been restored was still too congested. Too many people trying to use it all at once. Trying to call loved ones they knew outside of the area, to reassure them that they were fine. People trying to call into the area, to check on loved ones after they'd heard about the outbreak on the national news. And all the while, the texts I tried to send out all hovered at the top of my phone screen, uncompleted, suspended like that for what seemed like would be forever.

I told Mom I wanted to go down to the school, to see it for myself, to help look for people, even. "I can't stand just sitting here, doing nothing."

She wouldn't let me, though. "People have been told to stay home," she said. "It's too dangerous for anyone other than emergency crews to be out, Ellie."

And then, out of nowhere, late into the fourth night after the outbreak, after Mom and Dad had gone to bed, my phone vibrated back to life on my nightstand. I almost screamed, but what came out was something more like the hiss of a boiling teakettle. I stared at the phone for a minute, not believing it had done anything, and then when it vibrated again, I picked it up cautiously, turned it over, and began to read the messages that were finally coming through.

Messages from friends at school. Messages from people asking if I knew about all sorts of people who were still missing. People asking if I knew anything about Noah. (I didn't, and I hadn't been able to reach his parents when the cell connections were lost.) People asking if I knew anything about Becca. If I'd heard any word on Adrienne. If I'd heard anything about Rose.

Nothing. I knew nothing. And it was all I could do when I returned the well-intentioned, sometimes frantic texts of other survivors, hoping to trade information.

No, I said, *I haven't heard from any of them. And I can't reach their parents. Do you know anything?*

To which I received answers that were the sorts of things I didn't want to know.

Things like:

Oh. I thought you'd know. I was in the choir room when it happened. Other side of the school. We were safe there.

Or:

I thought for sure you'd know if anyone did. A bunch of us have been wondering.

And this, the absolute worst of them:

Everyone assumed you were with them. That's why everyone's asking, Ellie.

To which I tried to respond, *Noah and I had a fight that morning.*

In the end, though, I couldn't. I deleted those words, didn't respond to that last one at all. Decided I couldn't let anyone know that was why I wasn't there with them. The others. My best friends and my boyfriend. Instead, I looked up from the glowing screen of my phone into the dark of my room, where I'd tried to go to sleep hours ago, only to fail. I sat there with my knees pulled up to my chest, my arms wrapped around them, and tried not to think or feel anything about the messages that had started to find me in the middle of the night.

I knew what all of this meant, on some level. I just couldn't let myself accept it in the moment.

Later, though, I wouldn't be able to ignore what the messages meant collectively. I wouldn't be able to ignore the fact that, out of all of the texts I received, including the five my frantic mother had sent during the outbreak itself, none of them had come from Noah, Becca, Adrienne, or Rose. None were from *the rest of them*. The people I wasn't with on the afternoon of the outbreak.

In the days that followed, the names of the dead eventually began to circulate. Through phone calls and text messages and news report upon updated news report. Through Facebook and Twitter and any other kind of platform. The list of the dead was long, and it was ever growing. Already I'd seen the names of two of my teachers, Ms. Carlson, who taught Spanish, and Mr. Emory, who taught world history. Ms. Carlson was only twenty-five—less than ten years older than me. Fresh out of college. A fiancé waiting to marry her next year. And Mr. Emory had just become a grandparent for the first time recently. He had a gazillion pictures of his grandchild, a baby boy his son and daughter-in-law had named Zachary, after him. They scrolled across his laptop screen whenever the computer fell asleep.

There were others from school, and I knew them all, even if I wasn't necessarily close to all of them. A janitor. A school secretary. A teacher's aide, Mrs. Melvin, who volunteered as a calculus tutor. And classmates, too. Seniors and juniors. Most had been in the wing of the school the tanker had struck, leveling it like a bomb that had been dropped from the sky. All people I'd known since I was a child, my entire life.

With each addition to the list of the dead, a piece of something inside me seemed to wither and die, like a flower on a frost-stricken vine.

And still I waited, not calling Noah's parents, not calling the parents of any of my friends. Because as the hours and the days passed, I was afraid to find out what had happened to them. I was desperately trying not to accept what was most likely the truth.

But a person can only hide from the truth for so long, especially when everyone around her is trying to uncover it. And so it was on the sixth day after the outbreak that I saw their names on a website that had been set up to report on the status of people who were still unaccounted for. I'd been refreshing the page every hour, hoping that Noah and my friends would remain on the list of the missing. It was better if they were still missing, I thought. Because if they were still missing, they weren't dead and gone.

When I pulled up the web page on the sixth day, though, that's when I had to give up any hope I'd been clinging to. That's when I saw their names:

Noah Cady.

Rebecca Hendrix.

Adrienne Long.

Rose Sano.

I swallowed the hard lump that had been sitting in my throat for days, and I waited for it to hit me. I thought that at any moment I'd melt down into inexhaustible sobbing like I did after coming home from the lighthouse. But instead, an eerie web of calm seemed to settle over me, and I looked up from my laptop and over to my mom, who was working on her own computer across the room.

"All of them," I said very quietly, then shifted my eyes to the bookshelf next to her, where an old mantel clock my grandmother handed down to my mom ticked within its wooden frame.

Mom heard me and, without having to ask, she knew exactly what I meant. Immediately she came to sit beside me on the couch, pulling me into her chest.

"Oh, honey," she said, putting her cheek against mine. We stayed like that for a long time. And then, probably in a way she thought might console me, probably in a way she thought might help me recognize I wasn't alone in all of this, she said,

"The Barlows next door are having a terrible time right now, too. I spoke with them yesterday. They lost poor Timothy."

I stiffened a little in my seat, but didn't say anything. *How could the Barlows have lost Timothy?* I'd seen him right after I'd gotten home from the lighthouse, dribbling a basketball on his family's back deck.

I shook my head, slightly confused and suddenly scared in a different way than I'd been all week. I kept thinking, *How can that be? I saw him. I saw him.*

Rattled, I got up a second later, breaking away from her embrace. When Mom asked where I was going, I said I was just going up to my room to be alone for a while. I knew if I stayed any longer, she'd start to talk about them. She'd say their names—Becca, Adrienne, Rose, Noah—and right then I couldn't stand to think about them yet, let alone speak about them. Right then my head was filled with the screaming I couldn't let out.

"When you're ready to talk about this, Ellie," Mom said, "you know I'm here for you."

I nodded, then continued up the stairs. I couldn't talk about anything yet. My insides were completely hollow. It felt as if a gaping hole had opened up in the center of my chest, where everything good used to be. And now? Now nothing was there. It was just empty. I had barely enough strength to say meaningless things, let alone talk about the people I'd lost, and contemplating whether I'd seen the ghost of my neighbor was beyond me.

I shook my head as I went into my room, as if I could shake the static out of my thoughts. All I wanted to do was find the flannel shirt Noah had left in my car one night, the one that still held the scent of his cologne. I wanted nothing more than to stay in my room, holding that shirt against me like a blanket, closing up, curling inward, retreating from a world that had suddenly become impossible to live in.

And that's exactly what I did in the days that followed. Until nearly another week had passed and I saw him again, this time from my bedroom window. The next-door neighbors' kid, Timothy. He was out on the back deck again, nodding his head to music, the wires from his earbuds dangling on either side of his face.

"But, Timothy," I whispered, leaning closer to the window, fogging it with my breath. "You're dead."

And that's when Timothy Barlow—or Timothy Barlow's ghost, I should say—looked up, noticed me in the frame of my bedroom window, and smiled brightly, offering me a friendly wave.

4

The Last Will and Testament of Ellie Frame, cont.

I didn't tell anyone I'd seen Timothy's ghost listening to music on his back deck. I figured, why worry my parents more than I already have? I figured, why tell any of the people who had survived the outbreak and were trying to pull their own lives back together, who already had their own losses to deal with? A total of *forty-seven* tornadoes had torn across this corner of Ohio over a forty-eight-hour period, a record, according to one reporter, and in the following days, the president declared the region a federal disaster area, sending in the National Guard to help. Hundreds of families had lost homes. Whole streets and neighborhoods were leveled, the houses pulled apart brick by brick, plank by plank, their contents tossed into the sky and scattered for miles and miles across the Pennsylvania border. Debris was everywhere you looked: twisted pieces of metal that might otherwise be mistaken as sculptures, toilets and sinks surreally appearing in fields and ditches, bottles and wrappers and egg cartons from garbage cans littering the streets. Downed power lines slithered on roads for days, jumping and snapping out showers of yellow-hot sparks. A hundred and fifty-three people's lives had been claimed, and that was just in and around Newfoundland. After nearly two weeks, there were still people missing. With all of the fallout from the loss and death and destruction, I decided no one needed to hear from a girl who thought she'd seen the ghost of her dead neighbor boy amid the chaos.

Instead, I played a game with my parents and myself. It was a game I didn't realize I was playing then, but later I came to understand I'd invented it just to get me through each day. It was a game in which I had to act like nothing had gone terribly wrong, in which I would have to pretend to be well rested and perfectly fine rather than admitting to anyone, including myself, that I hadn't slept for days. It was a game in which, whenever my mom or dad asked how I was feeling, I'd turn to them and say, "I'm fine. Really." And then I'd do something incredibly ordinary, like set the table or wash dishes or pick up the remote and turn on the television to stare at the local news like it was the most interesting thing in the world, even though I no longer registered the images of ruined buildings and roads that had been pulled right out of the earth like loose threads, all scrolling across the screen in front of me.

This went on for a number of days, both before and after the funerals started. I played the *I'm fine, really* game like a pro after I saw Timothy Barlow's ghost on his back deck listening to music, then waving up to me in my bedroom window. And

I continued to play it the day my mom interrupted my very normal-seeming TV watching to say, "Ellie, I've spoken with a number of people for you over the past couple of days, honey. Noah's parents. Rebecca's and Rose's folks. They're going to have calling hours for them all soon. I don't know if you're up for going to them, but I think it might be something you should do, if you feel you can."

"I'm fine, really," I said, blinking up at my mom, who stood in the hallway between the living room and dining room with her arms folded across her chest, looking anxious and doubtful, as if she were waiting for me to finally break down in the big way that I sensed she wanted me to. Bigger than the intermittent sobbing I'd done on that first day, after the shock of returning home began to wear off. Big enough to encompass all of the death that surrounded us like a fog that refused to burn off when the sun came up.

I couldn't give her what she wanted, though. I couldn't let myself face everything that had just happened. I was afraid that if I let enough of that reality into my head, I might not just break down sobbing. I might break down for good.

So instead I said, "When are they?" as if she'd informed me of a series of graduation parties I'd been invited to attend. Graduation parties that would never happen. Graduation parties for dead friends. And though Mom frowned a little at my answer, clearly disbelieving my calmness, she listed off the days and times, many of which were back to back, due to the large number of the dead the local funeral homes had to process.

Process was a word I'd heard my dad use when he talked about the aftermath of the storms, about how much there was to clean up, to fix, to rebuild. It all felt overwhelming. "It will take a long time for us to process all of this," he kept saying. It was a word that felt safe, and it was the word I now chose to use when thinking about what I was being asked to do, because it made everything feel mechanical, and mechanical things could be used for something, or fixed if they happened to be broken. Mechanical things could be controlled.

The last thing Mom said before she left me to stare vacantly at the television again was "Ellie, you don't have to do this if you don't want to. I'm worried about you, honey. This is a whole lot . . . it's a whole lot to handle. Noah and Rose and . . . it's awful, I know. But you're not alone in it. Your dad and I are here for you, okay?"

"I'm fine, really," I said, hands trembling, gritting my teeth as I turned away, clenching them so tightly, I felt like I could have ground them down to powder.

On the day of the first two funerals—Noah's and Becca's—Timothy Barlow made another appearance. He'd been popping up every now and then, once I'd seen him from my bedroom window and understood what he was. Mainly I'd spot him out of the corner of one eye. I'd see a flicker of motion, then I'd turn to find him going around the corner of his house, or pulling up the Barlows' garage door, or bouncing up and down on the old trampoline that sat rusting under the tall pines in their backyard before letting himself finally fall flat on his back and lie still, like he used to do as a little kid, playing dead.

Then I'd blink and he'd be gone.

I'd put my fingertips to my temples and rub them a little, wincing, whispering to myself, "Ghosts aren't real," and hoping that I wasn't losing any more grip on myself than I'd already lost that day up in the lighthouse.

When Timothy appeared on the day of Noah's and Becca's funerals, I was standing on our own deck, staring out at the woods that lined the edge of our backyard. I noticed the flicker of motion out of the corner of my eye that usually accompanied Timothy's appearances, and slowly I turned my head to find him listening to music on his deck again. He was nodding to the rhythm of whatever song was playing on his phone, and the long black curls that fell over his forehead and ears swayed a little in time.

I was wearing the black dress my mom had bought for me to wear to my grandfather's funeral a year earlier. And around my neck, half of the heart-shaped Best Friends charm Becca had given me back in sixth grade shared a chain with Noah's senior-year ring, which he'd given me on the six-month anniversary of our first date. I'd be leaving for the funerals in a little less than an hour, so I shouldn't have done what I did, but I couldn't help myself. I'd been seeing Timothy's ghost far too often, and he was disturbing my concentration. I needed to maintain all of the illusions that had been propping me up or I'd never make it through the day. And every time I saw *him,* I thought of Noah or Becca or Adrienne or Rose. Saw their faces next to his, dissolving, as if they were made of smoke, within seconds. And afterward, all I could do was crumple up, knees to chest, in my bed, with the corner of a pillow stuffed into my mouth so my parents wouldn't hear me screaming.

Like I said, I shouldn't have done what I did, but as soon as I saw Timothy Barlow, I knew I had to do something to stop him. So I went down the steps of our back deck in my heels, wobbling a little as I crossed the yard, until I was standing at the foot of the Barlows' deck.

I waved up at Timothy, but he had his eyes closed as he rocked out to whatever song held his attention. It reminded me of when he was ten and I was twelve, and his mom and dad sometimes paid me to babysit him so they could have dinner somewhere fancy in one of the nearby towns. Timothy had loved music back then, too. He played the saxophone in the school band. But even when he was ten, he couldn't get enough of listening to his dad's jazz collections. I always thought it was odd, a little kid liking jazz the way Timothy did, especially when everyone else listened to whatever was popular. But it also made him easy to babysit, since I knew he'd zone out on music for most of the time I had to watch him.

"Timothy," I said now, after my wave didn't catch his attention. He looked up, startled to see me at the bottom of the steps, as if I were a ghost appearing to him.

"Oh hey, Ellie," he said, smiling after his initial surprise. "What's happening? Why are you dressed like that? Is there a dance tonight or something?"

Cocking my head to the side to stare at him even harder, I asked, "Are you real?"

A funny look came across his face then, like he thought I

might be joking and he wanted to laugh. But because I didn't smile back, he knew I wasn't kidding. "What do you mean?" he asked in a voice that sounded like he was suddenly afraid that he might be in trouble.

I felt bad now, hearing that flicker of fear in his voice, like it was me who was messing with his head and not the other way around. "Forget it," I said, and then I put one foot on the deck steps and started toward him.

He backed up a step for each one I took, as if he feared I meant to hurt him. And I suppose I may have looked like I might, because as soon as I took my first step up to him, I had decided I'd try to pass my hand right through his chest, and that would prove to us both that he was dead, and he'd go away instead of haunting me occasionally.

"What are you doing, Ellie?" he asked suspiciously, with his back pressed up against the sliding glass doors that led into the family's kitchen.

"I just want to see something, Timothy," I said, trying to sound non-scary, trying to reassure him, the same way I once had to approach him when he was little and had gotten a sliver of wood stuck under his nail. "I just need to look at it," I'd told him, then quickly pulled the sliver out with tweezers. He'd yelped in surprise, and I lifted the tweezers up to his eyes and said, "See? All done and over."

He could sense this was some kind of moment like that one, the sliver one, so I had to act fast, before he could escape. I reached out to put my hand through his shoulder quickly, curling my fingers inward to grasp the nothing I expected to find. . . .

And found that his flesh was as solid and firm as my own.

"Ellie?" he said, his mouth slightly parted, speechless.

"I'm sorry, Timothy," I said, shaking my head. "I don't know what came over me. I'm sorry."

Then I turned and hurried down the steps, stopping at the bottom to take off my heels, and jogged the rest of the way across the yard and back to my house, gasping for breath as soon as I got inside and closed the door behind me.

"Ellie?" My mom's voice floated down the stairs and into the kitchen to find me. "Are you ready, honey?"

I took one more deep breath, wiping sweat from my forehead, before I shouted back, "Of course!"

We left ten minutes later. It was just me and Mom. Dad had been working overtime for the past week, coming home only for eight-hour breaks to eat a quick meal with us before falling asleep. He'd started to look as ragged as I felt, with red-rimmed eyes and lines creasing his forehead. Neither of us were taking care of ourselves, but at least Dad had work to blame. He had to deal with clearing the roads of downed power lines and restoring service in places still so devastated, the National Guard had barely been able to get through to them. Me, though? No real excuses. I just couldn't stop thinking about my friends and Noah long enough for my brain to quiet and go to sleep.

The roads, while mostly clear, still looked bad. With pavement torn up in spots, as if a particularly severe winter had left humongous potholes dotting the landscape. Trees that had been cut up and cleared away still littered the sides of the roads. It felt like Mom was driving me through a foreign country as we left Newfoundland and headed for Cortland, the next town over, where Becca's family had arranged for her memorial service to be held. The two funeral homes in Newfoundland couldn't process the dead fast enough on their own.

When we pulled into the parking lot fifteen minutes later, Mom turned to me and said, "Ellie, if at any time you think you need to leave, just tell me. It's okay if that happens."

I nodded, but didn't say anything. Now that we were so close to Becca, whose body I knew was waiting inside the old Victorian house that served as a funeral home, I found that I couldn't play the *I'm fine, really* game as easily as I could in the comforts of my own home. I bit down on my lower lip gently, as if to pin my mouth closed, then unbuckled my seat belt and got out of the car to prompt Mom to stop talking about it.

The parking lot was filled with cars, and a line of people had already formed outside the funeral home, stretching from the front doors into the viewing room around one side of the house. As we got in line, Mom whispered, "So many people have come to say goodbye to Becca. Oh dear, her parents must be having such a hard time."

Stop talking, I thought. My mom meant well, I know, but there was something in her personality that gravitated toward vocalizing feelings, especially sad ones. I was more like my dad, maybe. I preferred to keep my feelings to myself, especially the hard ones. And in this case, there were so many hard feelings that it felt better not to acknowledge any of them at all. If I just pretended they weren't there, they might go away. Like I hoped Timothy Barlow's ghost would do eventually.

Mom continued to whisper more sad thoughts as we moved toward the front doors, which looked a little bit like what I imagined the witch's house in "Hansel and Gretel" might look like—quaint gingerbread trimmings, minus the candy and frosting decorations. And the closer we got to those doors, the more I wanted to tell my mom to wait in the car for me. She was messing with my ability to go through with this, because she couldn't stop narrating her own feelings. I needed to be able to walk through that viewing room like a ghost—unseen, invisible—say goodbye to Becca, and move through the back entrance before getting trapped by anyone who would want to talk at length about the tragic loss of Becca Hendrix, my best friend since elementary school. I didn't want anyone to show me to a room where others had gathered while waiting for the memorial service. That, at least, was how things had gone for my grandfather's funeral a year ago, and the small talk and sentiments were more than I could handle.

I made it to the front doors without bolting from the line, just barely, and as we pushed through into the foyer, I bit down harder on my bottom lip, hard enough to hurt, trying to create a different pain, a physical pain, so that the one inside me would go away for at least the next fifteen minutes.

"Remember, honey, if you need to—" my mom started to say.

And without looking at her, I cut her off, saying, "I know, Mom. Thank you."

The line moved from the foyer, where Mom signed a guest book, into the viewing room, where I was relieved to see Becca's parents standing beside a closed casket. Closed. Of course it was closed.

A large framed portrait of Becca stood beside her casket. It was her senior picture, the one with her curly red hair cascading over her shoulders. Her smile bright as diamonds, her brown eyes dark and deep, seemingly able to see right inside you. That was what I loved about Becca. She was the first person to know how I was feeling, in any situation, without me ever having to say a thing.

Now her eyes still burrowed into me, but in a way that made me uncomfortable. Now when I looked at her face in that senior picture, I saw her looking back and thinking, *Why weren't you there with me, Ellie? We were best friends. Why weren't you there?*

I took a deep breath, and Mom took hold of my hand and gently squeezed. I felt my resolve weakening, and she could sense it. But we were next in line to pay our respects to Mr. and Mrs. Hendrix and the rest of Becca's family. The only person I noticed missing was her older brother, Drew. Becca's parents had disowned him, Becca once told me, because he was gay. The Hendrix family was a pillar in one of Newfoundland's churches, the sort of family that drew hard lines in the sand, and was vocal about a number of issues I knew that Becca didn't agree with. She kept her feelings to herself; it was easier than contending with her parents. And as a result, she hadn't seen Drew since she was a little girl, though I knew that she'd hoped to find him after she graduated.

An organ played somewhere, its soft, sad music moving among the hushed voices, and the scent of lilies filled the viewing room. I hadn't noticed these things until it was my turn to go up to Mr. and Mrs. Hendrix, who stood with one arm wrapped around each other—Mr. Hendrix's draped around her shoulders, Mrs. Hendrix's around his back—looking utterly, utterly destroyed. I didn't really like the two of them, because of all the things Becca had told me—how controlling they were, how strict and sometimes harsh. But now I couldn't help but feel pain inside me as I looked into their faces and saw their own. It felt like a spear through my chest, leaving me breathless. And when I opened my mouth to say how sorry I was, a formless moan rose up and pushed its way out of my throat. Tears sprang to my eyes, fast and hot, making me frantic.

"I'm so sorry," I said in the next breath, and my mother squeezed me close to her. "I'm so sorry, I'm so sorry, I'm so sorry."

"Oh, Ellie," Mr. Hendrix said. "Please, Becca wouldn't want you to feel this way."

And Mrs. Hendrix came forward to pull me into her arms. "Shh, honey, shh," she said. Then her hand was on the back of my head, cradling it against her shoulder, and Mom was standing next to Mr. Hendrix, whispering something. "Shh, shh," Mrs. Hendrix said as I sobbed into her shoulder. "I know what you're feeling. I know. And there's nothing wrong with it. You were always such a good friend to Becca. Her best friend. She always said so. Shh. Don't cry, my love."

"It's so hard," I moaned, and it felt as if the words I spoke were not my own, were some kind of reflex and not how I really felt, or wanted to feel, or wanted to *not feel*. But all the same, I shook against Mrs. Hendrix's body, which smelled of lavender, the scent she always wore, and continued to cry.

"I know, sweetheart," she said, rocking me a little, and then she lowered her voice even more. "But you needn't worry. Becca isn't gone. She's still here with us."

I was waiting for Mrs. Hendrix to go on, to say the thing that everyone says after someone has died, the thing people say to comfort themselves. That the person who died isn't really gone. That they live on in our hearts and our memories.

Which is true. I knew I could look inside and pull up a memory of Becca laughing at one of my corny jokes, or huddled next to me, watching a scary movie on the couch at my house, since she wasn't allowed to see them at hers. Her favorite had been *Paranormal Activity,* and she'd jumped each time the spirit in the house moved something while being video recorded yet still went unseen. And there in my memory, Becca would indeed be alive again. The sound of her voice, the familiar smell of her coconut-scented shampoo.

But no. What Mrs. Hendrix whispered into my ear next wasn't that. Instead, she said, "Why, I've seen her nearly every night since she passed away. And the next time I see her, I'll tell her that she should pay you a visit."

5

The Last Will and Testament of Ellie Frame, cont.

By the time Mom politely excused us from the scene I played a part in making at my best friend's memorial service, I was running down a hallway covered in Victorian-style wallpaper depicting winding vines and thorny roses, and I was starting to hyperventilate.

Breathe in, breathe out, I kept telling myself. *Get out of this place. Don't think. Make your mind into a white space. Pretend that a nuclear bomb just went off and everything in your world was wiped out of existence.*

Which was a strangely comforting idea, dark as it was, considering almost everything and everyone in my world had been wiped out already. My best friends. My boyfriend. My school. The ice cream shop where I always asked to have gummy candies mixed into my strawberry ice cream, and the little boutique where my mom took me to buy my prom dress and didn't even balk at the price tag. The Italian restaurant everyone went to for special occasions. Anniversaries. Birthdays. Prom. Wedding parties. Blankness was what I craved, but I didn't need a nuclear explosion to wipe out my world. My world had already been wiped out by an outbreak of tornadoes.

And it was that phrase, too, that kept bothering me. *An outbreak of tornadoes.* It was how everyone described what had happened: the meteorologists, so grave, so severe as they talked about climate change and how our *outbreak* might be the beginning of new weather patterns; the local and national newscasters, who were still covering the *outbreak* and its aftermath two weeks later. Even in newspapers near and far, you'd see reporters pick up the phrase. An *outbreak of tornadoes* was the line even locals used when they were interviewed. And the more I heard the words, the more surreal it all felt. Like the storms were something I'd dreamed about instead of something that had actually happened.

I'd run from the viewing room after Mrs. Hendrix leaned in to whisper that my best friend, her daughter, had been visiting her almost every night since she'd died in the collapse of the high school. I knew Mom, always the expert smoother-over-of-awkwardness, would have immediately launched into an apology for my dramatic exit, explaining quietly how badly I was taking everything, obviously. And after relaying one more apology and condolence, she'd follow me, pleading for me to slow down.

Which is exactly what she did.

"Ellie," she called behind me, in a voice loud enough for me to hear yet restrained enough not to draw attention. But I kept hurrying through the mazelike hallways of the old house. "Ellie. Ellie, honey! Please stop."

"Not here," I hissed over my shoulder, between gasps of breath. "Please. Let's just get out of here."

Then finally I located an exit and burst through the door to find myself in the rear parking lot, in the light of day, away from those dark and mournful rooms shrouded in misery. And it was there that I leaned over, bracing my hands on my knees, and continued to gasp, thinking I might throw up, hiccupping eventually, until finally my heartbeat slowed and my breath started to come back.

Mom emerged a few seconds later, and came directly over to bend down in front of me and put a hand on one side of my face. I looked up to meet her eyes, those eyes that mirrored mine, both of us tearing up and reflecting one another. Between gasps, I said, "Mrs. Hendrix. Said. She. Sees. Becca. Every. Night."

"Oh my God," my mother said, shaking her head slowly, eyes widening as she took in Mrs. Hendrix's secret. And right then I knew that if that was Mom's response, she understood exactly why I'd run out of there so frantically. "That poor woman," she continued. "Ellie, I'm sorry I encouraged you to come here today. I thought it would be a good way to start getting closure, but this is all too much. It's too much for everyone, obviously." She looked away then, and wiped tears from her own eyes, trying not to let me see. And when she turned back, she said, "I'm not sure if we should go to Noah's services now."

I stood, and Mom stood with me, putting one hand around

my arm to brace me if I seemed like I might faint. I straightened my dress with the flats of my hands, trying to shake off the awful dread Mrs. Hendrix's words had sent crawling through my body. "No," I told Mom. "You were right. I need to do this. I need to say goodbye to them. Somehow. Otherwise—"

I stopped then, felt a sob start to form in my throat, but pressed my lips together long enough to contain it. Swallowed it back down.

"What, honey?" Mom said, her eyes searching my face with worry. "Otherwise, what?"

I didn't tell her right then that I'd been seeing a ghost myself. I didn't tell her that Timothy Barlow, whose memorial service Mom and Dad had attended several days ago without me, had been appearing to me for the past two weeks. As if the tornadoes had never happened, as if he wasn't one of the people crushed in the west wing of the high school or burned by the explosion. If I told her that, she'd freak out, and I didn't want her to look at me and say, *Oh my God,* and then stand in shock, disturbed by what I'd shared, the same way she did when I told her what Mrs. Hendrix had whispered.

So I kept all of it inside, and instead said, "Otherwise, I don't know what will happen to me. I need to go to Noah's. I can do this. I have you with me."

It was the truth, mostly, so at least I didn't feel like I was lying to her. Not like whenever I played the *I'm fine, really* game. I wasn't saying I was fine. I was just saying I could do something. Or that I thought I could do something.

"You are so strong, my beautiful girl," Mom said, brushing a curl of hair away from my forehead. "Okay, then. Let's go."

I wasn't strong, like Mom thought, but it wasn't really the time to debate the qualities of my character. And besides, I thought, shouldn't someone be able to look into the eyes of another person and see something good, even if it was just for a moment? If my mom wanted to see me as strong, I wouldn't stop her. She was stressed enough. I had smelled cigarettes on her clothes nearly every day since the outbreak, so I knew she'd gone back to them after that first day, when she thought I was dead.

On our way back to Newfoundland, I closed my eyes and tried to put myself in the right frame of mind for Noah's memorial service. Tried to put myself in the right frame of mind to say goodbye. I watched the passing scenes of what would ordinarily be peaceful fields of new corn growing taller, and cringed at the way entire fields had been decimated, the earth turned up like God's own plow had pushed through them. Telephone and electrical poles had fallen onto some of them, one after the other, like crosses snapped at their bases. *All gone,* I kept thinking as Mom drove past the wreckage. *All gone.*

And then, when we got back to Newfoundland and took a route that had been cleared to the funeral home where Noah's service was scheduled to start within an hour, a different thought—a terrible thought, really—suddenly sprang into my head.

Why Timothy Barlow? I thought. *If Mrs. Hendrix can see Becca, can I see Noah?*

I shook off the thought a moment after I had it. And yet it was a thought that somehow held out a kind of hope to me—even if it was a hope that came with a particular frustration. Because if it was really possible to still see Noah, why hadn't he already shown himself to me? Why Timothy Barlow?

No good answers come from thinking like that, though, and after Mom pulled into the funeral home in Newfoundland, I tried to unwind my thoughts, to put them away in some dusty, easily forgotten box.

"Listen," Mom said as she turned off the car engine, letting the keys sway and jingle from the ignition. She looked over at me with her game face back on. She'd used the trip back to Newfoundland to pull herself together like I'd intended to do, though I'd been unsuccessful. "The services for Noah don't start for twenty minutes, but I see his dad's car over there. We could go in, pay our respects. You could probably say goodbye to Noah privately, and then we could leave before anyone else gets here. How does that sound?"

I thought about it for a moment, pursing my lips, torn between doing the safe thing and the thing I felt was right. "I should stay for the service," I told Mom. "But I wouldn't mind going in and having some privacy first."

Mom nodded. I always tried to get the best of any decisions in front of me, she once said. When I was ten and she told me I needed to choose between going to camp or taking dance lessons over the summer, I asked her to send me to a dance camp instead. When I was fifteen, instead of choosing between the popular options of cheerleading or the marching band, I decided to cover sports for the school newspaper so I could be at all the games without having to be out in front of other people.

It's how I got started taking photos for the school paper, and how Mrs. Englund, our art teacher, eventually corralled me into working for the yearbook, which she taught every year as an elective.

"That's a good compromise," Mom said now, perhaps unsurprised that, even in all this mess, I was still trying to travel the road between what others saw as black-and-white choices. "Okay, then. Let's go in. And if you change your mind, just give my hand a squeeze."

She gave me her hand and squeezed mine once, then twice, as if to demonstrate, smiling softly. Then we got out of the car and headed up the front steps of the funeral home.

Here we performed the same rituals we had at Becca's service. Mom signed us into the guest book, and afterward we headed for the viewing room around the corner, where a minister stood in the entry, talking to someone just out of sight. As we turned the corner, though, I stopped suddenly when I recognized Noah's dad—his salt-and-pepper hair, his broad shoulders that reminded me of Noah's—and I put my hand to my mouth. Just the sight of him was enough to shock me into stillness. Mom grabbed my free hand and squeezed. I dropped the one covering my mouth and looked at her. "Sorry," I whispered.

"There's no reason to be sorry, Ellie," she whispered back. "I just want to make sure you're okay."

I nodded again, clenching my teeth, and we moved into the viewing room, where a closed casket was waiting for people to pass by, to say goodbye to Noah, to weep in mourning. Or, in my case, to feel regret burning me from the inside out over the last things we'd said to each other on the morning of the outbreak.

Beside the casket, Noah's senior portrait had been placed on a wrought-iron stand. It was a formal shot, a head-and-shoulders photo that was going in the yearbook. Navy-blue blazer, white shirt, royal-blue tie with pink and white stripes, his icy eyes highlighted because of it. His chestnut hair blown back a little. His teeth, straight and gleaming. My stomach clenched. Just looking at his face beside his casket, where recessed lights surrounded his portrait with an aura, made me stop. I wanted so badly to apologize, but that was impossible. Instead, all I could do was stand there and hate myself as his face stared back at me, smiling.

Beside me, Mom gave my hand another squeeze. I looked over, and her brows were raised in question. I nodded my okay, and we moved further into the viewing room, where Mrs. Cady sat in a chair while Mr. Cady and the minister talked quietly. And it was Mrs. Cady who finally noticed Mom and me, immediately standing from her chair to say, "Ellie, you've come," and waving me to her.

Both Mr. and Mrs. Cady looked horrible. Although they were dressed for their only child's funeral—very put together, very formal—their faces betrayed what the last two weeks had done to them. Waiting through the early days as rescuers sifted through the wreckage, waiting to find out if Noah was a survivor, then discovering he wasn't, and waiting again for this dreaded day to lay him, somehow, to rest. Dark pouches of skin sagged under their watery blue eyes. Those Cady eyes, usually so bright, showed no hint of life in their faces the way you could still see light behind Noah's eyes in his portrait. Wrinkles had appeared out of nowhere, seemingly etched across their faces overnight. Mrs. Cady had always looked younger than forty-seven, yet here she stood with a wrinkled brow and crow's-feet spreading out from the corners of her eyes. Now she looked more like she might be going on sixty.

I went to her and let her take my cold hands in hers, let her lean in and hug me, even though I worried she might whisper something terrible in my ear like Mrs. Hendrix had, not even thirty minutes earlier. I said the things I needed to tell her. That I was sorry. So sorry. That I was sorry I hadn't called. That I was sorry I hadn't come to see them yet. "I'm so sorry," I kept saying, and found new tears at the ready, although I didn't find myself sobbing uncontrollably like I had at Becca's memorial.

Afterward, Mr. Cady held me for a moment with his hand on the back of my head, my chin on his shoulder, while both he and Mrs. Cady reassured me that they weren't upset and that they completely understood they weren't the only people to lose someone. I heard Mom choke up behind me. Was she dealing with her own guilt, maybe, for having a child who survived? But she quickly recovered and said that she was sorry, too. Then, sniffing, she excused herself, saying she'd be right back.

The pastor came over after Mom's exit, apologizing before saying he had just a few more things he needed to speak to Mr. and Mrs. Cady about before people started to arrive. "Of course," the Cadys said, nodding. Then they looked back at me with the kind of smiles that seem more like frowns, the kind of smiles I imagine people make only when they're trying to show courage in the face of incredible devastation. "We'll see you soon, Ellie," Mrs. Cady said. "And please, don't be a stranger. Be good to yourself. Noah would want that."

I moved on from the viewing room to find seats for my mom and myself in the chapel, already feeling like a stranger. Already feeling like I was outside of the Cady family circle without Noah there to connect us. Nothing made sense anymore. *This wasn't supposed to happen, not to Noah, not to . . . any of them.* I had learned what it was to lose someone I loved when my grandpa died, but all of this death surrounding Newfoundland like a black cloud, choking everything within it, made me feel like the world had suddenly become a wasteland.

I found two chairs behind the first row, which was reserved for Noah's family, and sat to wait for Mom, willing myself not to look at Noah's portrait in the viewing room, trying to win at the *I'm fine, really* game, which I realized I was starting to play against myself. It was as if two versions of me were seated, and I could look over at the other chair and see myself looking back, saying, "You're fine, really. Don't think about any of this." And as that me, the *fine* me, continued to try to persuade the other me, I reached over and took hold of the back of her chair, pushed it over in one hard heave, and watched as it clattered to the floor, empty.

The Cadys and the minister turned to look at me from the viewing room, and I apologized, excusing myself while pulling the chair back up and into place. My face flushed, and I looked toward the foyer, where the front doors had opened and people had begun to enter, forming a crowd as they waited to sign the guest book.

Piped-in organ music began to play in the background. I sighed, welcoming the distraction. Closing my eyes, I told myself to get it together. For just the next hour. And when I opened my eyes again, determined to do just that, a woman had appeared in front of the crowd in the foyer, as if she'd manifested by way of magic. She wore a little black dress that looked more appropriate for a cocktail party or a wedding reception, and her dark hair curled over her shoulders in long waves. Her eyes were lined with a dusty green color, and the only thing those eyes did was fix me in their stare from across the room the same way her daughter had done whenever I came across her in school hallways.

It was Mrs. Mueller. *Ingrid* Mueller's mother. Ingrid Mueller of the spooky, spaced-out, gloom-filled stare. Ingrid Mueller of the jealousy so palpable, it seemed to roll off her in waves whenever she saw me.

Mrs. Mueller held my gaze for what seemed like an eternity, while I struggled to look away. But no matter what I told myself as I attempted to free myself from her icy stare, I remained frozen in my chair. It wasn't until I felt a warm hand land on my shoulder that I was able to look up, and found my mom. She stood beside me, carefully returning Mrs. Mueller's stare. "Hello, Calliope," Mom said. "I'm so sorry for your loss. If there's anything—"

Mrs. Mueller shook her head, though, cutting Mom off with a grimace. Then slowly she turned to enter the procession to pay her respects to the Cadys, her neighbors whose son had devoted so much of his time to her and her daughter after the loss of her husband.

"Don't mind her," Mom said afterward, even though I hadn't said anything to make her think I might have been bothered. "She must be having a difficult time right now. First her husband, now her daughter. The poor thing."

"I wonder how Ingrid's services were," I said.

And Mom said, "I hear it was a private service. Calliope wanted it that way."

As the line of mourners grew longer and those who passed through began to fill the seats around us, a group of girls came around the corner, heading in my direction. Girls from my class, girls I'd known since we were in kindergarten. Alicia Beckwith, Toni Kennedy, and Stacy Marsh. At first sight of them, I drew a sharp breath, worried I might be seeing their ghosts appear before me. But then I reminded myself that more than half of the senior class had survived. Had been in some safe part of the building or had been absent for some other reason, like me. These girls weren't ghosts. They were alive, breathing the same air I breathed, crying tears I fought to hold back when they came up to me, saying, "Ellie, where have you been? We've been so worried. Why haven't you texted? Are you okay? Oh God, this is so hard, isn't it? He was so good. So good. I can't believe it."

As their words swarmed around me, I started to feel suffocated by them. I shook my head, tried giving short answers, then apologized for not being in touch, anything to make them go away. Apologizing seemed to be the only thing I could do anymore. "I'm sorry I haven't returned your texts," I told them. "Yes, this is hard. He was so good. I don't . . . I don't know how to feel. . . . I don't know what to say."

I looked down at my hands in my lap, one of which my mom still held between her fingertips. My breath had begun to burn in my throat, and my eyes started to well up as the girls filled my sudden silence with more words, more memories, more reminders not to cut myself off from them. And with each word, each memory, each reminder, I could feel them tugging at me, trying to pull me out of myself.

"You need other people right now," Stacy Marsh insisted. "We all do."

"You need your friends, Ellie," Toni Kennedy declared.

And before Alicia Beckwith opened her mouth to add in her feelings, I squeezed Mom's hand.

Nothing more was said after that. At least nothing more by me. Because Mom stood immediately, pulled me up with her, and told the girls to please excuse us, she needed to talk to me in private.

I took her cue and followed behind, heading for the foyer, where we pushed through the ever-growing throng, and left the funeral home before the memorial service could properly begin.

After we'd put ourselves back into the car, Mom took hold of my chin between her thumb and forefinger, turning my face to hers. "Ellie, love," she said. "We won't be going to any more of these, okay?"

I nodded, wishing I could have gone through with it the way I'd hoped I could, as the tears I'd been holding back started to stream down my face.

"Also," Mom added as she used her thumb to wipe the tears away, "I think you should see someone. Someone special."

"What do you mean?" I asked, helping her wipe the tears away now.

"There's a woman, part of the team the governor sent to Newfoundland," Mom said.

"A woman?" I said, squinting.

"A psychiatrist," Mom said. "Someone who specializes in trauma in communities like ours. I've already had some exchanges with her and some of the other counselors. I think you should see her. I think you're exactly the sort of person she's been sent here to help."

6

Eva Arroyo—The Gone Away Place

The girl who sat slumped over in the metal folding chair in front of me wasn't sure if she wanted to live or die. She couldn't articulate her problem in those words, but after two decades of treating people who've suffered sudden catastrophic loss, I find it easy to recognize the signs. She'd survived when Death came on dark wings and slid his sword through the earth around her. And though she'd survived, she didn't understand that the sword had cut a wound deep inside her as well, in the most sacred of spaces, where, unless we could help her, it would fester for a long time.

"Eleanor," I said, after her mother left my makeshift office in a two-story downtown building. It was the only space this devastated town could offer my team to construct a community center. "Is it okay if I call you Ellie?" I asked.

The girl nodded, but she had yet to speak a word, other

than when her mother said she'd be right outside the door, and then the girl had simply said:

"I'll be fine, Mom, really."

Despite her blond hair and blue eyes, the clear white skin, she reminded me a bit of my daughters back in Columbus. My oldest was only a year younger than her, and from what the girl's mother had said over the course of our initial phone conversations, Ellie Frame and my oldest daughter both shared a devotion to their friends. "She has a lot of friends," her mother had said, and then started to tell me about the girls who had made up her daughter's circle before she suddenly went quiet. *"Had,"* she corrected herself a moment later, sounding embarrassed. "She's lost the best of them, as well as her boyfriend." And I had promised that I'd do my best to help, however I could.

On the outside, Ellie looked fine. She was still taking care of herself, washing her face, doing her hair, selecting clothes that weren't the sort she could hide inside of. Sometimes, people who are disturbed fail to maintain even the basics of caring for themselves. Where she wasn't fine was in her silences, and in her eyes, which told a different story. I knew she'd taken refuge far back inside herself, as though her body were a cave. You could see her peering out of those eyes with fear and uncertainty. When she looked up from her lap to say, "I'm fine," her eyes betrayed her.

"I'm Dr. Arroyo," I said. "But please call me Eva."

"Eva," she said, testing the name, nodding slightly.

"Your mother told me your story, Ellie," I said, "but I don't believe anyone can know our stories as well as we can. Our stories belong to us and us alone, and others will always have a different understanding of us, even the people who love us. So. I'm wondering if you'd like to tell me *your* story yourself?"

She squinted then, as if she didn't understand what I was asking, but she sat back in her chair, rather than slumping. "I don't have a story," she said, shaking her head. Just that. She didn't even ask me to clarify.

"I could start with what I know from your mother," I said, "if that's okay?"

She pursed her lips, but nodded. This was how her spirit was responding to what happened, I realized then. She was letting the world move around her now, instead of moving within the world.

So I began to tell her story to her, based on what I'd already been told, beginning not with the day of the outbreak but with other details her mother had provided. About her past. About the daily rituals of her previous existence. The fact that she was about to graduate, that she was the editor of her yearbook, that she loved writing stories and taking photos for the school newspaper, that she and her friends had spent the last three years planning to attend the same college so they could stay together after high school, and that she was in love with Noah Cady, a self-described geek for video games and comic books, who was also a member of the soccer team. I told her I knew she planned to pursue photojournalism in college, and that she'd been awarded a partial scholarship. "Your favorite photographer is Steve McCurry," I added at the end, "who's known for the *Afghan Girl* photo made famous in *National Geographic,* and who's best known for saying about photography and storytelling that—"

" 'If you wait,' " Ellie interrupted, " 'people will forget your camera and the soul will drift up into view.' "

"Yes," I said, smiling, glad that she'd decided to join my version of her story with a bit of her own. It was a good sign: she was still in possession of herself, even if her grasp of that wasn't steady. "I've always loved that quote. What draws you to it?"

She looked just past my shoulder, as if she'd seen something through the window behind me, though I knew there was nothing to see out there but broken concrete, twisted metal, and the remains of a vehicle still wrapped around a telephone pole, waiting to be hauled away to a salvage yard. I wondered if this looking away was normal behavior for her, or if it was an avoidance tactic that had only started since the disaster. Finally, though, still without meeting my eyes, she answered.

"It's about people, I guess," she said. "I mean, it's how I've always felt since I started taking pictures and writing. That there are ways to really see people, to connect with them in a way that allows you to see their real selves. To witness their most vulnerable feelings. Taking pictures and writing does that for me."

"So you are the real deal," I told her, and she swung her gaze back, suddenly at attention.

"What do you mean?" she asked, looking suspicious, entwining one of her fingers with a lock of hair that lay across her shoulder.

"I mean that you aspire to be a real artist. Taking pictures and writing stories for you are meaningful activities, not just hobbies. You do them because you're driven to, not just because they're fun. Right?"

"That's right," she said, not breaking away. Finally, I had her in the room with me, not floating somewhere between past and present, between here and wherever else her occupied mind kept going to.

"And have you been taking pictures or writing any stories lately?" I asked.

She was silent for a long time after that question. "No," she eventually said. "I haven't felt up to it."

"I can understand that," I said slowly, and I could.

"I guess," she started, "I guess I've just not been myself lately. I've been, I don't know . . . distracted."

"By what's happened here, surely," I said, assuming that her reason would be the most likely one, the one in which she described how scattered she'd been since discovering her friends had died in the school without her, and how attempting to go to their funerals had proven to be too much, too soon.

She shook her head, though, said no. And then the answer she gave surprised me.

"I've been distracted by a ghost," she said, her voice weakening a little on the last word.

"A ghost?" I said, trying not to betray any feelings I might have on that subject, so that she could continue to speak freely.

"Timothy Barlow's ghost," she said. "He was the boy who lived next door to us."

"I've heard his name," I said. "I've heard his story."

"The story about how he died?" Ellie said, looking at me, and I nodded for her to continue. "Yeah, well, like you said. No one can understand your own story like you do. But right now I can say with confidence that Timothy Barlow isn't dead. Or at least he's not all the way dead, the way people think he is. I've seen him four or five times in the last few weeks."

I asked for more information, and she continued to elaborate, guardedly. Were there patterns to when or where she saw him? Just the area surrounding his house, but mostly on the back deck, when he was listening to music. Did she have any interactions with him? Yes, she'd gone up and spoken with him on the day of the two funerals. None of this really surprised me. People who have lost loved ones—even those whose deaths weren't unexpected—often report hearing or seeing the person for weeks, months, sometimes years, after they've died. I told Ellie all of this, trying to reassure her that what she was experiencing wasn't unnatural.

"I kind of thought the same thing," she said, nodding in an almost agitated way. "But then something else happened that day. At Becca's services. Her mother was trying to calm me down, because I'd started crying so hard, and while she was hugging me, she told me that she's seen Becca almost every night since the outbreak."

"So she's been confronted by her own grief as well," I said.

"Yes," Ellie said, "but no. I mean. Here's the thing that keeps getting to me. The thing that won't let me sleep. I've thought about it, and it makes sense for Becca's mom to see her. Becca's her daughter; that kind of bond is supposed to be strong. But I'm going to say something that might make you think I'm a terrible person. And I have to do it because it's the only way to explain why it doesn't make sense for me to see Timothy Barlow. I mean, I feel bad for him and his family, I do. I feel bad for everyone right now. But the idea of being haunted by someone seems like it only makes sense if it's someone you had a super-intense relationship with. A relationship that you can't accept is gone. And I'm sorry, but for me that wasn't Timothy Barlow."

"I understand what you're saying," I said. And I confess, in that moment, talking to her about ghosts, I couldn't help but think about my daughters back home, and about the child who had come before both of them: a son I brought into this world when I was just twenty-three, married for only a year. He'd lived for five months until the night he suddenly stopped breathing.

I could suddenly feel tears behind my eyes, as fresh as if it were that day again, over two decades ago. I put my fingers to my temples to rub them a little. That time—the time that came after his death—was the worst in my life. For nearly a year afterward, I would wake each night, hearing him cry, calling to me. And then I'd stumble out of bed and down the hallway, only to find his crib empty in a room I could not bring myself to touch after his death. It eventually came between my first husband and me, my inability to move on, my belief that our child was still with us in spirit. A year and a half after his passing, we divorced, and it was only then that I entered into therapy, as well as into college, and decided to study psychology.

"I also understand how you feel," I simply told Ellie now, after I pulled myself back into the time and space we shared.

"You have a place inside you that has been hurt. Or maybe *destroyed* is how it might feel. A gone away place. A place you must heal. A place you must fill again. There are only two ways to do this that I know of. One is to remember the story you were a part of before the place inside you was destroyed, and begin to live within that story again. Or, if that doesn't seem possible, you must start a new story to live within. And the only way to do either of these is to begin talking. To begin telling your story, even if you're unsure of it at the beginning."

"Tell my story?" she asked, with her head beginning to tilt to one side, curious.

"Yes," I said. "Tell it as many times as you have to. To me. To your mother. To your father. To whoever you want to tell it to, really. You're existing without a story at the moment. Or you're existing in a story that no longer makes any sense. Without a story to live within, life feels meaningless, without purpose. It isn't where you want to stay for very long, I think, that gone away place."

"Where else is there?" she asked.

"Here," I said, looking around the room. "I know it's not much, but I think it's a start, don't you?"

7

The Last Will and Testament of Ellie Frame, cont.

Mom was quiet when I came out of Dr. Arroyo's office. I found her sitting in the makeshift waiting room of what used to be an empty storefront in downtown Newfoundland. The building had been vacant for as long as I could remember, and I couldn't help but think now how weird it was that a vacant building was one of the few to survive, as if the tornadoes had known there was no life inside it and ignored it.

"Everything okay?" Mom asked as she got up from one of the folding chairs Dr. Arroyo or her assistants had arranged against the bare wall, trying to make the front of the place feel more like a lobby than an empty store.

"Yep," I said, nodding, and just then Dr. Arroyo appeared in the doorway behind me.

"Thanks for bringing Ellie in to see me, Patty," Dr. Arroyo said. "She's a fine young woman. Very intelligent, just like you said." I blushed and looked away from both of them, focused on a corner of the floor opposite to where we stood. Being talked about in the third person only made me feel like more of a troubled person than I wanted to be, especially after I'd had a decent conversation with Dr. Arroyo. I half expected them to start pantomiming *call me* gestures while I wasn't looking. But when I turned back, they were both just watching me, as if waiting for me to join the discussion, which had moved on to some of the community programs Dr. Arroyo was organizing. To pool physical resources, she said, but also to pool emotional resources. She wanted to hold a community wake at the Newfoundland Lighthouse, she said, where everyone could come together.

The place where Noah and I had come together. The place where I'd watched everything fall apart.

I snagged on to the mention of the lighthouse and couldn't make sense of anything Dr. Arroyo said afterward. Eventually, though, when I realized she'd stopped talking, I pulled myself together again and told her, "Thanks for everything you said in there." And that was sincere. I appreciated her way of seeing things. Especially because she didn't make me feel like a head case for telling her I'd seen a ghost.

"I'm looking forward to hearing the stories you might tell in the future," she said as Mom and I headed for the exit. "And remember, you can see me anytime you want. Just give me a call."

I nodded, giving a brief smile while Mom thanked her again, saying we'd be in touch. Then we walked out the front door and into the daylight shining down on the ruins of Newfoundland.

It felt wrong somehow, I thought as we picked our way down the street, literally walking along the yellow line in the center of it, since the area was still not open to through traffic. The bright light, the huge white clouds drifting like dreamy islands through the watercolor-blue sky. It felt so wrong to have such beautiful weather above, while below, everything was gray and brown and broken.

As we were turning up the street where Mom had parked the car, I saw a flicker of light in the air. Possibly just a sunbeam bouncing off broken glass. But where it reflected was what stopped me cold.

My school. The school where they had all died. It was like the photographs you see online of war-torn cities, the building just a shell of itself. Half of it still there, the other half a pile of blackened rubble, exposing pipes and beams, the remains of the hallway that joined the west and the east wings together. If I squinted hard enough, I could almost see where the trophy case for Newfoundland High School sports teams once hung on a wall that was no longer there.

The area had been taped off, but at this point some of the tape had fallen and now lay across the glass-littered ground. At the curbside, a pile of flowers, stuffed animals, and teddy bears had started to grow, brought down here by mothers and fathers and grandparents, by neighbors and friends, by classmates who had survived that day. People who, unlike me, had been there with everyone. People who weren't safe inside a lighthouse on a hillside, watching while others' lives were taken from them.

"Honey?" Mom said, and I blinked, then looked back to where she stood waiting for me. "I'm sorry," she said. "We shouldn't have come this way."

"I want to look at it," I said, surprising myself even as I said those words. "I need to see it."

"Well," she said, a hesitant tone edging into her voice.

"Alone," I said. "Don't worry. I'll be fine. You'll be able to see me."

She nodded, biting her bottom lip like I do whenever I'm anxious. "Okay," she said. And then, after a moment, she said it again, as if she were trying to convince herself of it. "Okay."

I reassured her and then left her clutching her purse at the corner, a sentinel watching my every step.

What I hadn't told her was that I didn't just need to see the remains of the school. I needed to know if *he* was there. Lingering, maybe. Confused, like poor Timothy, not even aware of his death. If I found him like that, it would explain why he hadn't come to me. I hadn't thought beyond that imagined moment. But as I picked my way across the rubble and came as close to the ruins as I could without crossing the yellow tape, I thought for one long moment that I could feel him in there. His spirit. Waiting for me to find him.

"Noah," I said. Whispered, really. "Are you here?"

I closed my eyes and thought of his voice, the sweet rasp of it, and the way he'd turn when I called to him in the hallway with a smile that always managed to make me happy, even on my worst days. A test I hadn't done well on, an argument

I'd had with my mom or dad. Nothing could stand up to that smile. It crushed everything bad around me. I needed to see it now, more than ever. I needed it so I could smile back, the first smile I hadn't faked since the outbreak.

A breeze picked up, lifting my hair from my shoulders a little, stirring dust and grit on the ground around my feet. But as I opened my eyes, nothing more than that happened. No one emerged from the shadows of the ruins.

I stayed for a little longer, hoping as hard as I could. But eventually, I turned, saw my mom still waiting patiently in the distance where I'd left her, and made my way back to her.

On the way home, Mom acted funny. She was tight-lipped, facing forward, never looking over at me, not trying to spur any conversation between us. This wasn't like her. Even before the outbreak, she was the sort of mom who was always playing twenty questions. *What happened at school today? How is the yearbook coming? How's Noah? Did you tell Becca she could come over for dinner this Saturday?* That sort of thing. And in the weeks after the outbreak, she'd hovered and chattered even more than usual. I didn't blame her. I knew she was worried about me. Dad was worried about me, too. People from school I hadn't talked to in weeks were worried about me. Even I was worried about me. But when my mom went silent that afternoon, I started to worry about her instead.

At home, she started cleaning up rooms that she'd already cleaned that morning. And then she began to pick her way through each of our hampers, despite having finished the majority of the laundry the night before. She was scavenging for distractions, I realized, and when she took out a can of furniture polish from a cupboard, I said, "Mom, what's the matter?"

She looked up and, wide-eyed, said, "What do you mean?"

"None of this stuff needs to be done," I pointed out. "You dusted in here already. And you haven't said a word since we left downtown. Something's wrong. Go on. You can say it. What? Did Dr. Arroyo tell you I was a lost cause or something?"

Mom put the furniture polish back in the cupboard and turned to me, clasping her hands together in front of her waist, closing her eyes, and sighing. I started to think I'd hit on the truth there, and for a moment my worrying turned away from Mom and back to myself. *Was I a lost cause?*

"Just the opposite," she said, opening her eyes, giving me a weak smile. "Dr. Arroyo didn't say anything. You could see that for yourself. You were there."

"So," I said, "isn't that a good thing?"

"I hope so," Mom said. "It's just that, well, she either thinks you're going to be fine and I don't need to know anything, or else . . ."

"Or else she just doesn't know what to do for me yet?" I offered.

Mom closed her eyes again, and tears trailed down her cheeks suddenly. That's when I realized why she seemed so worried. She wasn't upset by anything Dr. Arroyo may have said or not said. She was upset because *she* didn't know how to help me.

I went to her and hugged her, I told her not to worry. I told her that I liked meeting Dr. Arroyo. I told her that she'd given me a different way to look at things. "I'm not really fine," I grudgingly admitted. "But I think maybe I can see a way to move forward through all of this at some point."

"Oh my God," Mom said, letting me hold some of her weight up for her, her arms squeezing me tight. "That is so good to hear, Ellie."

"What's good to hear?" I asked, pulling back to look at her face, all of the muscles in it starting to relax a little. "That I think I'll eventually be fine?"

"No," Mom said, smiling weakly as she shook her head and pushed a lock of hair away from my face. "It's good to hear you finally admit that you're not fine."

I didn't tell Mom that I hadn't shared absolutely everything I'd been experiencing with Dr. Arroyo. I hadn't told Mom about everything, either. She didn't know I'd been seeing Timothy's ghost. And she didn't know that every night, when she and Dad fell asleep, I lay awake, staring up at my ceiling, trying to replay every second, every detail from the day of the outbreak—from what I pulled out of my closet that morning until the moment I saw the tanker fly out of nowhere and hit the west wing of the school like a missile. I'd fallen backward and hit my head on the stone floor of the lighthouse. And I'd blacked out for a couple of hours afterward. But I was starting to remember things. Feelings. Realizations I'd had in the moment that I instinctively wanted to unrealize, like a movie on

79

rewind, until the event hadn't occurred at all. I spent my nights like that, replaying and rewinding, trying to understand, trying to take it all back. The stupid fight. The name-calling. The idiotic drama of feeling jealousy toward Ingrid, a girl who had nothing, just because Noah cared about her.

I didn't want to be me, not how I was that day. But it seemed like the only impression I had left of myself. I couldn't see any other part of myself but *her*. That girl. That stupid, selfish girl who should have been with her friends but instead was safe and sound in the lighthouse, nursing her stupid, trivial feelings.

I hadn't told Mom any of that. How small and stupid I'd been. How shallow. How I didn't deserve to have survived while other, more deserving people had lost their lives.

I also hadn't told Dr. Arroyo something else about Timothy's ghost. I could tell from the way she had talked about ghosts that she saw them as metaphors, strong memories that had taken on a life of their own, at least for the person who felt haunted. It was the same way my English teacher, Mrs. Hammond, talked about ghosts that appeared in a book or a play. They weren't real. They felt real to the characters they spoke to, but they were really there to move a plot forward, and they were always a metaphor for something else. For something the haunted person needed or desired.

So I hadn't told Dr. Arroyo the one thing that actually proved, at least to me, that Timothy's ghost was real and not just a figment of my imagination come to life out of despair and grief. I hadn't told Dr. Arroyo that I'd seen Timothy Barlow bouncing a basketball on his back deck before I even knew who was dead and who wasn't.

Timothy Barlow died in my high school that morning, but I hadn't known that, and I'd still seen him.

I couldn't tell Dr. Arroyo or my mom or dad or anyone, except maybe Becca's mother, something like that. It would only serve to make my mom more upset than she already was, and Dr. Arroyo would probably say I needed more intensive intervention. Clearly, she'd say, I was having auditory and visual hallucinations. Clearly, I'd had a psychotic break. That's probably what I would have thought before the outbreak, too.

So I left Mom downstairs to continue distracting herself with her unnecessary cleaning efforts and went up to my room, letting her feel relieved about me for the first time in weeks.

I sat on my bed but didn't look out my window for fear that Timothy would be out there waiting, as if he knew I'd been talking about him to Dr. Arroyo. Not that him knowing something like that would matter. From what I could tell, Timothy didn't even know he was dead. He just kept on living, at least in his own mind, seemingly impervious to the reality of his circumstances.

Across my room, my laptop was open, its screen blank with sleep. Next to it was a flash drive I hadn't touched in weeks. A flash drive that contained all the contents for the school yearbook. That is, all the contents except for a few remaining senior wills—of the members of the yearbook staff itself—that we were planning to record for the digital edition. We'd left ours for last, and now I couldn't bring myself to open the files, knowing our words would never be recorded like the rest of our classmates' had.

Not that I even knew what would happen with the yearbook, now that nothing in Newfoundland was certain. The rest of the school year had been canceled after our town had been declared a disaster zone, and besides, we really had only a few weeks left. There was talk of a belated graduation ceremony for the surviving seniors, but according to Mom, there was pushback from various people who thought it in bad taste to proceed with one, out of consideration for the parents of the dead. I agreed with those pushing back, whoever they were.

We surviving seniors didn't need a graduation ceremony to feel like we'd moved on to the next big phase in our lives. The outbreak had marked that change for us. And that mark would never leave us.

I got up and went over to my desk, stroked the red flash drive with the tip of one finger, wishing I could go back in time and record Becca's and Noah's and Adrienne's and Rose's senior-will videos. Regret and guilt. Those were the two feelings my entire existence revolved around, and I didn't know how to put either one to rest. I didn't know if there was even a real way to do that. According to Dr. Arroyo, there was, and I wanted to believe her. But knowing that a way forward exists and knowing the way itself are two different things.

I took last year's yearbook off my shelf, lay down on my bed with it open in front of me, and started to page through the junior-class pictures, stopping to look at the photos of my smiling friends. They were good photos, of course, but they were school photos. Nothing like the kind of photos Steve McCurry meant when he'd said, "If you wait, people will forget your camera and the soul will drift up into view." These were photos staged to capture the kind of smile every parent expects their children to have in a school yearbook. But they weren't *real*. These weren't how I knew my friends. My God, looking at Becca's fake smile, you'd never know how suffocated she felt by her family, by her mom. You'd never know this was a girl who couldn't wait to graduate so she could leave home and Newfoundland forever. Her soul wasn't in these pictures.

I heard the slow and brassy notes of a saxophone just then as I was looking at Becca's picture, and knew that Timothy Barlow had come to haunt me after all. I wasn't disturbed or frightened by his appearances; he wasn't a threat to me. He was just hanging around, clueless.

I didn't get up to go to the window right away, deciding instead to see if he'd stop and go away if no one came around to pay him attention. But after a few minutes, as the jazzy saxophone notes kept slipping through my open window, it became clear he wasn't going to stop.

What would Dr. Arroyo do, I wondered, if I showed her the truth of what I'd been experiencing?

I got up from my bed, leaving the yearbook pages to flutter behind me, and went to my window. Timothy was on his back deck, leaning into his saxophone, playing a slow song with a sad and winding rhythm. I felt my front pocket to make sure I had my phone on me, and then I went downstairs, where Mom was vacuuming the living room and didn't notice me leaving by the back door as I carefully closed it behind me.

I walked slowly across the backyard to the Barlows' house,

cautiously fingering the cell phone in my pocket, unsure if I was maybe somehow wrong for doing what I planned. But I needed to know if it was possible. For myself, for my sanity, for evidence, if it ever became necessary. So I recommitted myself to my initial impulse and didn't waver from my path.

Up the steps I went, one, two, three, until I was on the Barlows' back deck, standing behind Timothy, who faced the sliding back door of the house, watching his reflection in the glass, as if he were practicing to look cool and sexy at his next jazz recital. And when he eventually spun around and saw me there with him, lips still locked on the saxophone, his eyes went wide and he removed the sax from his mouth immediately, running the fingers of his free hand through his shaggy hair.

"Oh hey, Ellie," he said, voice cracking. "I didn't see you there. What's up?"

"Nothing," I said, trying to sound normal. "I just heard you playing and thought I'd come over to listen."

"Oh," he said, smiling awkwardly. "I wasn't bothering you, was I?"

"You weren't," I said. "I like to hear you play. In fact, I was thinking of doing a profile on you for the yearbook, for our digital edition. You know, get a video recording of you playing, maybe a short interview? What do you think?"

"Me?" he asked, blinking in disbelief. "You should do something on Matt Bauer. He's a senior, after all."

"We still need content on the junior and sophomore classes, too," I said. "Come on. Please? I think it'd be great."

He thought about it for a few seconds, then finally broke

into a smile, saying, "Okay, sure. Why not? How should we do it?"

"I have my phone with me," I offered, slipping it out of the front pocket of my jeans, clicking the camera on, and holding it up so that he fit within its frame. "We can do it just like this."

But over the next few minutes, while I asked him a handful of profile questions, recording his answers, I didn't see anything on the screen of my phone other than the Barlows' sliding glass door, with my own image reflected in it. I asked for his full name, his birth date and age, how he wanted to spend his senior year, how he first got into playing the saxophone, and if he had any special plans for his music after high school. All of that took no more than three or four minutes, and by the time I'd finished with my impromptu line of questioning, I still couldn't see Timothy on my phone's camera. I sighed, both frustrated and disappointed that this wasn't working. But then again, I don't know what I'd been expecting. Some kind of movie hocus-pocus?

"What date is it today?" I finally asked, scrambling for more questions to keep him talking, hoping that I would at least be able to capture his voice if not his image. And though the question was lame, since my phone had a time stamp on it, and though Timothy revealed how lame he thought it was by raising his eyebrows, he answered me.

"Um," he said, thinking about it a little. "May fifteenth."

I blinked, and looked up and away from my phone's screen to stare at Timothy for a long moment. May fifteenth was nearly *three weeks ago*. May fifteenth was the day of the outbreak.

May fifteenth was the last day Timothy Barlow had been alive and breathing.

I licked my lips, but I didn't want to call any more attention to myself than I was sure I already had. He was starting to act funny, too, to seem suspicious, and I didn't blame him. I was acting pretty suspicious. So I did what I could to wrap up my false yearbook profile and said, "Great, thanks. Why don't you play that song you were just playing when I came over? Let everyone else have a chance to hear it, too. It was really good. *You're* really good."

"Okay," he said, and then he lifted the saxophone to his lips, launching back into the same jazz melody that had drifted over our backyards, up high enough to slip through my bedroom window and reach me. It was a slow, sad song—something I recognized now, "My Funny Valentine"—and as I listened to him play it again, the sound made me regret having had the idea to come over here to record him to begin with. Every note he played sent a shiver through me, especially after I started to recall some of the song lyrics. The singer imploring the person they love to not change, to stay, to please stay.

But despite my regret for doing this, as I stood there listening, determined to finish my task before leaving Timothy's ghost alone once again, I began to see something on my screen. At first, I thought it was just a thumbprint on the camera lens, but slowly and steadily the blurry spot began to take on a shape and details. It was like watching one of those old Polaroid photographs develop. There was nothing to see of him during our entire interview and then suddenly there he was— Timothy Barlow—swinging his hips slowly to the melancholy tune, his shaggy hair flopping over his forehead into his closed eyes, looking as though no one had ever played that song better than he did. And as far as I was concerned, no one ever had. I was privy to something special, being there to record it. I'd just had to wait for the right moment.

And then I understood: Timothy Barlow was his truest self when he was making music. I was witnessing his soul drift up into view.

When he finished playing, Timothy lowered the saxophone from his lips and looked at me with a satisfied grin, like he'd just scored a touchdown or tossed a winning free throw into the basket with only seconds left in the game.

I wiped a tear from the corner of one eye, and then clicked the camera off on my phone. "That was beautiful, Timothy," I told him. And I meant it.

"Thanks for giving me a chance to play it for your video," Timothy said.

I was about to tell him that it was no problem, that it would make an amazing addition to the yearbook, and that I couldn't wait to hear whatever he'd end up playing someday in the future—not lies, really, so much as momentarily forgetting that Timothy was *dead,* that there was no future for him. But before I could say anything, I saw what looked like snowflakes surrounding his body, even though it was early June. As I continued to stare, though, I realized it wasn't snow falling around Timothy so much as Timothy himself fading into the air around him. Bit by bit, molecule by molecule, until he was just the softly amorphous blur I'd first seen on my phone's camera. And then, all at once, he was drifting up in a swirl, up and up, coalescing one more time to look like Timothy again, laughing as he hovered above me, looking down, and saying, "Ellie! I'm sorry for bothering you, but I have to go now! I have to go home!" And then he shot like a star into the bright blue sky above our houses.

Timothy Barlow had left, finally. And his soul—the soul that had drifted up into view after I'd waited for it to reveal itself—was gone now. Gone home.

8

The Last Will and Testament of Ellie Frame, cont.

After Timothy Barlow's spirit disappeared, all I could think about was Becca. My best friend since kindergarten, the girl who held me as I sobbed after my first real boyfriend broke up with me in the tenth grade. The girl who patiently listened to my constant complaints about Ingrid Mueller being weird to me over the last few months. The girl who always said I looked fantastic on days when I felt sick or sad about something. The girl who gave me one half of a heart-shaped charm that spelled out the words *Best Friends* when you put the pieces together. I'd been wearing the charm every day since the outbreak, reaching to hold it between my thumb and forefinger whenever a memory of one of my friends would surge up out of the dark and set me crying. I'd stroke the letters of my half of the heart, the side that spelled out *Friends,* as if by doing that, I could bring all of them back to life again.

I kept thinking about what Becca's mother had said at the memorial service. How she'd been seeing Becca nearly every night since she died. And because I'd been seeing Timothy Barlow's ghost, I had to wonder if Becca had really been appearing to her mom so regularly. I wondered because I knew with certainty that the person Becca Hendrix wanted to spend the least amount of time with in life had been her mother.

It was no secret to anyone that Becca's mom was domineering, especially when it came to her children. For years, Mrs. Hendrix had been trying to mold Becca into a younger version of herself, dictating the kind of clothes Becca wore, the way she did her hair, the extracurricular groups Becca could join, even the boys Becca could date—if she let her date anyone, which was rare. It's like Mrs. Hendrix saw her and Becca as those nesting dolls that open up to reveal a smaller version of the bigger doll inside. And if Becca didn't fall in line, if she didn't at least pretend to, there was always hell to pay for it.

One time, when we were thirteen, Becca's mom locked her in a closet after Becca confided to the school guidance counselor that Mrs. Hendrix had a drinking problem. Becca told me she'd done it because her mother would sometimes drink heavily at night, and if she drank too much, she'd get mean and start fights with Becca and even with Mr. Hendrix, who always looked away instead of meeting your eyes. Even in his own house, Mr. Hendrix seemed to spend all his time sitting in a reclining chair in the living room, staring at the TV, not seeming to care what was going on around him, as long as he didn't have to talk. The guidance counselor, it turned out, knew Mrs. Hendrix from church and doubted Becca's story. So she asked Mrs.

Hendrix to come in and discuss how to handle "Becca's lying." Mrs. Hendrix had gone straight home and grabbed Becca by her ponytail, called her an ungrateful, worthless slut, no better than her brother, who would never again be welcome in their home. Then she pushed Becca into a closet, locked it, and left her there overnight.

Another time, when we were fifteen, Becca texted me at two in the morning, asking if I'd help her run away. *What's wrong?!?!* I'd asked, and she'd replied, *Everything*.

After twenty minutes of texting back and forth, she eventually told me that her mom had seen her commenting on the Facebook wall of Marcus Benge, the track-star son of the only black family that lived in Newfoundland, congratulating him on going to the state finals. Mrs. Hendrix had come into Becca's room and asked Becca if she was "keen on him," because no daughter of hers would ever be seen with someone like that. She didn't explain what she meant by *someone like that,* but Becca knew; her mother had said racist things before. When Becca argued back, told her that Marcus was her friend, Mrs. Hendrix calmly took Becca's homecoming dress off the back of her door and cut it up with a pair of scissors. Then she made Becca phone Alex Marshall, a boy as meek as Becca's father, who also attended their church, to call off their homecoming plans.

I knew Becca's mom was horrible, but hardly anyone else in Newfoundland did, because she always came across as pleasant, if a bit awkward, in public. It was just me, Adrienne, and Rose who knew the real story. Becca lived in fear of others finding out, especially after she'd reached out to that middle school counselor, and instead of helping, the woman had gone straight to Mrs. Hendrix. After that, Becca trusted only the three of us, and we did the best we could to help her endure whatever her mother was putting her through at any given moment.

That's why I had a hard time believing Becca had been visiting her mother every night since she'd died. Why, I wondered, would she want to see the woman who in life had been her tormenter?

The need to know the answer to that question grew bigger and bigger, taking up more and more space inside me, displacing the days and weeks of anger and guilt and the sheer horror I'd felt up until then for still being alive. For having survived when I should have been in that school with them. The need to know grew so big that, eventually, after I'd bitten my nails down to the quick and started to wear a circular trail into my bedroom carpet from all of my pacing, I knew I'd have to do something.

Which I did. Something that surprised even me.

The only way I could get the answers I wanted, I decided, would be to visit Mrs. Hendrix.

It was nearly mid-June when I finally went to see her. I wasn't exactly sure what I was about to do, but I told myself to be prepared for anything. I walked, even though the roads were clear, so I'd have time to think, to pull myself together.

The Hendrix family lived in a burnt-red, two-story house

that sloped down to one story in the back. Three black-shuttered windows faced the road from the second story, and two windows on the first floor bookended the front door. Mrs. Hendrix had always called their home a saltbox, which I'd eventually learned was an architectural style. But when I was little, it always made me think of a box of saltine crackers. The house was Mrs. Hendrix's pride and joy, one of the oldest homes in Newfoundland. It had belonged to her great-grandparents and was passed down through the generations until it came into her possession.

When I came up to its driveway that day, I stopped to look at the place for a moment, taking in the tall, old maples and oaks that grew around it, casting shadows across the house and yard where Becca and I used to play as kids. The house hadn't been touched during the outbreak, while just one street over, an entire cul-de-sac had been wiped out. Mrs. Hendrix said in a local TV interview that their house being spared was "the will of God," never thinking about what that must sound like to the people just on the other side of the woods behind her.

I made my way up to the front door and knocked, hoping I wouldn't lose my nerve once she answered. I'd already envisioned a scene in which she'd open the door, bring me into the kitchen, and offer me something to drink, after which she'd ask what she could do for me. And instead of telling her the truth, I'd break down crying, which was what I felt like doing most days in general. And I'd say something like how I wasn't sure, that I was just missing Becca and I didn't know who to talk to. Mrs. Hendrix would pat me awkwardly on the back a few times, because she was never a particularly warm person, and then she'd say how hard things were right now for everyone, how she understood, and how I shouldn't cry like that, because Becca wouldn't want that.

Which is close to what actually happened.

The door opened after I'd knocked three times, and there Mrs. Hendrix stood, in faded blue jeans and a pink T-shirt and an apron I knew she wore whenever she was cleaning. The apron had a picture of a black cat licking its paw on the front, and embroidered beneath it were the words *Make it purrty!* Becca and I used to make fun of the apron behind her mom's back, and had developed an entire language around it to crack ourselves up. *Purrfect score! What a great purrsonality. Are you feeling supurrior? Purrhaps, purrhaps!* Or my *purrsonal* favorite, *What a purrvert!*

"Ellie!" Mrs. Hendrix said, looking surprised but in this way that seemed almost excited, almost . . . gleeful. It unnerved me. I hadn't experienced a basic emotion like happiness for the last few weeks, forget about glee. How could she, the mother of a girl who died in the school's collapse, possibly feel something like that? I had a hard time believing it was just because her daughter's best friend was on her doorstep.

"What can I do for you, dear?" she asked, like I'd imagined she would.

So I played my part, too.

"Hi, Mrs. Hendrix," I said, feeling hesitant and awkward. "I was wondering if you might have some time to talk. I've just been . . . I've just been thinking a lot lately . . . about Becca."

Mrs. Hendrix made a face, her lips twisting in concern, then nodded quickly. "I know what you're going through, sweetheart," she said. "It's terrible to lose someone you love. I've been hoping you'd come to see me. Believe me, you don't have to feel alone in all of this. Come in. Let's talk."

After walking me into the kitchen, Mrs. Hendrix turned on her electric teakettle, then brought out a plate of pink, heart-shaped sugar cookies, which she set in front of me as if I were a five-year-old. She even took a moment to stroke the top of my head, making me stiffen a little under her touch, before she turned to go back to the teakettle on her kitchen counter. She was humming some sort of melody as she put tea bags into two mugs and then poured hot water over them after the kettle whistled. And, I swear, she was swaying her hips in time to whatever song she was humming. It was a happy sort of song, like something out of a Disney movie.

With the tea ready, she put my mug down next to the plate of cookies, then sat across from me. She was still smiling, beaming in this odd way. "Let me guess," she said. "You're feeling awful. You're feeling left alone, because Becca and the others are gone. Am I right?"

I nodded, and though I was completely weirded out by the joyful vibe that surrounded her, I found myself fighting off the tears that burned behind my eyes whenever anyone said the names of my friends.

"That's right," I said, my throat clenching as I tried to keep myself together. Mrs. Hendrix must have noticed this and, in yet another moment of strangeness, flashed me an even bigger smile.

"I see your sadness, Ellie," she said. "And I want to tell you, you don't need to feel that way. The people we love aren't

95

gone. They're still here with us. You can even see them, if you want to. If you know how to call for them. If you want them and need them hard enough, they'll come to you. I can guarantee it."

I squinted at her. It was as if she'd gone out of focus, and I needed to narrow my eyes in order to see her more clearly. "Mrs. Hendrix," I said, "you said something to me at the funeral. Something about seeing Becca at night. Is that what you're talking about?"

She had started to nod even before I could finish the question, her already animated gestures seemingly able to grow even more energetic. "It is," she said. "It is. Let me tell you, I had a dark night of the soul in those first few days after the storms, especially after they told me about what happened to Becca." Here she paused to pat her chest several times before going on, unwittingly patting the head of the black cat on her apron. "I thought my heart was going to burst into pieces, it hurt so much. But on the fourth night, after Mr. Hendrix went to bed, I stayed up, crying into one of the couch pillows so I wouldn't wake him, and all I could think as I sobbed was *Becca, I need you. Baby, I need you.* And then suddenly she was there, sitting on the couch."

"Becca?" I said, cocking my head to the side, probably looking incredibly doubtful. After my own experience with Timothy Barlow, though, I had no reason to be a skeptic. I think I just didn't like the idea of Becca coming to see her mother and not me.

Mrs. Hendrix nodded again, then pushed the plate of

heart-shaped cookies closer to me. "Go ahead," she said. "Have one, sweetie."

I took one to be polite, brought it to my mouth to give it a mandatory nibble, but immediately I wanted to gag from the taste of sugar. It was too sweet, and the sweetness felt wrong, considering the topic of our conversation. Still, it seemed to make Mrs. Hendrix happy, because after I'd taken that nibble, she started to tell me about how Becca had sat on the couch in the clothes she'd worn on the day of the outbreak—she would know, considering she kept a constant inventory of Becca's wardrobe—and how Becca had simply asked, "Why are you crying, Mom?" And how after Mrs. Hendrix had gotten past her initial astonishment, Becca had consoled her for more than an hour, rubbing her back while Mrs. Hendrix thanked God over and over for delivering her daughter to her, and how Becca had said, "Shh, Mom, shh. It's okay. I'm here. You don't have to cry anymore. Just calm down. I'm here for you."

I sat there, listening with the unwanted tears starting to fill my eyes, and dropped the heart-shaped cookie onto the table. It broke in half upon hitting the plate, and I began to apologize for my clumsiness, as if that mattered.

"It's nothing," said Mrs. Hendrix. "You're just feeling what I felt when Becca first came to me, that's all. You're shocked. That's natural, Ellie."

I wanted to tell her that wasn't the case. My tears weren't from shock or because of my own sadness at losing Becca. My tears were entirely for Becca, for her somehow being forced to haunt the person who had made her so unhappy in life.

She came around to my side of the table, swept the broken cookie into her palm, then deposited it in a waste bin. Afterward, she turned around with the gleeful expression back on her face and said, "Why don't you try it, Ellie?"

I narrowed my eyes and said, "You mean . . . you mean try calling her?"

Mrs. Hendrix nodded excitedly. "Yes," she said. "She comes to me at night, when Becca's dad is asleep. Why don't you try calling her now? You could go up to her room, if you think that would help. You know, to recall her. To feel how much you miss her. Think of all those nights you two spent up there, over the years, for sleepovers."

I couldn't believe what I was hearing. Was Mrs. Hendrix really offering to let me go into her dead daughter's room so I could attempt to call her up from the beyond, as if she were some kind of genie in a bottle?

For a moment, we just stared at each other "Go *on,* Ellie," she said finally, waving one hand in the air like it was no big thing. "Don't be shy. I know how important Becca was to you."

As she stood there, nodding her encouragement, I realized she wasn't going to budge from the idea. So I slowly scraped my chair back from the table and looked hesitantly at Mrs. Hendrix once more before I passed by her and took the stairs up to the second floor.

⌒

It was strange going up those old steps, each one sounding out its own specific creak under my weight. When we were little, Becca and I used to pretend those stairs were a musical instrument, like a xylophone. She'd play the bottom half while I played the top, and we'd try to figure out how to make music out of them. It never worked. It always sounded like badly done horror-film sound effects, no matter what combination of creaks we tried. And in the end, Mrs. Hendrix usually yelled at us to stop within a few minutes.

Hearing the creaks beneath my steps now, though, I couldn't help but find them more nostalgic than eerie. Which shouldn't have been the case, I thought. I was going up to my best friend's bedroom, where I would attempt to call her ghost to me on her mother's insistence. That *should* have felt eerie. Somehow, though, I wasn't afraid. In fact, I found myself hoping that Mrs. Hendrix's story might even be true. Because right then what I wanted more than anything was to sit down next to Becca, the person I'd shared everything with since as long as I could remember. And just talk as if nothing horrible had happened. As if there hadn't been an outbreak. As if she'd never been taken away.

When I got to the landing, I turned toward Becca's door and reached out, placing my hand on the doorknob for a moment before finally pushing it open. It squealed a little, just like it always had, no matter how often Mr. Hendrix oiled it. And beyond it was Becca's room. The room she hated because she'd been given no say in it. It was still bubble-gum pink, a garish, un-Becca-like stereotypical little girl's room, on Mrs. Hendrix's insistence, and where the walls met the ceiling, a white wallpaper border with curling roses sealed the room off like the lid of a Victorian hatbox.

I moved slowly into the room, closing the door behind me, taking careful steps across the white carpet, as if I might disturb something, even though the floor was clear and everything was in its place, just how Becca would have left it so that her mother wouldn't yell at her for being messy. There were her Academic Challenge trophies from the past three years, lining the top of her desk. There was her collection of Andrew Lang's fairy-tale books on a shelf above her bed's headboard, probably the only things in the room that reflected who Becca was. I'd always thought those books could have set Mrs. Hendrix off, because they were filled with magical happenings. But they'd escaped her notice over the years, probably only because they seemed appropriate for a little girl. There was the handmade quilt Becca's mom had paid an Amish woman to make, using the same pattern of roses on it that lined the walls.

It was awful to be in that room, Becca's pink-and-white prison cell. I could almost smell the suffocating scent of roses coming from the images of them throughout the room, and wrinkled my nose, remembering the time Becca and I had secretly colored a wallpaper rose black with a marker. I'd suggested it. "To stake your claim," I'd told her. Even if it was a secret claim. To make the room hers without her mother ever knowing. The rose was hidden behind the fairy-tale books above her bed. And when I reached up to pull several out, I smiled, seeing the black petals and thorny vine still growing there.

My smile was brief, though, because almost immediately I felt that ragged hole inside my chest start to throb around its edges, and then my breathing started to come quicker and quicker, as if I couldn't take in enough air. Then I was crying, the tears running hot down my cheeks and over my lips, erasing the smile that had just formed a second before.

"Oh, Becca," I said, and my voice came out like the tiny squeal of Mrs. Hendrix's electric teakettle. "Why you? Why you?"

I sat down on the edge of her bed and put my face in my hands, crying harder with each passing moment, unable to stop the memories flickering through my head. Becca flashing a satisfied, wicked grin as she filled in the last wallpaper rose petal with black ink. Becca rocking back and forth on this bed, laughing hysterically, as we invented *purr* jokes and puns about her mother's cleaning apron. Becca's arm around my shoulder as I cried through my first heartbreak, her warm cheek pressed against mine as she whispered to me that everything would be all right. Now I was crying so hard, I could hear myself moan, and I rocked back and forth until the only words that came out of me were "Not you. Not you."

"Yes, me," a voice said quietly, and I looked up, my crying interrupted, to see her kneeling right in front of me. Becca Hendrix. My best friend. The girl who gave me one half of a heart-shaped charm when we were eleven.

"Yes, me," she said again, now that I was looking at her and had gone silent out of shock. "It happened, Ellie. You have to accept that. You have to be okay with it."

I bit my bottom lip and nodded, even though I didn't want to believe what I was seeing, and wiped tears away from my face as I looked at hers, taking in every detail of her because I'd wished so hard after she was gone that I had done that. Just looked at her. Studied her. Not taken anything about her for granted. Not her coils of coppery hair, not her brown eyes or her pale skin patterned with tiny freckles. "I'm trying, Becca," I said. "It's just so hard."

"I know," Becca said. "But you can't just stop like you've been doing, Ellie. You can't freeze up and stop living. You have to keep moving."

"You . . . you've seen me?" I said, blinking, surprised, yet not at all afraid of that idea, either.

Becca put her arms on my legs and took my hands in hers, nodding.

"When?" I asked, still finding it hard to somehow believe her.

"Over the past few weeks," she said. "Some of the others have, too."

I looked up and away from her for a moment, taking in a few quick, deep breaths to stop myself from hyperventilating. When I got myself under control again, I looked back to Becca and whispered, "What do you mean, some of the others?"

"Adrienne," she said, softly, as if the name were sacred and shouldn't be spoken too loudly. "And Rose."

Adrienne and Rose and . . . I could feel my lips trembling with the question I wanted to ask, but I was afraid of the answer. Becca knew what I wanted, though. She could see the truth in my eyes, like always, like I could always see the truth in hers.

"I don't know about Noah," she said gently now, "if that's what you're wondering. I haven't seen him for a while. But I can't help but think that if Rose and I have looked in on you, so has he."

9

The Last Will and Testament of Ellie Frame, cont.

Becca got up and sat next to me on the bed. Knowing that she'd been watching me had turned me into a mess.

Impossibly, I felt her weight beside me. "I don't understand," I said. "How can I feel you sit down like that? How can I feel your hand on my back?"

"I'm in a . . . gray area right now," Becca said.

"A gray area?"

"This whole place. Newfoundland. The area around it. It's thin right now. It's like the boundaries between the living and the dead aren't as strong as they usually would be."

"I don't understand any of this."

"I don't understand much of it, either," confessed Becca. "I've learned some things in the last few weeks, though. Things I can do. Things the *dead* can do, or things that the living can make the dead do. This—us being together like this—is just one of them."

"There's more?"

"Yes," she said, nodding.

And then Becca began to tell me what she'd learned about life after dying.

⁓

"There's a lot I don't know," Becca said, curling up beside me on her bed, our hands resting on each other's hips, foreheads almost touching. Just like how we used to do when I'd spend the night, telling stories and sharing secrets in the dark for hours. It almost felt as if Becca hadn't really died. Because here she was, telling me what she'd learned so far about what the dead can do, saying, "It's all really confusing. But I'll tell you what I've learned since I woke up outside of my body."

There was rubble strewn around her, Becca said. And smoke everywhere, thicker than the thickest fog. She didn't know where she was, but she could hear voices around her at different distances. People moaning. People crying. Names being shouted, and the grind of engines, or something that sounded like engines. Her head hurt, as if she had a migraine, and she remembered looking down and being able to see her hands and forearms through the smoke when she lifted them up. Otherwise, though, it was like she was packed away in a cloud.

"I started to climb out of the wreckage," she said, "and

bumped into someone. It was Rose. I knew because I could smell her perfume, the kind that smells like rose blossoms that her grandmother always sends from Japan for her birthday."

"*Hamanasu,*" I said, remembering. For years, Rose had tried to teach us little bits of Japanese. We used it to speak to each other in code when we were kids, and that seemed cool. And later, after we were in junior high and high school, we tried to learn more because we knew some of the other kids made Rose feel out of place as one of the only Asian American girls in our school of pale midwestern faces.

"That's it," Becca said, nodding. "*Hamanasu.* Wild rose." Becca chuckled then, because Rose was anything but wild. While Becca had to toe a pretty strict line at home, she always found ways to quietly flout her mother's controlling measures. Rose, though? Rose was always the one of our group who wouldn't break any rules, wouldn't test any boundaries. "Anyway," Becca said as her laughter faded.

She told me that they'd been kneeling in front of a wall of lockers, their fingers laced and clasped behind their heads. "All I can remember is kneeling there and people crying, and wondering when it was all going to stop, and then there was this momentary burst of light and heat before everything went dark. A part of me could sense the school collapsing on top of us, and Adrienne and Noah were right there beside us, too. But later, no matter how much Rose and I called for them, we couldn't find them."

I opened my mouth to interrupt Becca then, got one guttural sound out, but failed to form any actual words. Just hearing her say his name, hearing her say he was right there with them, sank a hook into me and pulled at me. Pulled at the jagged, empty space inside me.

Becca touched her forehead against mine, not saying anything at first. And when I didn't manage to say anything after all, she continued with her story.

"After a while we gave up looking," she said. And then they decided they should just walk in one direction, hoping that if they walked long enough, they'd find the end of the cloud of smoke surrounding them. That acrid fog that, for some reason, didn't burn their eyes or make them cough and choke. And that did the trick. Eventually, the smoke thinned and, to their surprise, they found themselves not on a nearby street during the afternoon, but on a hillside with the stars spread out above them, pinpricks sparkling across a clear black night, not too far from the Newfoundland Lighthouse.

They wandered for a while, and saw others from school emerging from the smoky cloud at various places. Timothy Barlow was one of the first people Becca recognized. He came stumbling out of the smoke, landing on his hands and knees, looking up and all around like a lost child.

"I still don't know why he came to me," I interrupted.

"You saw Timothy?" Becca asked. When I nodded, she said, "Probably his mom or dad was calling to him without realizing it—or maybe both of them were—and you were just near enough to tune in to his . . . frequency."

"He seemed really confused," I said, thinking back to my encounters with him. "Like he didn't know that he was dead."

"I think some people are still like that," Becca said. "They're just wandering. Or they're returning to the places that were familiar to them without realizing that's what they're doing." Becca paused for a moment, as if she didn't want to talk about it anymore, and then a change passed over her face. It seemed almost deliberate, like she was changing the subject, because then she grinned. "Ellie, you do know that Timothy had a huge crush on you, right?"

"Stop," I said, shaking my head. Then I felt bad, because I actually *did* know that he'd had a crush on me. I'd always thought it was cute, but had never taken it seriously. He was just my neighbor, two years younger, the kid I'd babysit when he was still too young to stay home alone. "No, you're right," I said a moment later, feeling like I should at least acknowledge the truth of it, especially now that Timothy would never be able to have a crush on anyone ever again. "I knew that. I did know that."

"Thought so," said Becca, still grinning. "It might also have been why he was appearing to you, confused as he was. You were nearby. That makes it easier."

"What about you?" I asked finally, hoping the question wouldn't make Becca close up. "Why are you coming to see your mother every night? I don't get it."

"It's not because I want to," Becca said, looking down and away a little, as if she were ashamed. "It's because . . . it's because of . . . I don't even know how to describe it."

"What?"

"This . . . thing," she said. "This feeling, like there's this rope or something anchored in my gut, and it pulls on me whenever she calls."

"A rope?" I asked.

She looked back up and shrugged. "Something like it. A rope or a line," she said. "I'm not sure, but it feels that way. I think it might be whatever it is that connects people, even after death. All of us. When my mom calls, it's like she pulls so hard on that rope, I have no choice but to come to her. She's so strong, I can't fight her. That's what I meant when I said maybe Timothy's mom and dad were doing that, and that's why you saw him."

"So do you think other people are seeing ghosts," I said, "not just your mom and me?"

Becca looked hesitant at first, but eventually she said, "I'm pretty sure of it, Ellie. They just might not be talking about it. Even your dad has seen a ghost."

"My *dad*?" I said, shaking my head in disbelief. Dan Frame wasn't the sort of guy who believed in such things. "Are you sure?"

Becca nodded, looking down a little again. When she looked up, she said, "I'm sure. Because the ghosts he saw were Rose and me."

"What?" I said, and pulled back a little in shock. I shook my head once, then looked hard at Becca and said, *"How?"*

"It was by chance," Becca said. "It was a few days after the storms, and Rose and I were still getting our bearings. Trying to find our way back to her house. It's not like how it works in the movies, you know. It's not like we can just disappear and reappear anywhere we want to. Well, not like that, at least. And right then we didn't know how to fly yet."

"Fly?" I said, blinking and blinking.

Becca nodded, like this was no big deal.

"Something like that," she continued. "I'm not sure how else to describe it. Once you've been somewhere, you can go there fast, and it feels like flying. And I'm sure, to the living, it does feel like we're just appearing and disappearing out of nowhere. But anyway, we were on foot, and we were trying to find our way back to Rose's house. Which is how we ended up passing your dad's work crew on the road. The line between here and there was almost nonexistent, so . . . he saw us. In fact, I'm pretty sure his whole crew did."

I didn't know what to say to that. How could my dad have seen my friends and not tell me? Was it because he was embarrassed or worried that Mom and I would think he'd lost his senses? Or was he being typical Dan Frame, husband and father, protector of his family? Did he think he was somehow shielding us from this by not talking about it? As I sat there, trying to absorb all of it, Becca continued.

"Your dad and his crew seeing us was different from how it happens with my mom," she said. "My mom . . . her need is strong. I think I was all she had left, after she and my brother stopped talking, and you know she and my dad . . . Well, it's complicated. I can't help but come to her. Especially when she's been drinking, which seems to make her need even stronger. And she's been drinking *every* night. She starts with wine at dinner, moves on to my dad's bourbon after he goes to bed."

"I'm so sorry, Becca," I said, squeezing her forearm.

"I didn't come to you when you called in the first few weeks because your need was . . . well . . . to be honest, Ellie, it was muffled. Or something like that. I could see you, and I could *feel* your need, but it was like you were calling from deep down inside a well or something. Somewhere far away."

"I think I know why," I said, taking a deep breath and sighing. "I was playing a game with myself. A head game. It hurts so much, Becca, everything that's happened, all of you just . . . going away. So I kept telling myself and everyone that I was fine. And I *could* be fine, or at least seem so, if I didn't leave the house or think about any of you for very long. For the first couple of weeks, I thought I actually *was* fine. But when the funerals began, I realized I wasn't."

"I know," Becca said. "I saw what happened at mine. I understand. Don't feel bad about it. And shutting yourself off might have been a good thing."

"Why do you say that?"

"Because," Becca said, "that rope I told you about? Well, we can tug on it, too. The dead. I think we can bring the living over to our side."

"Your side?" I said, repeating the word Becca kept using, the word that made it impossible for me to pretend she wasn't really dead. "You can . . . bring us over?"

"I'm not sure exactly," said Becca. "But I think so. That's why I said that you have to move on. I don't know how long this place will be thin like it is right now. I don't know if it'll ever change back. But there's nothing for you where I am, trust me."

"Are the others okay?"

"Rose is fine," Becca said immediately. "Her father has been doing these rituals they perform in Japan after someone dies. I don't understand what it all is, but Rose does. She never leaves their front porch, and when I've gotten near enough to speak to her, she says she wishes she could let me in the house with her, that it's safe there. Dying changed some people, I think. They don't want to move on, or they're trying to figure out how to stay. Rose and I saw it before we found our parents."

"What about Adrienne?" I said, raising one eyebrow. I'd noticed that Becca hadn't mentioned her yet, and it was starting to feel weird.

"Adrienne," Becca said, looking up to the rose I'd convinced her to black out with a marker all those years ago. "Adrienne's one of the ones who've changed. I think she's with Ingrid Mueller."

"Ingrid *Mueller*?" I said immediately. In all of this time since the outbreak, I hadn't mourned Ingrid Mueller's death. I hadn't felt anything in the last three months before she died but creeped out by her. And before that, a kind of automatic sympathy. "Adrienne never gave Ingrid Mueller the time of day," I said. "Why are they together now?"

Becca turned onto her back to look up at the ceiling. "I don't know for sure. Adrienne's changed, Ellie. She and Ingrid have been acting strange."

"Strange how?" I asked, even though I could tell Becca didn't want to go into any detail.

"I don't know how to explain it, Ellie," she said again, shaking her head back and forth on her pillow. "You think people on your side of things have been having a hard time since the storms? You can't imagine how some of us who died have been taking it."

"I'm sorry, Becca," I said. "I didn't mean . . ."

"I know what you meant, Ellie. It's okay. I don't *want* you to understand how things are on this side of things. Just trust me. If you see Adrienne or Ingrid, don't talk to them. Just look away as if you never saw them."

"What about Noah?" I finally asked.

And Becca rolled back over, her face serious. "You need to forget about him, Ellie," she said. "It's in your best interest. He won't come to you, no matter how hard you call."

I felt the pressure of tears building behind my eyes then, and my bottom lip began to tremble. "But why? Is it because of the fight we had? Is it because . . . Does he hate me?"

Becca stroked the top of my head like her mother had earlier, then shook her head. "No," she said. "Nothing like that. Trust me."

I wanted to ask more, to press her for answers, but I could tell by the look on Becca's face that she wouldn't let any more slip than she had.

"I wish I could leave," Becca said after a while.

"What do you mean?"

"I mean, it's this feeling I have. When my mom calls to me, it's like being tugged at in the center of my body. But there's another feeling, a different kind of calling, and it never stops. I can't tell where it's coming from, but it's like it's telling me to fly away. Except that I can't. It's like I'm anchored to this place, and no matter where I've looked, I can't get past the gray area. Rose and I spent our first few days trying to find a way out, and I thought it was just smoke, but it's not that. It's like there's a gray wall surrounding us."

"Fly away?" I asked, thinking about my last encounter with Timothy Barlow.

"Yeah," said Becca.

"There's something that I should probably tell you, too," I admitted. "I did something. To Timothy Barlow. Something that made him fly away, I think."

"What do you mean?" Becca asked, her eyes narrowing as she studied me.

So I told her how I'd recorded Timothy with my phone, and how afterward he rose up and up until I couldn't see him any longer, seemingly freed from whatever was keeping him here on earth. "The gray area," I said, "or whatever you called it." I told her that I'd done it because I'd wanted proof to show Dr. Arroyo that I wasn't crazy, and that I hadn't expected it would turn out like it did.

A strange look came over Becca's face when I'd finished my story. Her eyes went wide, her jaw tightened a little. "Ellie," she said, "would you do it for me, too? Please?"

I couldn't believe what she was saying. "Didn't you hear what I just told you?" I said. "I have no idea what happened to Timothy. What if I . . . what if I accidentally destroyed him?"

It was something I'd considered ever since I'd recorded Timothy, but I hadn't let myself dwell on it. It was too pain-ful to consider: What if I had caused even more harm to a soul who had already suffered enough? Becca and I had always told each other everything, the whole truth, no matter what. But if I'd known this would be her reaction, that she'd want me to do to her what I'd done to Timothy, I would have made it the first secret I ever kept from her.

"I can't keep on like this, Ellie," Becca said. "I have no idea what's going to happen. I'm being pulled back to my mom every night, and I don't know if I'll ever be free if you don't at least try it. I'll take the chance. Please, Ellie. Do this for me. Do me this one last favor."

Tears spilled down my face, and my throat closed up as I wiped them away. I could feel myself slowly shaking my head at the very idea. I'd just gotten her back. How could I lose her again?

Becca undid her necklace then, taking off her half of our heart-shaped charm. "Please, Ellie," she said again, slipping the charm into my hands and squeezing.

"Okay," I said at last, through my ragged breathing.

Then I took my phone out of my front pocket, and told Becca to think of this as her last will and testament for our unfinished yearbook.

10

The Last Will and Testament of Becca Hendrix

You want me to tell you a story? A story about myself? I'm not really good at stories, Ellie. You know that. I'm even worse at talking about myself. You know that, too.

Okay, okay. I get it. I do. It's for the yearbook. It's for me. It's for whatever I want to leave behind, before everyone forgets about me.

I know you won't forget me, Ellie. I already knew that. You're the bestest friend I ever had.

So. If I'm going to do this, you're going to have to indulge me. Because the story I'm going to tell isn't about just me. It's about my brother. Drew. You remember him, don't you? You used to think he was cute, in a best-friend's-older-brother sort of way.

Sorry, right. I forgot. I need to talk to the camera. Okay, then. Don't worry.

Just keep shooting.

I was nine when my brother, Drew, left home for college. Our parents had us far apart, not because they wanted to but because it's just how things worked out. My mom had several miscarriages between our births, and the doctors had told her the probability that she'd be able to carry another child full term was something around one in a hundred thousand. Not good odds, but my parents kept trying. Mom always told me I stopped moving in the eighth month, and she thought that was it, that I'd died inside her. But a few weeks later, she was holding me in her arms in a hospital room, sobbing, mostly for joy, but also because she and my dad hadn't thought about names. They were trying to avoid becoming attached, since her last few pregnancies hadn't concluded happily. They ended up choosing Rebecca, which Mom once told me means "captivating, to be tied up, a knotted cord." She always said the cord between us could never be severed. I guess that's true, considering how she's still pulling me back to the house to be with her, even though I feel this other tug in the center of my body, as if there's a second cord attached there, pulling me in a different direction, away from this place, away from her and this world.

But back to Drew. When I was growing up, he felt more like an uncle to me than a brother, mainly because of our age difference. He treated me like a little sister, though, believe me. Called me names he knew I hated (brat, carrot-top, short-cake). Tousled my hair whenever he walked past, which I also hated. Bounced a basketball against the wall between our rooms when Mom and Dad weren't home, which I hated more than anything.

Don't get me wrong, though. Drew could be seriously nice, too. For my seventh birthday, he gave me a bicycle he'd bought with money he'd earned mowing lawns and baling hay at nearby farms. He was only sixteen, and when I look back on it, it's hard to believe a teenage boy would do something like that. It's the sort of thing you expect more from your parents.

Above all else, though, beyond being occasionally annoying or generous, Drew was talented. Mom always said, "That boy has the voice of an angel and the hands of God." When he was six, he started playing piano. By the time he was thirteen, he'd been invited to sing with the Cleveland Boys' Choir. Mom had used my aunt Donna's address in Cleveland to get him an audition. It was the only thing I think she ever did that was, you know, kind of illegal. "But I'll do anything," Mom said (to my dad, when he questioned her actions), "to make sure Drew gets what he needs to fulfill his God-given talent." What Drew needed were opportunities, and Mom said opportunities of the artistic kind wouldn't be easily found in Newfoundland.

She probably regrets doing all of that for Drew now. Actually, I know she does. I've heard her say as much a couple of times. At church, when any of her friends ask if she has news from Drew, she'll shake her head, tell them that she's still praying for him. The other time I heard her say she regretted helping him with his musical ability, I was too young to understand what she meant.

I was ten then, and at that point Drew had been away at

college for a year. He was a classical voice and opera major at New York University. He'd received several scholarships—some on the basis of his audition, others academic, and, of course, his financial need—and in the end, the money he was granted covered nearly all of his expenses. He still took a part-time student job on campus, though, to make spending money. I knew all of this despite being uninterested in the lives of college students. I knew because whenever Mom and Dad took me with them to run errands, they'd inevitably see friends from church, who would always ask about Drew, and my parents would beam with pride as they listed his accomplishments. Dad in particular was unable to fill people in on Drew's doings without saying, "My boy's a hard worker. Think of that. Still working a part-time job, even with all of those classes he's taking."

Having spent my entire life hearing my parents describe Drew like he was God's gift to the world, I knew it came as a complete shock when they turned on him. And even worse, when it turned out to be my fault.

It happened on a Sunday the summer after Drew's first year in Manhattan. Drew had been home for just two days, and my parents insisted he come to church, where they had a surprise in store for him. They'd made arrangements with the choir director to have Drew lead the congregation in singing "Amazing Grace" (my mom's favorite song, the very first one she taught Drew how to play on the piano), and of course Drew handled it with his typical humility and ease. I sat in the first pew and smiled so hard, I could feel the skin pull back on my cheeks. It was the first time I felt like I'd really heard my brother sing and was old enough to appreciate it.

Drew was a pretty boy. I could tell that about him even as a little girl. Some of my friends (ahem) had told me they thought he was cute. He had curly brown-blond hair, this nuclear bright smile, green eyes, and skin like porcelain. No wonder my mom poured herself into him. He might as well have been her doppelgänger. He sang like her (though better). He played piano like her (also better). All those years she'd devoted to him, the opportunities she gave him to develop his abilities? That was just like giving things to herself, but pouring them into another vessel.

I'd known all of that about Drew for years. You know, that he and my mom looked alike and how his musical talent set him apart. It was hard in some ways. Sometimes I felt like a shadow on the walls of my house, compared to all the space his legend took up, even after he was gone. My being a good reader who occasionally wrote poems didn't really inspire my mom in the way Drew's music did. And yet it took me a superlong time to put it all together. How Mom really did see herself in Drew. And how that was what drove her pride in him. It all suddenly clicked for me when I watched her in church that day, seeing her beam at the notes he was able to produce and hold.

I spent part of that service holding on to Drew's phone. He'd given it to me when he went up to sing. I guess he'd been checking his text messages because the phone was unlocked, and I started to look through it, curious, hoping I might find a glimmer of what Drew's life away from home looked like. And as I thumbed through his photos, I kept seeing photos of Drew and this other boy, whose name I found out later was Craig. Pictures of Drew and Craig singing karaoke. Pictures of Drew and Craig in the back of a taxi with a couple of other friends. Pictures of Drew and Craig at a park with fountains turned on behind them. Pictures of Drew and Craig sitting on a bench beneath the bough of some kind of flowering tree, the petals framing their faces, their faces turned toward each other, their lips just barely touching.

That last picture stopped me, and the mix of happy surprise and shame for having found it made me gasp aloud. My mom turned to look at me then, in the middle of Drew's song, and saw the phone in my hand, the picture of Drew and Craig kissing right there on the screen. I looked up, afraid at the sight of her eyes widening and her skin tightening around her mouth as she pursed her lips a second later. But all she said was "Give that to me, Becca. You shouldn't look through other people's things. It's rude."

When the service was over and the handshaking and catching up among community friends had finished—when we were all at home again and the picture on the phone hadn't been brought up by anyone yet—I started to think nothing bad might come of it, and began to set the table for our Sunday afternoon meal as usual. I was wrong to think nothing bad would come of it, though, because it was just as I was putting silverware beside the plates that Mom called Drew out of the living room, where he'd been watching football with Dad, to ask him directly, with no gentleness in her tone, if he "had become gay in New York City."

Drew's face fell while my mom's expression was firm. But I did notice her hands trembling at her sides a little as she waited for his answer. And that answer came, matching her directness with a quiet defiance. Drew said, "I didn't become gay in New York City, Mom. I've been gay for as long as I can remember," and I saw a look of utter destruction tear across her face.

You think those tornadoes were something, Ellie? You should have seen how fast Drew's confession leveled the entire foundation of my mother's existence. Everything it once carried—her hopes and dreams bound up in Drew's future— fell in one moment. And all of it, everything about that horrible moment, was because of me.

"I've always been gay," he said once more, after no one responded immediately. I was still standing at the dinner table, clenching the fork I'd been about to lay next to a plate. I knew instinctively that what Drew had admitted would change everything in our lives, but I wasn't exactly sure why. I was ten, okay? I knew what being gay was, but in the same vague way that I understood anything about sex or love at that point. And I knew that, in my parents' house, because of their beliefs, being gay wasn't a good thing to admit. But there was Drew, admitting it. And there were my parents, shocked into silence: my father staring up at the ceiling in his recliner in the living room, as if he'd just noticed a crack that needed to be patched over, my mom staring down at the palms of her hands, which she closed and opened as if she were just discovering the use of her fingers. "I hope that you can still love me," Drew said, trying to bring a human voice back into the room. "Because I still love you, and I want you to love me, all of me, as I am."

My parents still didn't speak. They just kept staring off into various spaces, as if they'd received the news that Drew had been killed in some kind of freak accident. And because

I saw tears starting to fill in Drew's eyes right then, I couldn't hold myself back any longer. I said, "I love you, Drew." And while that made Drew smile at me from across the room as he lifted the back of one hand to wipe at his eyes, it actually made things worse in the end, my saying that.

"Becca," Mom said in the voice she used only for seriously messed-up moments, for when she felt she needed to command everyone in the family like some kind of drill sergeant. "Go to your room. Right now."

"But I want to stay," I said.

And my dad shot out, "Becca, goddamn it, listen to your mother," which set me to crying. I threw the fork down on the plate, ran to my room and slammed the door, then threw myself onto my bed, burying my face in my pillows.

I heard a lot of things afterward, even though my door was closed, even though I was still crying in jags off and on for the next half hour. They weren't good things, and my parents' voices were harsh as they said them.

"Your poor little sister saw those awful pictures on your phone!" I heard my mom say, scandalized. "How dare you?"

"You know that this isn't good, son," I heard my dad say. "This is a sin, what you're doing. What you are. You're going to have to get right with the Lord. He'll fix this for you."

And Drew pleading, asking, "Why can't you see me? Why can't you *see* me?" as if he were a ghost in the room, unable to communicate to the very people whose love he needed at exactly that moment.

And he *was* like a ghost, really. Because on that day, for my parents—who knows, maybe even for Drew—the boy they'd previously known as Drew died.

They gave Drew one chance—one single chance—to take back the change he'd initiated, to undo everything bad, and told him that everything would be okay, that we could all still move forward together, if he would just see a church counselor. Which, of course, Drew refused to do. "I don't need to be fixed," he told them. And as he turned from wounded to "hostile"— as my mother would later put it to friends at church, who were told of the terrible fate that had befallen her son—my mom told him not to darken their doorstep in the future (my mother *actually* said this) unless he was coming home to tell them he'd been momentarily insane and that God had brought him back around to them.

I heard Drew thump past my bedroom door after that, and he was sobbing, which made my own crying jag start up again in sympathy. "Cowardly assholes, ignorant fuckheads," I heard him say through the wall between our rooms. He was packing some clothes into the suitcase he'd brought them in. A few minutes later, my door swung open, and he stood there, face red from crying, eyes swollen. I immediately started to say I was sorry for playing with his phone, but he shushed me a little and said, "I love you so much, Becca. This isn't your fault. Don't ever forget that. I'll see you again someday, okay?"

"Leave her be," my mother said from further down the hallway, and I nodded quickly at Drew so he knew I was making a silent pact with him. I wanted to go with him right then, but I knew that wasn't possible.

"I love you, Drew," I told him one last time, and then he was gone.

The very next day, my mom sat me down when my dad was at work and told me why they had needed to ask Drew to leave. She explained how he was choosing to live in a way that God couldn't approve of, and how it broke her heart to do what she and my dad had done. "But it was necessary, Becca," she said, sniffing away tears. "You understand that, sweetheart, don't you?"

I knew only one thing at that moment, after witnessing what had just gone down with Drew. And that new knowledge was that my parents couldn't be trusted. Not with anything truly meaningful, that is. I made a quick decision not to ever let them know anything they might disagree with, especially if it was something to do with some major part of who I was.

So I looked up at my mom and said, "I understand," and let her squeeze my hand gently, maybe even with affection, for being such an agreeable daughter. And though what I was doing right then and forever after was a matter of protecting myself from them, I hated having to do it. The lie went down my throat, thick and bitter, making me suddenly cough a second later.

"Are you okay, Becca?" Mom asked.

I coughed a little more, nodding. "Just an itch in my throat," I said.

"It's all the pollen," Mom said, nodding. "You're sensitive to it, like me."

I don't think I'd ever heard my mom draw a comparison between us before that day, or at least not in a long while. Long

124

enough not to remember when the last time was. And though I still didn't completely understand why they'd told Drew he was now a stranger to them, I was even more confused when it seemed that my mom had decided, seemingly overnight, to put her remaining energies into me, despite my not having any obvious talent to nurture. For the next eight years of my life, she'd throw herself in regardless, and her support would almost always feel suffocating.

Drew's twenty-six years old now. He sings in the New York Metropolitan Opera Chorus. He has a website with his bio, a list of upcoming events, his résumé, his photos and reviews, and sound clips. For years, I used to visit that site and watch videos of him I'd find on YouTube. I always did this on the school computers, so I didn't have to worry about Mom prying into my search history at home. I'd stare and stare at his contact information for what seemed like hours, wishing I could bring myself to click the email button.

I finally did that, about a year ago. I'd played by my parents' rules until I was sixteen and hadn't contacted Drew, like they'd ordered. At sixteen, though, I was starting to feel like I needed to talk to someone about what I should be doing to make sure I could get out of Newfoundland, and out of Mom and Dad's world, after I graduated. Drew replied to my email within minutes. *Oh my God, Becca,* he said. *I've been waiting so long for this.* He said he knew one day he'd hear from me, he just didn't know when, and he asked me if I was able to talk on the phone without Mom and Dad finding out. If not, then we'd keep talking by email. My whole chest felt like it was going to explode as I read his words—my *brother*'s words on the screen of my phone—and I released that breath only when I called him from the school parking lot after classes were over the next day and heard his voice for the first time in years. I think we both cried for at least five minutes before either of us could say full sentences that made any sense at all.

I'd been talking to Drew every week since then, for the past year, before . . . before, well, you know what happened. I was going to get on a bus to Manhattan a few days after graduation and move in with him. That was my big escape plan.

And now it'll never happen.

I've only seen him once in the past month, since I died. My mom and dad, I'm betting, wouldn't let him attend the funeral. But I felt him a couple of days after the ceremony. It was like the tug I feel in the center of my chest whenever my mom pulls me to her.

When I felt Drew tugging at me, it was a little like that. A tug of desperate need. A need for me to be there with him. And because I could sense it was Drew, I flew to him in an instant.

He was at my grave, in the one cemetery the tornadoes didn't touch when they destroyed Newfoundland. He was wearing a black suit, a white button-down, and a black tie, like he was holding his own private funeral for me. "Oh, Becca," he was saying through his tears as he looked down at my headstone. The words *Beloved Daughter* had been inscribed on it. No mention of *Beloved Sister*. "Oh, Becca, we had so much we needed to do together."

I didn't want to haunt Drew. At least, I didn't want to be forced to haunt him, the way my mother forced me, keeping me around in her typically selfish way. And if I didn't want that kind of entanglement with Drew, I knew I couldn't call out to him, that I shouldn't turn him in my direction. I worried we'd be bound in the way I was bound to my mother, making it that much harder for me to find a way out of this world.

So instead of calling him to me, I flew home and found a photo Dad had taken of me standing proudly next to the bike Drew bought for my seventh birthday. I brought it back to the cemetery, right as he was turning away from my grave. I left the photo on his dashboard, and waited far enough away to watch without being seen as he discovered it.

After his mouth stopped hanging open in shock and after he stopped crying a few moments later, Drew looked around, as if checking to see if there was something unearthly in the car with him. Was his sister a ghost now? Was she there with him, invisible but present, trying to reach out to him? Trying to tell him, "I love you, Drew," one last time? I could see these thoughts on his still-angelic face as he scanned the headstones and then the skirt of the woods surrounding the cemetery.

In the end, he just nodded, the way I'd nodded to him the day my parents threw him out of the house, to let him know I'd find him one day. Drew must have decided right then that he knew how the photo came to him, that he didn't need to see me to believe that I was there. He just propped the photo back up on the dash before leaving.

⌣

You're probably wondering why I'd tell this story when I have only this one chance to leave something of myself behind.

There are so many other stories I could tell, it's true. But that's the story that means the most to me, because it's the one time in my life when I feel like I was a whole person, doing what I wanted, seeking out my brother despite being ordered not to. I didn't care about the potential consequences. Because it was right, and it was true.

I'm telling this story not just for myself, though. I'm telling it for my mom and dad. Make sure they watch this, Ellie. Make sure they watch it all the way through.

My mom and dad named me Rebecca. It means something like "captivating," but it also means to be tied up with a knot, and my mom has managed to make that definition more than true. She's kept me here with her. She's tied me up with so many knots, because she doesn't want to lose her last child, and I don't know how to free myself.

She and my dad do have another child, though. They just refuse to see him. They refuse to cut the cord to me, but now I'm going to do that myself, if what you say is true, Ellie. And what I need them to hear from all of this, my last will and testament, is that if they want to keep any part of me in their hearts after I go on to wherever I'm headed next, they need to find Drew. They need to love him. Because he's the only family left on earth who'll have a piece of my heart after I go away.

If they want to keep me alive in their hearts afterward, too, they need to see this. They need to hear this. And they need to pray that Drew will forgive them.

That's all I have to say. Otherwise, I'm ready to go. And I hope that, whatever happens next, I never have to return to this world.

11

Dan Frame—Ghosts Passing By

The first time I saw them was five or six days after the storms, and I was out with my crew, cutting up fallen trees. It seemed as if at least half of the trees around Newfoundland had snapped like twigs in the high winds of the outbreak, and now they crisscrossed the roads. Each time my crew finished clearing a path, we'd move to a new road and just find more trees waiting to be cut up and thrown off to the side.

It wasn't me who saw the ghosts first. It was Joe, a young guy, maybe nineteen. He was lugging a large wheel of tree trunk to pitch across the ditch into a field, and suddenly he stopped, made this weird sound I can't even imitate. It was like some kind of animal was caught in his throat, scratching and clawing to get out. Joe dropped the chunk of tree, and it bounced once on the pavement before rolling a few inches away. "What? What's *that*?" Joe said to pretty much anyone in hearing distance. So I turned with a couple of other guys to look.

Joe was pointing toward the hayfield he'd been pitching pieces of trees into all morning. And in the middle of that hayfield, we saw two girls walking toward us. There was something wrong with them, but I couldn't understand what, exactly, at the time. Something about them seemed fuzzy, like the outlines of their bodies weren't very defined. I chalked it up to having worked sixteen-hour days for the past week, helping the National Guard clear roads and secure downed power lines. As the girls came nearer, when they were no more than thirty or forty feet away, I finally recognized them as friends of my daughter: Rose Sano and Becca Hendrix. Ellie would be so happy, I thought, knowing they were okay. She'd been so worried about them. But what were they doing out here? It wasn't a good time to be walking around Newfoundland, with all of the storm debris, some of it dangerous, littering the place.

Relieved, I sighed and said, "Rose, Becca! You're safe! Thank God!"

The girls didn't say anything in response, though. They just kept walking through the ankle-high grasses of the field, staring ahead as if they hadn't heard me.

"Rose!" I said as they came even nearer. "Becca!"

But still the girls didn't seem to hear me.

A few moments later, they stepped cautiously down into the ditch near the roadside, then climbed up the other side, where I was standing with the rest of the guys, who had stopped whatever they'd been doing and were now watching openmouthed, same as I was. It was then that the girls paused beside me for a second, and Becca Hendrix looked over at me to say, "We're just trying to get to Rose's house, Mr. Frame." They stood there for a moment longer, staring at me quietly, and it looked like the outlines of their bodies shimmered or wavered, went out of focus.

I shook my head and blinked, rubbed my eyes, and when I looked up, the girls had started walking again, crossed the road, stepped down into the ditch on the other side, then came up into the soybean field on the other end, which I knew was owned by Rose Sano's family.

The Sano house stood in the distance, a white clapboard farmhouse with forest-green trim. From my vantage point, it looked small, more like a cottage than the many-roomed place I knew it was, from various visits over the years when they had Patty and me over for dinner or to play cards on a lazy weekend.

Now, in silence, my crew and I watched the girls head toward the Sano house, and kept watching until they were so far away, they seemed to wink out of existence. *Blip!* Here now, gone the next moment.

After that, I blinked and blinked, rubbed my eyes, looked around at the shocked faces of the men. Young Joe turned to me and said, "I know those girls. They were just two grades below me. They . . . they . . ."

Before he could say what I suspected he was thinking—that he'd seen their names released on one of the casualty lists that were circulating—I looked away from him and at the rest of my crew and said, "Listen up, guys. I'm not sure what we just saw, so maybe we should keep a lid on this until I can check into things. There are . . . there are a lot of legal things we need to pay attention to right now. Legal protocols for disaster-zone maintenance. So I appreciate your cooperation in getting back to work. Can I rest assured that everything that just happened will stay between us for now?"

I was making it all up on the spot, of course. The disaster-zone legal issues, I mean. And I wasn't even sure why. It's not like I had anyone to protect. It's not like anyone had done anything wrong.

But I instinctively wanted to tamp it all down, regardless. To deny what we'd seen. What *I'd* seen. We'd been working too many overtime hours at that point, with barely a chance to eat and sleep in between shifts, that I figured a collective hallucination was, you know, a possibility. And if we'd hallucinated the ghosts of those two girls, I thought the best thing to do was pretend it never happened in the first place. To make it go away.

"It's cool, Dan," one of the guys said. Muttered, really. "No need to worry about us. Right, boys?"

And that was that. Everyone nodded in silence, except Joe, who still looked a bit shaken up by it all as he stared toward the spot in the distance where the ghosts of my daughter's friends had headed.

———

There were more sightings after that first one, of course. Everyone in town would eventually come to know about the hauntings, because you can only see so many ghosts in a short span of time before someone breaks down and says they can't take it anymore. They have to say something. They have to tell someone. They think they're going crazy, and so they decide that they're going to talk to those psychologists or psychiatrists, whichever they are, who the governor sent to Newfoundland to help our community heal. Like the woman my wife took my daughter to see, because Ellie was clearly not coping with the loss of her friends and boyfriend.

The woman I eventually went to see, too, to confess what I'd witnessed on the road that day, as well as a few times after, in other circumstances. Once, the neighbor boy, Timothy Barlow, out on his back deck, knocking on the sliding glass door and calling to his parents. The other time, it was Ellie's boyfriend, Noah, standing just at the edge of the woods in our backyard, hidden in the evening shadows. I blinked, and then his back was to me as he moved into the trees. I saw a number on the back of his shirt, though, right before he disappeared from sight. It was his number from the soccer team. "Lucky number seven, Mr. Frame," he told me once, back when Ellie finally brought him over to have dinner and I was trying to get to know him better. "A winger," he'd explained. That was his position. Someone who comes in from the wings to take care of things. Not so lucky a number after all.

Noah was a good kid. Treated Ellie like gold, from what I could see. I trusted them together. Around him, she seemed to come to life even more than usual, and it reminded me of how Patty and I were together, back when we were kids just getting ready to graduate high school and figure out what to do with the rest of our lives. There's nothing I love more than seeing my little girl happy, and that's what Noah Cady did for her. Made her happy. After he was gone, it was like he took some part of Ellie with him. And no matter how much Patty or I tried to comfort her, to take away her pain, there seemed to be no way to reach her.

The psychologist told me that I shouldn't be concerned about what I'd seen. She said that, under the circumstances, it was completely normal to experience something so extraordinary. She told me it wasn't just me. Others in Newfoundland had been seeing things of this nature, too, she said, and she was trying to figure out a way to organize a group where people might come together to talk, to help one another move through those experiences and back into their regular lives. I nodded, and thanked her for telling me all of that. It truly was a relief to know it wasn't just me. But I'm not one for group therapy, either, I told her, and she nodded and said she understood, and that she'd make sure to let me know about whatever happened, in case I changed my mind.

When I was standing at the door of her makeshift office in the ruins of downtown Newfoundland, about to leave, I paused and looked over my shoulder. "I don't know if you can answer this," I said, "but you talked to my daughter not too long ago. In your opinion, is she okay?"

And the doctor gave me a brief smile before saying, "She is as okay as you are."

That gave me some relief as well, and I thanked her again before leaving.

It wasn't until I came home from work one afternoon, a week or so later, that I realized maybe that doctor had been trying to tell me something else when she said Ellie was as okay as I was. Because when I opened the front door, Ellie was waiting for me in the foyer with her arms crossed, her eyes seeming to spark like blue gas flames, and what she did next was say, "I know what you saw, Dad."

At first, I tried to play it safe, to pretend like I didn't know what she was talking about, but she continued. "Becca and Rose," she said, not moving from her spot in front of me, blocking my way to the kitchen. "You saw them."

I knew right then she'd somehow found me out. And I knew as well that if my daughter was anything like her mother, I'd have to tell her everything—every last detail, down to every single feeling I had in the moment—before she'd let me be, and let me put my days of seeing ghosts behind me.

12

The Last Will and Testament of Ellie Frame, cont.

Before she disappeared—right as she started to develop that strange aura I'd seen around Timothy Barlow's ghost while I recorded him—Becca said, "Oh my God, Ellie. It's so beautiful. So beautiful. You won't believe it."

Then she rose up and up, seemingly passing through the ceiling, passing through the attic and the roof, and I went to her window to watch as she continued to rise up into a sky so blue, no gray wall could ever keep her out of it.

Then Becca was gone, and I was alone in her room again, holding my phone, the camera still running. There was nothing for it to record, though, except for the desk chair where she'd been sitting the moment before. I almost couldn't believe I'd done what she'd asked of me, and for a moment I wished I had refused. Then I felt horrible for having that feeling, because in that last second before she rose up and went to wherever it was she felt she needed to get to, she had smiled with happiness and relief, a smile like I'd never seen her truly wear before.

Reluctantly I turned the phone off and slipped it into my pocket, then carefully put everything in the room back into place so Becca's mom wouldn't see the black rose behind the shelf of fairy-tale books unless someday she decided to pack Becca's things away.

Afterward, I crept down the creaking stairs into the kitchen, where Mrs. Hendrix was sitting at the table, drinking a fresh mug of tea. "Well?" she said, smiling her weirdly excited smile, clearly waiting for me to report in detail on my experience with Becca. "How did things go?"

For a second, I thought about telling her the truth. I thought about telling her how she'd been right. That Becca had come to me. That we'd talked. That it had made me feel better to be able to do that. That it had given me some kind of relief to be able to say goodbye to Becca properly, instead of feeling locked up in my guilt for not having been there with her and the others that day. But also that I'd been able to help Becca find peace. As I stood there, though, looking down at Mrs. Hendrix, knowing that I'd released Becca from her mother and from the gray area Newfoundland had become following the outbreak, I realized Mrs. Hendrix would probably resent my having done that. She'd been calling Becca to her every night for weeks now. Like Becca had said, her mother's need for her was strong. I didn't want to face any reaction Mrs. Hendrix might have after learning that Becca was free of her now.

So instead I said, "I'm sorry, Mrs. Hendrix. It didn't work for me."

She squinted, hearing this, as if she couldn't believe Becca hadn't come to see me, and said, "*Wh-what?* Are you serious?"

"I tried," I said, nodding. "I tried to call her to me like you said. I even tried talking to her as if I believed she was in the room with me. But she never came. I'm sorry. I wish she would have."

I could see Mrs. Hendrix working through all of this information, trying to come up with some kind of reason for why I hadn't been able to call Becca to me like she could. And very quickly, she must have arrived at an explanation for my failure, an explanation that simultaneously made her happy, I could tell, by the return of her blissfully obsessed smile.

"It must be because she'll only come for me," she said, twisting her smile into a sort of pout that made it seem like she felt bad for me, but you know what they say about a mother's love. It's stronger than any other. I could just imagine what she was thinking: *It's because of our special bond, the reason Becca only comes to me.* And while she was right, in a way, I remembered what Becca had said about her name, how it was a braid her mother had knotted around her, to hold her down, to keep her like a pet on a leash. That's a kind of bond, but not the sort Mrs. Hendrix could ever fathom her daughter felt about her.

So I said, "That must be it," and nodded, glad that we could part ways on this note. And when I eventually left a few minutes later, I looked back just once from the end of the driveway. I could hear Mrs. Hendrix calling for Becca. "Becca? Becca, love?" she kept saying. Her voice climbed higher each time Becca didn't come to her. "Becca, where are you, sweetheart?"

Hearing her like that, her voice so full of need, made me feel bad, but my sympathy for Mrs. Hendrix wasn't as strong as my relief for Becca, who had finally been able to fly away, the way she'd wanted to, free as a bird on the wing.

At home, I paced around my room the way I'd done after helping Timothy Barlow's ghost. I kept thinking about my dad. I kept thinking about how Becca said she and Rose had seen him a few days after the outbreak, when he was out with his crew, working overtime to aid in the relief efforts, to clear the roads of trees and downed power lines. He'd seen them. He'd seen the ghosts of two of my best friends, and he hadn't told me.

I wanted to shake him, to scream at him for keeping quiet. But I knew that would just make me a hypocrite. I hadn't told Mom or Dad that I'd seen ghosts, either. I had to remind myself of this as I paced, clenching my fingers into the palms of my hands, my nails digging crescent-shaped red marks into my flesh. I had to remember that anyone who'd seen a ghost might not want others to know. Except, of course, Mrs. Hendrix, who clearly felt seeing Becca made her special. She was, after all, the same woman who claimed that God had turned the tornadoes away from her house in order to protect her. She wasn't the most thoughtful person, obviously, and that's probably why she was the only person in Newfoundland talking about something others hoped no one would ever discover.

So I let my anger go. I shook it off by flicking my fingers

toward the floor, as if my anger were drops of water. And by the time I heard Dad's car pull into the driveway, I was mostly calm again, and I went downstairs to meet him as he came through the front door.

My dad is a big guy. Tall. Broad-shouldered. He has wavy black hair and blue eyes, with just a few recently acquired worry lines radiating from their corners. Sometimes my mom calls him Superman, and based on photos of my dad when he was young, I agree he looks like him, at least a little. He has no awkward Clark Kent features, though—just the Man of Steel swagger. He's the sort of guy who immediately comes to the rescue when he hears someone in trouble. So when I confronted him in the living room before he even had a chance to pull off his work boots, demanding he tell me why he hadn't mentioned seeing Becca and Rose weeks ago, and tears fell down his stubbly cheeks, I gasped. I was horrified to discover that my superhero wasn't invulnerable. That I actually had the power to hurt him.

We talked for a while in the living room, sitting on the couch together. Dad had a hard time looking at me while he told me about the day Rose's and Becca's ghosts cut across the road his crew was working on as they headed toward Rose's house. He seemed almost embarrassed to admit it, as if there was some kind of shame in what had happened. And he admitted that he'd even gone to see Dr. Arroyo about it, because he knew Mom had taken me to visit her, and Mom had told him she was more at ease about how I was doing afterward. "I guess that's how you found out, huh?" he eventually asked.

"What do you mean?" I said.

"Dr. Arroyo," he said. "She told you what I said in her office."

"I haven't seen her in a couple of weeks," I said, not thinking my answer through completely, because Dad looked confused and asked, if not Dr. Arroyo, then who? He hadn't told Mom, so how did I know? Was it one of his crew?

It was time for me to confess some things myself, I realized, especially after Dad had been so open with me. So I told him about Timothy Barlow, and I told him about seeing Becca, too. I didn't tell him every single detail, because I was still having a hard time understanding everything that was happening to me, that was happening to Newfoundland. And I especially had a hard time keeping my thinking straight when Dad turned to me and said, "I saw Timothy and Noah, too."

My skin shivered and my breath caught in my throat when I heard that. My hands began to tremble in my lap, and my face must have looked how I felt, because Dad said, "Ellie, what's the matter? You've turned white as—"

"A ghost," I said for him, still unable to stop my hands from trembling, even though I clasped them together now, trying to hold them steady. After a long pause, I faced him again and said, "You saw him? You saw Noah?"

Dad blinked. "I think it was him," he said. "He was standing at the edge of the woods out back. I didn't get a good look at him, but I saw the seven on the back of his shirt as he walked away, so I figured it was him. Why? Haven't you seen him?"

I shook my head, unable to even say no. My entire body felt as if it were ice or stone at that point. I felt colder and heavier than I had even in the first week or two after the outbreak.

"It might not have been Noah, then," Dad said quickly; he was clearly trying to make me feel better. "I probably didn't see anyone at all that day. It was so fast, more of a flash. Not like when I saw Rose and Becca."

"No," I said, shaking my head again. "It was him."

"How do you know?"

"Because," I said, "Becca told me that others have seen me. That they've kept their distance but have looked in on me."

"Honey," Dad said, putting one of his big hands on my clasped-together hands. "We probably shouldn't mention any of this to your mom. She's already been worn out by all of the volunteer work she's doing at the shelter. I don't want her to worry about us on top of that."

I wasn't able to respond right away, because my mind was still turning over the fact that my dad had seen Noah . . . and I hadn't. Becca had told me not to expect to see him. She wouldn't say why, said I had to trust her. And because it was Becca, I believed her. But now, knowing Dad had seen Noah, I couldn't help but feel betrayed. *Why* not *me*, I kept thinking. *Why won't you let me see you, Noah?*

"Honey?" Dad said.

And I snapped out of my daze, looked back at him, and said, "I don't know if it's a good idea not to tell Mom."

"Why?" Dad asked.

"Because," I said, "you and I have both seen ghosts and didn't tell each other about it. What if Mom has, too? It might actually be a relief for her to know she isn't the only one."

When Mom came home an hour later, Dad and I were both in the living room, sitting on the couch with what must have been the weirdest looks on our faces ever, because Mom's brows immediately went up when she found us staring at her in silence. "Hi," she said, looking confused. "What's up, you two?"

⌒

It was a long night, with what seemed like endless discussion. It turned out my mom actually hadn't seen anything remotely like a ghost, she said, but she'd met a lot of people at the shelter—people who had lost their homes in the outbreak and had no family to take them in afterward—who claimed they'd been seeing the dead, too. "I thought they were just traumatized," she said.

And I said, "Seems like we all are, even more than we thought."

"Yes," Mom agreed. "We are. Some of those folks, Ellie, they've lost *everything*. Loved ones, their homes, *everything*. Some of them have nothing left but the clothes they came in wearing."

I nodded. It's so hard to see outside of your own grief. It's easy to feel as if no one is experiencing the smothering darkness of loss like you are. It was no wonder, really, that my mom was the only person I knew at that point who *hadn't* seen a ghost: she's the one person in my life who, no matter what, seems able to keep a mostly selfless perspective. She could move through her own grief without being blind to others'. She was able to put things in her own life aside in order to help other people get theirs back together.

Suddenly I wished I could be more like her.

Mom was good about hearing everything Dad and I had to tell her, but it was clear she was concerned at the same time. She'd already been worried about me, but in the middle of listening to Dad tell her about what he'd seen, she reached out to take his hand in hers and started to cry a little.

In the end, Mom said, "I don't want what's happened to Newfoundland to happen to my family. We're going to be okay. All of us."

After that, there was a lot of sighing and hugging, and I told myself that I needed to be more like Mom instead of just wishing I was. I told myself that I needed to stop thinking about what I'd lost or why I hadn't seen Noah. I told myself to focus on what still remained: my family, my home, a future.

It was a good realization, but realizations can be fragile when they're still fresh. Which is what happened to mine not even an hour later, when I went upstairs to my room to find the screen of my laptop brightly lit in the dark of my room, with a search engine bar already filled with these words: *Friend Pulling Day*.

I looked around, knowing that someone—the ghost of someone—had been in my room or might even be there still, invisible, not showing themselves, and wanted me to find this.

So I placed the cursor over the magnifying glass icon, and pressed it to search for whatever meaning those words might lead to.

13

The Last Will and Testament of Ellie Frame, cont.

Friend Pulling Day. In Japanese, it's *tomobiki*. On the Japanese calendar, the days of each month that are considered "friend pulling" are clearly marked so that people can decide how to schedule weddings, funerals, and other important events. On a Friend Pulling Day, it's good luck all day, except at noon. You can have a wedding on a Friend Pulling Day, but you should never have a funeral. Why? Because *tomobiki* literally means to pull your friends into the same spirit world or situation you find yourself in. Good for weddings, because you pull your friends into the spirit of love. Bad for funerals, when you could be pulled away from the land of the living and into the land of the dead.

Or into a gray area, I thought as I looked away from the glow of my laptop. Just like Becca said Newfoundland had become after the outbreak.

Rose, I thought. She must have been here. In my house. In my room. Who else would leave me a ready-made search term that, with one click of a button, would lead me to information about a Japanese superstition?

I was about to close my computer when my cell buzzed, notifying me about a new email. I didn't bother looking at my phone and instead opened my email on the laptop, and what I found was a message from Alicia Beckwith, whom I hadn't seen or heard from since Noah's memorial service. Her message came with this subject header:

Newfoundland is now famous for more than tornadoes.

I thought about not even opening it up, which I'd been doing with most emails for weeks at that point, the same way I'd been ignoring text messages from people until they eventually stopped reaching out. But something made me pause. Maybe it was because I'd just been left a cryptic search term from the ghost of my friend, or maybe it was because the subject header itself spiked my interest. Maybe it was both of those things. Whatever the reason or reasons, I decided to open Alicia's email, and what I found inside were three simple sentences:

Guys, look at this. Newfoundland is famous. And you'll never guess what for.

They were followed by a link that swept me away from Alicia Beckwith's email to an article that had been posted earlier on the website of the *Plain Dealer*. "The Haunting of Newfoundland, Ohio" read the headline, and the story that followed was an account of the aftermath of the tornado outbreak, detailing the lives of six Newfoundlanders who claimed they were being haunted by the ghosts of their lost loved ones.

It was a long article—the cover story of the print newspaper, which I drove into Cortland the next morning to pick up at a convenience store. A large photograph of a devastated Newfoundland cemetery took up a quarter of the page. The headstones in the picture leaned toward one another like crooked teeth, and the head of a cherub lay at the base of a marker that had been broken in half like a wafer. I knew that cemetery. It was on the north side of town, near the lighthouse; it was where the Cadys had waited to bury Noah once the cleanup and repairs to the cemetery had been taken care of, and new grave beds could be excavated for those who had died in the outbreak.

The people featured in the article were all anonymous, but if you were a Newfoundlander (and, in particular, a Newfoundlander who paid attention to others), you could easily guess who some of them were. And as I read, I guessed at the identities of three of the interviewees, just by noticing certain details the reporter included.

One, I thought, was our school librarian, Mrs. Sparks. The library was on the east side of the high school, and while some photos I'd seen online showed it looking a wreck—with shelves turned over and books scattered across the floor, their pages fanned open, as if they'd all been shot—it had been mostly untouched by the storm and the explosion. At least, compared to the west wing of the building. The interviewee I thought was Mrs. Sparks was quoted as saying, "I keep hearing their voices.

The kids. The students. They keep asking me questions. Where they can find certain things they need. How to use certain databases. I've tried to ignore them, though it hurts to do that. But as soon as one leaves, I'll open my door and find another one waiting on my doorstep, wanting to ask me a question."

The second one, I thought, was probably Mrs. Hendrix. The woman was quoted as saying, "Every night, my daughter comes to me, and every night, we talk. It's like she hasn't died, not really. She'll sit across the table while I sip my tea, and we'll carry on a conversation as if nothing ever happened. No, I don't feel afraid at all. I feel blessed, actually. Truly blessed. This is a gift from God, to make up for what was taken from me."

Leave it to Mrs. Hendrix, I thought, to make it seem like the creator of the universe had picked her out for special reparations.

And as for the third interviewee: I guessed him to be Mr. Armstrong, the husband of our French teacher. She had reportedly shielded several students with her own body when the tornadoes began to rip the roof off the building. She'd hoped, it seemed, to be able to spare them if the roof were to cave in. In the end, though, they were killed, all of them. And I reasoned this was Mr. Armstrong because, in his section of the article, he was quoted as saying, "My wife speaks another language now, the language she loved most of all. The *language of love,* she used to call it. I don't understand what she's trying to tell me, but I listen and listen, writing down the words I can pick out, and later I try to translate them with a dictionary."

I sat in my car outside the convenience store, shaking my head, feeling both like the privacy of my friends and neighbors had been invaded, and somehow relieved that it wasn't just me. That it wasn't just Dad. That we weren't in the same category of thinking as Mrs. Hendrix, who somehow seemed to gloat over her circumstances while others around her suffered. That we were, weirdly, the normal ones.

I remember driving home that morning from Cortland, after reading the paper in private, and pulling into my driveway, planning to show it to Mom. To put it down on the breakfast table, where she'd be having coffee before taking off for her shift at the shelter. *Here,* I was going to tell her as I put the paper down in front of her. *Look here. There are more than we even thought. More people like Dad and me.* I instinctively wanted to drive the point home to her that sometimes there were no rational reasons for things, and that she'd simply been lucky not to have been haunted. Not to have ghosts knock on the door or sit across the table from her long after their bodies were broken and buried beneath the rubble.

Instead, what I found as I opened the front door was Mom kneeling in front of the television, wiping tears from her cheeks. She looked over her shoulder as I came in and said, "Oh, Ellie, it's worse than we even imagined."

And then, as I looked at the television screen beyond where she knelt on the living room floor, I realized the news of our ghosts had reached even further than the papers.

⌒

For the next hour, Mom and I watched as a local channel ran segments on Newfoundlanders telling their stories. Stories all about hauntings. All ghost stories. The paper from Cleveland was just the first to dig into the wreckage of our community and unearth the strangeness that we'd all been hiding behind closed and broken doors.

They showed footage of our ruined cemeteries, of our half-collapsed high school, of the pile of rubble and pipes and wood that had been our town hall. They showed helicopter views of neighborhoods that had been wiped out completely, as if they'd never existed, and of the places where the woods that wove their way through and around Newfoundland had been reduced to fields of splinters. They showed footage of our funeral home parking lots packed tight with cars. Footage of people crying in shelters and in the housing units the government had erected at the county fairgrounds. And all the while, between these flashing images, they ran interviews with people around town who were being haunted.

Toward the end of the hour-long report, they interviewed Dr. Arroyo, introducing her as a community-trauma specialist. She was sitting in the chair behind the old steel desk in her make-shift office, talking about the hauntings from a psychologist's point of view. Granted, a psychologist who, as the interviewer noted, had been trained in Jungian psychotherapy—which is sort of old-fashioned, according to Mom—but it was that particular philosophy, Dr. Arroyo said, that provided her with the skills a community like ours needed at a time like this.

"I've been speaking with people for weeks now," Dr. Arroyo said, "who claim to be seeing ghosts. Young people, middle-aged people, the elderly. Men and women alike. There is no particular pattern to who is experiencing this phenomenon. It is the community as a whole that is being haunted, and that is not entirely unexpected, if you have studied other communities around the world that have suffered great losses. I have traveled to and have lived within communities that have been destroyed by earthquake, ravaged by tsunami, or affected by environmental disasters. In each of those cases, phenomena such as this are present."

"And what's become of those communities?" the reporter asked next.

"Some have moved on. Some are in the middle of rebuilding. Some are still afflicted many years later, if the community was unable to put itself back together."

"What do you think will become of Newfoundland and the surrounding towns that were hit hard, here in Ohio?" the reporter asked.

For a second, Dr. Arroyo seemed to wince, but then, with a sudden air of conviction, she said, "I believe the people of Newfoundland will be able to move beyond what's occurred here. People here are struggling, but it's still early. And they're already going about repairing various aspects of their lives. In the end, it will be a long process. A long struggle. Only time will tell the final story."

⌣

Only time will tell. Only time will tell. I kept repeating those words in my mind like a mantra, as if they held the key to everything. The secret I'd been trying to uncover. A way to release my friends and family, to release myself and everyone, the dead and the living, from the gray embrace that gripped us. How to release us all from the gray area Newfoundland had become?

Only time would tell. But how long would it take before it gave up the ending to Newfoundland's story? And would it be a happy one, or sad? Would it be something else entirely? Or something in between, maybe, like the gray area we were in now? And if that last possibility turned out to be true, would those who died be cursed to stay here on earth forever, unable to attain whatever kind of heaven might be waiting to receive them? And would it mean that people like my dad and me would be forever haunted?

Only time would tell.

But there might be others who knew something about it. *Rose,* I thought, who'd left me the search terms for Friend Pulling Day. Rose might know what I needed to understand. Becca had alluded to that in our conversation. She'd said that Rose was with her parents, being well protected. What did that even mean? Becca had seemed afraid to tell me certain things, had held back on revealing what she knew of the other side. She'd asked me to trust that there were things I shouldn't know, because if I knew, I might attract the wrong attention.

But maybe I was already attracting the wrong attention. Otherwise, I would never have seen a ghost at all. Or I would hope that I would have at least been able to attract the right attention. Like Noah's.

Where was he? Why wouldn't he show himself to me? The

question continued to linger, especially after my dad told me that he'd seen Noah standing at the edge of the woods behind our backyard. I would have even taken some kind of invisible communication from him. Anything at this point, really. Why wouldn't he brush his hand against my cheek, making me look in his direction? Why wouldn't he whisper something into my ear during a sleepless night, something only I would understand, while I stared across my room at a bookshelf I'd lined with framed photographs of him and me?

Becca might have thought not telling me everything would protect me, but I didn't feel safe at all. Not when, no matter where I was—in my bedroom, in the kitchen, as I drove my car into Cortland to pick up groceries for Mom, walking in those aisles of canned goods and boxes of crackers—I could feel the presence of invisible others surrounding me, their fingertips practically brushing against my arms and shoulders, lifting a lock of my hair for an instant, letting it fall before I could catch sight of them.

No, I thought. Not knowing wasn't a form of protection.

So I decided to visit Rose.

The Sano farm lay on the outskirts of Newfoundland, on an old back road called Messenger Run, which was named after Mrs. Sano's family. My mom always said that the Messengers must have been among the first settlers of Newfoundland, as the farmhouse had looked ancient even when she was a kid, back when my grandparents moved to Newfoundland in the

1960s, when it seemed like it might be the sort of small town to invest in before it grew into a suburb. The Messenger family, Mom said, went back and back in the town library's historical records. The records had probably been lost in the wreckage of the town library, at least the original documents, but hopefully one day they could be resurrected if the librarians had begun to transfer them to electronic files.

The Messenger farmhouse was white with forest-green trim, and it sat behind the wide, arcing loop of a gravel drive. On either side of the driveway, towering pine trees stood like guardians, and surrounding the farmhouse itself were far-ranging fields, where Rose's dad, Mr. Sano, grew soybeans and corn. It was such an old-fashioned kind of place that whenever I'd come over to visit or stay the night as a kid, it felt like stepping back in time. Rose and I would play *Little House on the Prairie* after we'd read the books, because the farmlands surrounding the house seemed straight out of the stories.

Standing before the front porch now, I could still see Rose and me as little girls, playing with dolls I'd brought over, eating the unfamiliar treats her grandmother in Japan would send to her, like green-tea chocolates and moist cakes that tasted like melon. I was always in awe of Rose's life, even though I knew she felt like she didn't fit in because she was one of only a handful of Asian American kids in our town. But to me, it always felt like she had access to another world, a much bigger world beyond our small-town life. During the winter break each school year, she and her parents would fly to Japan to visit her father's family, and each summer, her parents would send her to stay with her aunt Miyuki and uncle Ren, who lived in the house where Rose's father had grown up and still took care of Rose's grandmother. When she was gone, Rose would email and text photos from Ibaraki, the prefecture where her family lived in Japan: Rose standing in the middle of an arched red bridge with a waterfall behind her; Rose wearing a midnight-blue kimono patterned with cherry blossoms, a festival of orange lanterns and men twirling fire sticks in the background; a cooked fish with its silvery scales still on, and small bowls of rice and pickled vegetables surrounding it; Rose with her grandmother standing beside her, smiling, so proud of her American granddaughter, which Rose once told me was how her grandmother would introduce her to the other people in the rural village where they lived: "my American granddaughter."

I saw us up on that front porch, playing, eating treats from faraway Japan, and tears sprang, hot and prickling, into my eyes. I looked away, but wherever I turned, there was another memory waiting for me, and one in particular nearly made me drop to my knees. A memory from just a couple of months ago: Rose and her prom date, Danny Trier, on one side of me, all of us laughing as Rose struggled to pin his boutonniere on. Noah standing beside me, wearing a crisp tuxedo, the boutonniere I'd pinned onto his jacket an hour earlier, at my house, tickling my chin whenever I leaned in to hug him. Mr. Sano and Mrs. Sano taking pictures of us on the lawn, with the towering pine trees behind us. Noah leaning down to whisper, "You're the prettiest girl at the prom," and me saying, "We're not there yet," and him saying, "I'm psychic. Just wait. You'll see once we get there."

"Ellie?" a voice said, freeing me from that moment in time, which threatened to freeze me inside it, like a figure in a snow globe.

I blinked and looked back to the porch, where Rose stood, holding the front door open behind her.

"You found me," she said, smiling down at me, her black hair falling around her shoulders like silk ribbons. "I'm so glad you got my message," she said, pulling the door open wider. "Quick. Come inside where we can be safe."

14

Rose Sano—A Family Spirit

My grandmother once told me that when I was born, she added my name to a list at the shrine in her village, making me into what people in Japan call a "family child." After I died, she told my dad on the phone that I was now a "family spirit." Her voice was frail and shook as she talked. I could hear her because I was standing right next to my dad in the kitchen, leaning in to listen to my grandmother whispering across the airwaves, across the ocean, and across the continent, all the way from her village in Japan to our small town in Ohio.

It was an old tradition, putting a newborn child's name onto a shrine's list. It was supposed to guarantee a person a warm welcome into the afterlife once they have passed on into that space that exists beyond the earthly world. It was my grandmother who taught me that your earthly birth—your incarnation in flesh and blood and bone—makes you into a family child. When you die and shed your earthly condition, you become a family spirit.

After the outbreak, that's what I'd become: a spirit that roamed the old farmhouse I'd lived in from the time I was three years old.

I was lucky, really. From what I could tell, most of us who died in the outbreak had nowhere to go while we waited for the gray area to fade, to allow us to leave this world. Or at least nowhere safe to go to. Becca hid at her house, but it was just another kind of danger, a prison built by her mother. For me, though, I was able to reveal myself to my parents a few days after I found my way back. I was lucky that my dad knew things—things his parents had taught him about how to protect a person who's died, when their spirit is vulnerable to the predators that roam the spirit world, looking for those newly born into it, who have no clue about how things work in the hereafter.

After I died, and as soon as the phones were working again, the first thing my father did was call my grandmother in Japan. *"Okaasan,"* he began in a shaky voice, and then he told her about the outbreak and the horrible fate I'd suffered.

My grandmother is a superstitious woman. The village where she lives—where she grew up and where I'd been born—still follows many of the old ways that most people in Japan had stopped believing in long ago. She had many superstitions, and she taught some of them to me when I went to stay with her and my aunt and uncle over the summer. Never stick your chopsticks straight up in a bowl of rice—that's reserved for funeral ceremonies. Never whistle at night—it will attract the attention of evil spirits. When you see a hearse, hide your thumb in your fist, or one of your parents may die. Don't sleep facing north, or you will have a short life.

So when my grandmother told my dad that I was now a family spirit, his first reaction was to sigh and shake his head. My mom was sitting at the breakfast table in the kitchen with him, her hands wrapped around a mug of green tea. She shrugged as if to say, *Don't argue with her. Let her say whatever she needs to.*

That's generally how my parents had talked about my grandmother for as long as I could remember. "She's old," my mom would say, whenever my dad grew frustrated with my grandmother's superstitions. And my dad would raise his eyebrows and say, "Amy, she doesn't think these things because she's old. She believed these things when she was young, too."

My dad took my mom's shrug as good advice, though, and let my grandmother tell him whatever she wanted to. And most of the things my grandmother told him were instructions he needed to follow to ensure my safety in the spirit world.

He nodded as she talked on and on, saying, "Uhn, uhn," over and over, a grunting sound that meant he was paying attention, like how when Ellie or Becca or Adrienne and I hung out and one of us was telling a story about something that happened to us that day, we'd say, "Uh-huh," a lot as we talked. My dad, of course, was just pretending to listen. "Humor her," my mom always told him, and that's exactly what he was doing as I stood next to him in the kitchen, desperately wishing that, for once in his life, he would listen to my grandmother.

Because I did need protection. I'd realized within the few days as I'd wandered through the Newfoundland countryside that my grandmother had been right.

There were dangers in the afterlife. There were things—I don't even know what to call some of them—that wanted to hurt me. It made me wish I had listened more carefully to my grandmother's old tales—stories of ghosts and demons—whenever I visited her during the summer.

Please, Dad, I kept saying as he brushed off my grandmother's instructions. *Please! Listen to her!*

But of course he couldn't hear me. Not then. Not that early.

It was only after my father actually did something my grandmother had mentioned during that first phone call. It was only after he went over to the family shrine—the *kamidana,* it is called, which means "the god shelf"—and closed its doors, covering it with a piece of white paper afterward, that he and my mother were able to see me.

My grandmother had given us our god shelf. It's a traditional thing in most Japanese houses. She'd brought it with her on her first visit to America, when I was four. I can still remember her unpacking its various parts in our living room, then setting it up on the mantel over our fireplace. It looked like a dollhouse to me, but in a Japanese style. It was a wooden box, really, with shelves that held little statues of foxes, tiny porcelain bowls of rice, and miniature vases with dried cherry blossom twigs poking out of them. Its two doors were always open to display these items, and with those items on its shelves, it reminded me of the shadow boxes my mom sometimes made as a hobby, filling the niches with trinkets that meant something to her.

My grandmother had filled our god shelf with traditional items, as well as some she said we should include since we were so far away from my dad's homeland. One of those items was a rock that could fit in the palm of my hand. It was speckled with some kind of crystal, and my grandmother let me examine it before she placed it into the god shelf, saying, "Rose-*chan,* after I put this into the *kamidana,* you should not touch it." The rock held, she said, a household god that protected our family. And she told my father that when the day came that she died, he should close the doors of the god shelf and cover it with a piece of white paper in order to keep out evil spirits and the spirit of death itself.

As usual, my parents had nodded and smiled, humoring my grandma even then. But in the days that followed the news of my death, my father must have decided to listen to her. For what reason, I couldn't tell. Probably out of nostalgia for the things he remembered from his youth, or maybe out of a lingering sense of family duty. Grief is a powerful emotion. It makes people do things they'd usually never think of. And as I stood watching my dad close the doors of the god shelf on our living room mantel, covering it with the traditional white paper, I felt a strange and powerful feeling of relief wash over me.

"Thank goodness," I said, closing my eyes and sighing.

My father spun around then, his mouth hanging open, eyes wide, and after a moment, said, "Rose. *Rose?* Rose! Amy, come here! Amy!"

My dad had heard and seen me, and when my mom came running downstairs to the living room, she did, too.

It was a surprise to all of us, really. I hadn't expected anything like that to happen. I'd mainly been hiding in the house, waiting for whatever was supposed to happen next, pulling aside the curtains in the windows just a sliver to peek outside from time to time, hoping I wouldn't see any of the strange, shadowy figures I'd seen with Becca as we'd wandered the fields and woods, trying to find our way back home. And I especially hoped I wouldn't see Adrienne and Ingrid.

The last time I'd seen them, Becca and I had come across them by accident, while trying to get back to our houses. Noah had been with them at that point, too, but he seemed shy and somewhat skittish. Adrienne did all of the talking. And she talked *a lot,* fast and rambling, telling me and Becca all sorts of things she and Ingrid were figuring out, now that they were dead. I didn't like some of the things she said. Like how she figured we could, as a group, collectively take over a human dwelling (she used those exact words, which made me shiver), if we wanted to stay on earth. Or how we could feed off the energy of the living. Becca and I had glanced at one another, recognized the fear in each other's eyes. This wasn't our old friend Adrienne. Death had done something to . . . change her.

I'd been hiding in my house ever since, hoping and praying that they wouldn't come looking for me. I didn't want to go back out into that world of shadows and strange beings I had no names for. I wished that I had listened to my grandmother when she tried to tell me about them as a child. Home was safer than anywhere, I figured. And the one time Becca showed up to see me, I told her she should do the same thing, go home, hide, even if it meant she had to put up with her mother. The gray area Newfoundland had become, and everything within it, wasn't safe for innocent spirits.

My dad called my grandmother a second time, after I'd appeared to him, and this time he took notes. After they hung up, he immediately began to do things. He made a paper lantern, painting Japanese characters onto it before hanging it on our front porch. He set up a table next to my bed, and placed things on it, like a candle, a vase of flowers, incense, and a small knife that he found in a box he'd brought with him when we first moved from Japan. He looked up several Buddhist sutras online that my grandmother recommended, and even though he wasn't a priest, he recited them over my bed every night.

I don't know if any of the things my dad did were of any real use, to be honest. But I took some kind of relief in him doing them, all the same. It was like how I felt in life whenever I got sick; it was a relief just to have a doctor suggest different things to make me well again. We were doing *something,* at least, and I felt less lonely being able to see and talk with my parents on occasion.

I made sure to tell Ellie all of this when she found her way to me and I took her up to my room, including how I really wasn't sure whether any of it was a true solution. I didn't want to lie to her. I didn't want to say, *If you do this, you'll be safe.* Or, *If you do that, you can protect yourself.*

Because I was afraid for Ellie. I had come to understand that it's not only the dead who are vulnerable right after their deaths. The living, too, can be affected. Mostly by the grief they feel about the people they've lost. But also because, if anything Adrienne had told us was real, then the dead had the ability to do things to the living. If they knew how to. If they wanted to.

We sat on the edge of my bed and talked for a while, Ellie and I. My parents were gone right then, Dad tending to chores around the farm and Mom running errands in Cortland, so we were able to speak freely. And at a certain point in our conversation, Ellie shared a secret of her own.

"Rose," she said, "I know how to do something, too. Something that could free you from all of this, if you want." And then she went on to describe how she'd freed Timothy Barlow and Becca, just by using the camera on her phone to record them telling a story. She offered to do the same for me, to record my last will and testament, if I wanted.

I sat on the edge of my bed, hands folded in my lap, and thought about it. The possibility was tempting; I didn't *want* to be here, trapped between life and death. But at the same time, I wasn't as afraid as I'd been at the start. No one and no *thing* had come looking for me in all the weeks that had passed since I died, like I'd originally worried would happen. And if my grandmother was correct, there was a period of time that I would have to wait until my spirit could leave this world. Forty-nine days, according to my grandmother. I was counting them eagerly. We were fast approaching the one-month marker since the outbreak, which meant I only had a few more weeks. Since I didn't feel afraid and since being with my parents was a comfort to me, I decided to wait, to see if my grandmother was right.

"But will you come back and check? Just in case?" I asked Ellie, and she nodded.

"Let me know however you can," she said, "if I can help you, Rose."

"I won't leave the house," I promised her. "I don't want to risk running into . . . anything out there."

"But you came to my house," she said. "You typed the words *Friend Pulling Day* into my computer."

"I wanted to see you one last time. And since you weren't there, I decided to leave that message. I knew you'd figure it out," I told her. "But it took a lot to do that. I didn't have Becca with me, and I was so, so afraid. I don't think I can take that kind of chance again. Not now that my dad is doing things here to protect me."

We sat on the edge of my bed, waiting. I held Ellie's hand between mine. We passed an hour like this, sitting and talking and trying to tell each other the things we wished we would have when I was still alive. And when it was finally time for Ellie to leave, I told her, "Wait," and she turned back around in my doorway. "If you see any of the others," I said, "try to ignore them. Don't worry about trying to set them free."

"Why?" she asked, looking puzzled.

"Because," I said, "I'm not sure they want to be helped in the same way you helped Timothy and Becca. They might not want to be freed."

"But Noah . . . ," she started to say.

"Forget about him," I said. "I know it's hard, Ellie. But, really, remember everything you loved about him. And after that, try to move on."

15

The Last Will and Testament of Ellie Frame, cont.

"Forget about him," Rose told me. Almost the exact thing Becca had said. But after hearing everything Rose had to say, I found that forgetting Noah wasn't possible. Not knowing that he might be in some kind of danger. Not after learning from Rose that there were other kinds of things on her side of the divide between the living and the dead. Things she had no name for. A shiver ran through my body as I drove away from the Sano farm, and it continued to roll through me on the drive home like waves, raising goose bumps on my arms as I gripped the steering wheel tighter, making my knuckles turn a sickly greenish white under the glow of the dashboard lights.

When I got out of the car back home, I stopped halfway between the driveway and the front stoop to look around, searching the woods that bordered the back and side of our property for any signs of ghosts or other . . . things. If Rose was right—if it was true that things existed in the afterworld besides ghosts—then I needed to pay even more attention. It wasn't just the spirits of my friends watching me, maybe.

I saw nothing and no one skulking in the dark, even though I did feel watched. It was a feeling I'd started to have in general, but I told myself that I couldn't trust it to mean that something or someone was actually watching me at any given moment.

So I turned and continued on my way up to the stoop and through the front door, swinging it open to find my mom and dad on the couch together, holding hands as if they were on a date. It turned out, though, that their hand-holding wasn't really a romantic gesture. Instead, it soon became clear they'd made some important decisions about how we should, as my mom said, "Go forward from here on out as a family."

I didn't move from where I stood in the front doorway, my keys still hot and sweaty in the palm of my hand. "What do you mean?" I said, feeling I wasn't going to like whatever my mom was going to say next.

But just like I couldn't trust the feeling that I was being watched, it turned out I also couldn't trust some of my other feelings. Because what my mom said next made me understand that I possibly had the best and smartest parents I could ask for.

"Your dad and I have been talking about things for a while now. About what he's seen. About what you've experienced. About what it seems like so many people around here have been going through." Mom paused for a second, looking as uncomfortable as she sounded, clearly not able to say words like *ghosts* and *haunted*. Finally, though, she made herself continue. "I know you've already gone to see Dr. Arroyo once, and so has your dad. So have I, to be completely honest, though I haven't seen or heard anything like you two have. I'm still bothered by what's been happening, though, and I'm even more bothered by how you and your dad have had to deal with this . . . other stuff. This stuff I'd rather you not have to go through."

My mom paused for another second. She didn't turn away, but I noticed her eyes lower a little, as if she preferred to look at the floor rather than at me for the next part.

"Mom, it's okay," I said. "Whatever it is, I know we're all in this together."

Her eyes flicked up at that, and she smiled in that way that looks a little more like a frown. "Your dad and I want all three of us to see Dr. Arroyo together. To see if she has any strategies for us to move through this. To get the both of you . . . well, frankly, to get the both of you not seeing these sorts of things anymore."

I took a deep breath and sighed. It wasn't what I'd expected. I think I'd been worried that Mom and Dad had decided to do something extreme, out of fear. Like packing up our things overnight and moving to another state or country. Like burning the house down before we even pulled out of the driveway. I wouldn't have really blamed them for something like that, because what was happening in Newfoundland was scary. But I couldn't leave, not yet. Not until I was sure Noah would be okay. Not until I could make sure Adrienne and even Ingrid Mueller—who I wished I didn't feel some kind of duty to save for Noah's sake—weren't in danger of being stuck like they were, forever.

"That," I said, "sounds like a good idea to me."

And then my mom sighed, too. "Good," she said. "I was worried you wouldn't want to. I know this isn't easy. We miss them, too, Ellie. Noah. The girls. It still doesn't feel completely real to me, either. I just want them back with us more than anything. But I know how hard it is to accept things like . . ."

She paused then, unsure how to complete her sentence.

"Hard to accept things like the idea that I might be losing my sanity?" I finished for her. Her eyebrows lifted, as if she was surprised by my willingness to say that without freaking out, then she nodded.

Dad beamed beside her, as if he wasn't surprised at all. "You're something else, Ellie," he said.

"Something else," I said, snorting, "is exactly how I feel. I'd much rather go back to feeling more like myself instead of like something else."

Dad closed his eyes and nodded. "I know," he said. "I know."

My parents were relieved and grateful that I was on board to see Dr. Arroyo again, but even so, I didn't tell them everything else I'd committed myself to beyond that. I didn't tell them that before I could go back to feeling more like myself— while I could still see what was ordinarily invisible, while I could still touch what was ordinarily untouchable—I needed to make sure Noah and the others would be okay.

I left my parents in the living room the way I'd found them, holding hands, and went upstairs, not mentioning that I'd seen Rose. And by withholding that from them, I began to understand how Becca and Rose must have felt when they were clearly not telling me everything. I began to understand why they thought that not knowing something could be a form of protection. I thought the same, I realized as I sat on my bed, holding my bottom lip between my teeth. If I told my parents about Becca and Rose, about everything I'd learned, it could set them off in the extreme direction of pulling up stakes and running as fast and as far away from Newfoundland as possible.

My mom emailed Dr. Arroyo later that night to ask if she could see us as a family, and by midmorning the next day, Dr. Arroyo had responded. "'Absolutely, Patty,'" Mom said, holding her phone up to read the email aloud to Dad and me at the breakfast table. Dr. Arroyo said she could see us after Dad got home from work that afternoon.

I spent the rest of the day in a semihaze. Mostly because I hadn't been sleeping well for the past month, and when sleep did come, my dreams were troubled. Not nightmares, exactly, but something a few shades away. The kind that felt too real, that sometimes made me forget about everything that had happened.

So I was exhausted enough from being up most of the night, before replaying my visit to Rose in my head, that I fell asleep right at my desk. One moment, I was typing random search terms about Japanese ghosts and demons into my laptop, trying to figure out something—*anything*—I might be able to do to help them. And the next thing I knew, I was opening my eyes and wiping sweat from the side of my face that had been pressed against my desktop for who knew how long.

I was rubbing my eyes when I heard someone clear their throat. The sound came from behind me, and I turned fast to find Noah, of all people, sitting on my bed. *Thank you, thank you, thank you, God,* I thought in one quick instant, before either of us could say anything.

Noah was smiling at me, just one corner of his mouth lifted shyly, and his head was tilted a little to the side, as if he'd been looking at me like that for a while, just staring at me in the way I'd sometimes catch him doing when he was alive and we were doing something ordinary, like watching TV. I'd turn to comment on a stupid character or a funny commercial, and find him looking at me like that—like how he was right now in my bedroom—smiling at me like I was more interesting than everything else, even when I wasn't doing or saying anything remarkable.

"Noah," I said, just barely audible. I was afraid if I spoke too loudly, he might disappear on me.

He kept smiling, but he didn't say anything. And then, when I stood from my chair to go over to him, my knees turned weak and my legs gave out beneath me.

That was when I actually woke up at my desk, where I'd fallen asleep at the laptop. I was leaning heavily to one side of my chair, about to fall out of it. When I realized what was happening, I quickly sat up and spun the chair around, only to find no one sitting on the bed behind me. No Noah smiling at me, watching me sleep. Nothing but my comforter and sheets twisted and rumpled into hills and valleys.

I hadn't had a crying jag in several days—at least not the sort where I shook and shook, unable to catch my breath as I tried to stifle my sobs so no one would hear me. But now one came on with the force of a train barreling down on me. I put my face in my hands and sobbed, trying to hold the cries in. And when I was afraid Mom and Dad might hear me, I got up and ran to the closet, closing the door, still cupping one hand over my mouth. I reached up and grabbed hold of the first thing I could find and pulled it from its hanger. It was a flannel shirt Noah had left in my car last fall, and it still held the faint scent of his cologne. I felt another wave of tears coming then, and I cried and moaned into the shirt over and over, until finally I felt empty. Empty and hollow, from head to toe, the way I felt after finding out how Noah and my friends had died without me. And just like then I couldn't feel anything. Just that place that had opened up inside me, that cold crevasse where my heart used to beat.

Get up, I told myself. I didn't have any tears left, and I wiped at my eyes, my cheeks. *Get up. Go downstairs. Make coffee. Drink it. Talk to Mom like nothing's happened. Now. Go. Now.*

And that's what I did. Forcing myself to act, to pretend. For the first time in weeks, I was playing the *I'm fine, really* game again.

⌒

At Dr. Arroyo's, Mom and Dad did most of the talking. I answered questions when asked, and tried not to seem hyper from drinking too much coffee as a way to stay awake for as long as possible, to avoid dreaming.

Dr. Arroyo looked exhausted, too. The skin around her eyes

sagged, as if she wasn't sleeping much, either, and her hair was pulled back into a simple bun, nothing like the long, carefully tended waves and curls she had when she first came to Newfoundland. "It's been a trying period," she said when Mom asked if she was doing okay. "There's so much work to be done, and my team and I only have so many hours in a day to do it."

"I'm so sorry," Mom said, and immediately thanked her for giving yet another one of those hours from her day to the Frame family.

"No need to apologize," Dr. Arroyo said. She smiled then, and I could see her sit up straighter. She knew how to play the *I'm fine, really* game, too, I realized. As skillfully as I did. "It's a pleasure," she said, "to see you all here together. That's the sign of a family that will not only survive their obstacles but become stronger once past them."

She went on to ask what Dad and I had been experiencing, and though Dad didn't hesitate to tell her about what he'd seen, I carefully omitted some details. I knew Dr. Arroyo didn't believe Newfoundland was haunted by real ghosts so much as by "the ghosts of our wounded psyches," which was how she'd phrased it in a TV interview I'd seen several days before. And I didn't need to convince her. Convincing her that ghosts were real didn't matter when nothing could be done about it anyway. We had no choice but to wait things out, like Rose had said. To hope that the gray area that spread over our small corner of the world would eventually lift—like fog from a field once the sun rose high enough—and things would go back to normal.

She advised us to hold open conversations every evening, to do it with purpose, to not let a night go by when we didn't sit down together and talk about anything we felt, even if it was just ordinary sadness, even if no one had seen anything remotely resembling a ghost. "Because," she said, looking at Mom, "I imagine that even though Patty hasn't had those same experiences, it must still take a toll on her to volunteer at the shelters every day. To be constantly surrounded by the pain of others."

Mom blinked, then nodded, a stoic warrior. "It does," she said. "But I'm grateful to be able to do it. I just want Dan and Ellie not to have to go through any of this any longer."

"Don't deny your own struggle because you think the struggles of others are worse, Patty," Dr. Arroyo said, leaning forward in her chair. "You're strong, but remember you're also human. You can't save everyone, especially if you wear yourself down."

Mom smiled and said, "That sounds like good advice for you, too," and then they both laughed.

"This is why it's a great pleasure to see your family," she said. "You bring good medicine for me, too."

She went on to ask more questions of me and Dad, but especially me. It was as if she had a pickax, and was trying to chip away at the walls I'd put up. Was I sure I was mostly okay? Were the things I'd been experiencing disturbing? Could I tell her about at least one incident so that she could get a better sense of what I'd been seeing?

I knew that at a certain point my vagueness might be the thing that gave me away, that it'd be obvious I was keeping secrets. So I decided to give her something to appease her. I had to think fast, though, to offer her something that was real but not so alarming as, say, sitting next to the ghosts of my dead best friends in their bedrooms. Something like that, I figured, or something like what happened with Timothy Barlow, would rate too high on the disturbance meter.

So instead I told her it was just weird little things. Like the search terms I found typed into my laptop's browser and how I felt sure that Rose must have put them there. And how I had trouble sleeping because I always dreamed about Noah. I told her I'd think it was real, that he was really alive, and when I woke up and had to face the truth, it was like finding out all over again that he had died.

"I just wish I could get one decent night's sleep," I said, sighing, which actually wasn't a lie. I did wish I could sleep; I just wanted to be able to do it without dreaming of Noah.

"You may have unconsciously typed those search terms into your laptop without realizing it," Dr. Arroyo said. "Especially if you've not been sleeping well. You might have remembered your friend telling you about that superstition and attempted to look it up while being in a semiconscious state."

I figured she'd say as much, particularly because I hadn't told her the rest of the story about the search terms. That Rose really *had* done it.

"The sleep avoidance is understandable," Dr. Arroyo said. "Especially because of the nature of your dreams. That is something I can help you with, if you and your parents would be comfortable with a prescription sedative."

I was glad to see her feeling useful, so to seal the deal, I nodded enthusiastically and said, "I'd try anything at this point."

Dr. Arroyo looked over to Mom and Dad, who were clearly still upset by my admission. "Oh, Ellie," Mom said while Dad stroked the back of my head. "Why didn't you tell us you weren't sleeping?"

"This is why you need to talk openly every day," Dr. Arroyo said. She pulled out a pad, put the nib of a pen against it, and scribbled out the name and dosage for the cure to my dreams. "I'm glad you're willing to try this. Your mind needs time to heal. When you feel up to it, I think it would be good for you to begin to build some bridges to those around you who are still living."

"What do you mean?" I asked.

Dr. Arroyo finished writing, clicked her pen shut, then ripped the prescription off the pad and handed it over to Mom. "I mean other classmates. Other friends you may have had, even if you weren't as close to them as the friends you've lost. Or even the parents of your friends, or one of their brothers or sisters. It could help, I think, if you are able to share your feelings of loss with others who have lost the same person. Does that make sense?"

"It does," I said, even though I wasn't sure if I believed what she suggested would really help me in any big way.

"What about Couri?" Mom said beside me, squeezing my shoulder. Then she turned to Dr. Arroyo and said, "She's the younger sister of Ellie's friend Adrienne. She was in the other wing of the school that day, the wing that was . . . spared."

"Couri," I said, nodding. Adrienne and Couri had never really gotten along, but I said her name again and kept on nodding, agreeing that giving her a call might be a good idea, if for no other reason than to make them feel like our meeting had resulted in some kind of progress.

16

The Last Will and Testament of Ellie Frame, cont.

For as many years as I'd known Adrienne Long and her little sister, Couri, I'd never once heard Adrienne say something nice about her. Couri was three years younger than us, a straight-A student, a cello prodigy, a star runner on the junior varsity girls' track team, and, in the opinion of pretty much anyone who set eyes on her, possibly the most beautiful girl they'd ever seen.

Everyone in Newfoundland thought Adrienne hated Couri. And it wasn't hard to understand why, considering the fights the two of them had gotten into over the years. Fights that Adrienne always started, and that could have been avoided if she had simply made it a point not to let her little sister's vast talent, abilities, and popularity get to her.

But no matter what it might look like, one thing I knew about Adrienne Long was that she didn't hate her little sister.

She *resented* her. There's a difference between those two feelings, and sometimes it's hard to see it. Especially if you didn't know their parents treated Couri like a princess and Adrienne like her handmaid. People like Rose, me, and Becca, though? We'd had special guest passes, first-row seats to the Long family drama ever since we were little girls. We were privy to the truth that fueled the public eruptions.

How it usually went was: Days would go by, then weeks, maybe even a few months, in which Adrienne would try her best not to let her parents' preferential treatment for Couri get to her. Her mom would ask her to pick up Couri's laundry from the floor. Her dad would say, "Hey, Adrienne, do me a favor and pick Couri up from her cello lesson tonight," which ordinarily would be a typical annoyance for anyone, but constantly having to work around Couri's schedule was what really got to Adrienne, especially when she'd already made it clear she had plans to hang out with me or Becca or Rose after school. Her time, the things she wanted to do, didn't seem to matter. She was asked, or told, to do any number of chores around the house that Couri never had to do, and she was never once praised for doing any of it. I once stayed the night at Adrienne's place, probably three or four years ago, and saw the *Cinderella, Cinderella* act for myself. I was shocked that the Longs were so oblivious that they'd call on her to do everything around the house, even when she had a friend staying over.

And it wasn't as if Adrienne didn't have her own gifts or talents. They just didn't stack up to the level that Couri's did. Second place in flute at regionals just wasn't the same as first place at state in cello, and then top twenty at nationals. The most congratulatory thing I ever heard come out of Mr. Long's mouth was: "Not half bad, Adrienne." And from Mrs. Long, it was: "I'm sure you'll do better next time, honey."

From the front seat now, my mom said, "What are you thinking about, Ellie?"

I paused for a moment, not sure if I should tell her.

"You're thinking about what Dr. Arroyo said, aren't you?" she asked, turning to look over her shoulder at me after I didn't answer.

I slid my eyes to the side, trying to avoid revealing just how much I was thinking about it, and said, "About calling Adrienne's sister? Yeah. A little."

Mom reached her hand over the front seat and gestured for me to give her mine, which I did, immediately feeling the comfort of her skin, warm and soft, better than any childhood toy or blanket. "Couri must be taking this so hard," Mom said, squeezing gently, while Dad glanced back at me in the rear-view mirror, checking to see if I was okay.

"Or something," I said, not thinking.

"What do you mean?" Mom said, brows knitting together.

I thought about trying to recover from that fumble, but instead I decided to shrug it off, as if it were a matter of my own general confusion over everything that had been going on in Newfoundland. "I don't know," I said. "I don't know why I said that. I think it's probably because I know Adrienne and Couri didn't exactly get along."

"Ah," Mom said, nodding. "Well, sometimes it's hardest on those who can't make up with someone any longer."

I nodded back at her, thinking of how right she was. How that was the exact reason I wanted to see Noah, how awful it was to know he was out there, unwilling to let me see him.

No one was in the mood to cook, and after leaving Dr. Arroyo's, Dad declared that comfort food was in order, and we picked dinner up at the One Red Light Diner on our way home. It was literally a diner located at the corner of Newfoundland's one red-light intersection, just a couple of miles up the hill from Main Street, where the school and library and town hall used to be. The diner had only sustained a few broken windows and roof damage during the outbreak, nothing that couldn't be repaired very easily. So once the roads had opened again, so did the One Red Light Diner.

Dad came out with a bucket of chicken and a side of potato wedges with gravy. It wasn't exactly comforting food, but then again, nothing had tasted good to me in the past month. I made a point of eating a little bit when we got home to assure my parents that I wasn't going to waste away right before their eyes.

A convincing enough dinner consisted of one chicken leg and a few potato wedges. I didn't take more than I thought I could actually eat, so that when I finished, it would at least seem like I was doing okay. And after wiping my lips with a napkin and taking my plate to the sink, I told them I was going upstairs to take a look at the flash drive of the school yearbook, which had gone unfinished.

When I had only one foot on the stairs, my mom said from behind me, "You should probably talk to the principal to see about having that released eventually."

"If you want, I can give her a call," my dad offered.

"Don't worry. I've got it under control," I said, giving them a quick smile, which forced them to smile and nod in return.

It wasn't as if I had much of anything under control, but I couldn't let them worry more than they already were. Dad had his own stress, and he was still working an unhealthy amount of overtime. Mom had started to say she should cut back on her volunteer work at the shelter, though. She said it was because she needed to get back into the groove of the real estate business—"such as it is"—but I knew it was because she wanted to be around in case I needed her. Thinly veiled behind her eyes was the real concern she wouldn't directly state: she worried that I was seeing ghosts only when she wasn't around. And she thought that by being at home, she could scare the ghosts of Newfoundland away from her daughter. It was a nice thought, but a little naïve. How could she think otherwise, though, since she seemed blind to their presence in the first place?

Upstairs, I pulled my phone out and opened up my list of contacts. I hadn't updated the list since the outbreak, and there were a lot of numbers in there that probably no longer worked. Noah's, Becca's, Rose's, Adrienne's . . . But theirs weren't the one I was looking for. The one I needed right then was Couri's.

When I found her number on my screen, I touched it, then held my breath as the call went through. A few seconds later, the lines connected. But before I could say anything, a voice that wasn't Couri's answered.

"Hey, Ellie," the voice said, tone casual. "Long time no see. I wondered if I'd ever hear from you."

"I'm sorry?" I said, confused. "Do I have the right number? I was looking for Couri Long. This is Couri's number, right?"

"Yep, it's Couri's phone, all right," the voice said. "But Couri isn't available at the moment. Ha ha ha. What? Don't you recognize my voice, Ellie? It's not been *that* long since we last talked."

I inhaled sharply, realizing that I recognized the voice on the other end, but hoping I was wrong. So I stood there for a long moment, hesitating, until I finally made the guess I didn't want to say aloud. "Is this . . . is this Adrienne I'm speaking with?"

Then suddenly my laptop came to life, lighting up as it shifted out of sleep mode, as if I'd stroked its keyboard with a finger. Then the sound of an incoming video call started to ring.

"Ding, ding, ding! We have a winner!" Adrienne said on the other end of the phone. "Go to your laptop so you can see for yourself."

I didn't move right away, just continued to stand in the center of my room, phone pressed against my ear, hot and sweaty, as I listened to the video call ringing and ringing on my computer. After a while, Adrienne said, "What's the matter, Ellie? Are you afraid?"

If Adrienne Long knew anything about me, it was that I caved whenever she challenged me. When we were twelve and

I wanted a pixie cut but my mom wouldn't let me, she dared me to cut my hair off in protest. And when I wavered, not sure I should go through with it, she told me I'd always do whatever my parents told me to. So I'd taken a pair of scissors into my bathroom and sliced off six inches of the long blond locks my mother loved so much. I couldn't help but hear that same kind of challenge in her voice now, and like then she was able to bait me, because as soon as she said that, I went over to my desk and sat down, fingers hovering over the keyboard. Before I could change my mind, I quickly clicked a key to accept her call. And as the screen opened to show the person calling, I shivered.

It was Couri, sitting at her own desk in her own bedroom at home, where a poster of Jacqueline du Pré, this English cellist from the 1960s who became popular for her talent, stared at me from over her shoulder. She was Couri's idol, the representation of everything Couri wanted to achieve with her music. She'd shown Adrienne and me some videos of the woman playing at some huge event that took place in a palace over fifty years ago. Du Pré had this weird way of playing—curling her body around the cello, throwing her head back and her elbows out in a wide arc—that had made her seem more like a rock star than a classical musician.

"Freaky Friday, huh?" Adrienne said through Couri's mouth, laughing lightly, the voice on my phone speaker doubling with the voice coming out of my laptop. "The old switcheroo. Pretty cool trick, huh?"

I turned my phone off and tried to nod, to seem unbothered by what was happening.

"Yeah," I said, "pretty cool trick. But . . . how do you do it?"

"Watch," Adrienne said.

And then my mouth fell open.

My mouth fell open because in a period of maybe half a minute, as Couri's body began to shake and then to convulse, as if she were sick and about to throw up, a shadow began to gather behind her. At first, it was a formless sort of thing, no more than a cloud of fine black mist. But slowly that mist began to take on the outline of a human figure, and then specifically a female figure, and then specifically it began to take on the features of Adrienne Long herself.

Short, spiky black hair, dark brown eyes, flawless skin— the one physical feature Adrienne shared with her little sister. She wore the same top I remembered her wearing the morning of the outbreak, where she'd stood not far from me and Noah out in the parking lot, watching as we fought. It was a black, lacy bodice that Adrienne had found in a vintage shop in New York City when she and Couri had gone with the school band for a music competition. She'd worn that top more than any other article of clothing in the past year, whenever the weather was appropriate, and sometimes even when it wasn't. Seeing her in it now made me feel weirdly relieved. Like, at least she still had that, I thought. This small token of happiness from her former life.

"So?" Adrienne said, spreading her arms out wide behind her little sister, who began to slump forward in the desk chair, forehead coming closer to me on my side of the screen. "What do you think?"

At first, I could only sit there with wide eyes and open

mouth, afraid and in awe. Mostly afraid, though, which is what kept me from forming a coherent response.

Adrienne started laughing, then shook her head like my reaction was the most hilarious thing in the world. "Well, look at that," she said. "I'm pretty sure this is the first time I've ever seen Ellie Frame, journalist extraordinaire, without a strong opinion."

"I can't," I said, nearly breathless. "I can't believe you can do that."

"It's not easy," Adrienne said, "but just like Mom and Dad always told me and Couri when it came to mastering our instruments, practice makes perfect."

She put her hands in the position I'd seen her take to play her flute and pretended to pipe a few notes before dropping her arms at her sides and looking down at her sister. Couri's eyelids were half closed, as if she were on some kind of sedative.

"Help," Couri said, slurring that sad little word.

A shiver ran down my spine. I could feel it hit each and every vertebra as it passed through. Then another ran through me as I saw Adrienne's face contort a little, as if she was holding back tears only seconds after she'd finished laughing, and the next thing she did was to lean down and put one cheek against Couri's, stroking her sister's hair gently. "Oh, Couri," she said. "I'm so sorry. I wish it could be some other way, too."

I didn't know what she meant by that, but I began to get an inkling as I watched Adrienne's form dissipate, returning to that fine black mist surrounding Couri, who began to choke and convulse again as Adrienne forced herself back inside her.

After it was over, Couri's eyes opened and, from somewhere inside her, Adrienne's voice said, "I really do wish there was some other way, but this is all I've been able to figure out so far."

She flexed Couri's fingers, cracking them like she might be prepping to play a difficult piece of music, then rubbed Couri's wrists, one after the other, as if she were making sure gloves had been pulled tightly over her own hands.

"Adrienne," I said, "where did you learn how to do that?"

"That's kind of hard to answer," Adrienne said, tilting Couri's head a little, as if she were trying to find the right words. "It was kind of by accident, actually. A little bird showed me, after I got to this side of things."

"What side of things?" I asked, even though I knew from Becca and Rose exactly what she meant. I wanted to draw her out. Whenever the Adrienne I had known got upset in the past, giving her the space to talk was the best way to get her to be reasonable.

"You know," said Adrienne. "The other side. The shadow side. The land of the dead."

"I was hoping you wouldn't have to do this sort of thing," I said then, giving out just a little bit of bait that I hoped Adrienne would take, which she did.

"What sort of thing?" she asked immediately. Couri's eyes narrowed, expressing Adrienne's suspicion. "What would you know about it?"

"It's all over the news," I said.

"What is?"

"The hauntings," I said. "So many of them. It's like half of Newfoundland is haunted."

"Oh, that," Adrienne said, shrugging. "Well, some of us aren't interested in haunting anyone. I'm just trying to keep myself alive."

"What do you mean?" I asked, leaning in a little, trying to show her that she didn't have to treat me like the enemy. "Is there something trying to hurt you? Is there anything I can do?"

Adrienne huffed in frustration through Couri's nose, then wrapped Couri's arms around her chest, hugging herself defensively. "Really, Ellie," she said, and right then the tears she'd previously held back started to well in Couri's eyes. "There's nothing the living can do for me now. Goddamn it. I didn't want to cry."

Couri's body suddenly began to convulse again, her shoulders jerking as she struggled through a fit of coughing. "Help," Couri said again, in her own voice.

Then her body returned to stillness, and Adrienne was back in the control booth.

"Please don't fight me, Couri," she said, wiping away her tears. "You know it just makes this harder."

"What are you doing to her?" I asked, disturbed by what I was seeing.

"I'm taking what she always had," Adrienne said. "I'm going to get what I always deserved but only she was given."

"What's that?" I asked.

"A life," Adrienne said. "Attention. And respect. I was talented, too, you know."

I could tell at that point that Becca and Rose had been right. Adrienne wasn't the person I remembered. Sure, she'd always been a bit resentful of the attention her parents and everyone else showered on Couri, but she'd always been gracious about it. Used us, her friends, to vent about her problems so that she didn't make any more issues than there already were between her and her family. But she'd never been like this. Never once while she was alive had I seen her become so unhinged, so vindictive.

"I know you were talented, Adrienne," I said. "We all knew that."

"Having friends who understood the situation made things better, Ellie," she agreed, nodding a little, her voice cracking from the pressure of trying to hold back her tears. "But that's all gone now. A month ago, I still had a future, where things could have gotten better, you know? Where it would have been enough for me to just be me. Now, though?" She shook Couri's head, rubbed Couri's red eyes, thumbing away the tears she wouldn't let fall. "Now things are different. It's all over. There are no second chances. There's no wide-open future for me. I'm sorry if you don't understand. But trust me. You'd feel the same way, if you were in my position."

"What's your position, Adrienne?" I said. "Help me understand."

"My position?" Adrienne said, sighing, rolling her eyes. "Not a good one, really. I just want my life back, you know? But I can't have that. And yet I can't leave this godforsaken place, either. So this"—here she paused to hold Couri's arms out in front of her, turning Couri's palms upward, clenching and unclenching Couri's fists before looking up at me again—"is the best I can do. I'm not going to hide or try to wait things

189

out like Becca and Rose. I may be dead, but this—what I'm doing here with Couri—this is the one choice I've been able to make on this side of things. Screw that gray-area bullshit. If I can't leave, I'm going to figure out how to live, somehow."

"You don't have to do this, though," I said. "Not like this."

Adrienne snorted. "Oh, really?" she said. "I'm sorry, Ellie, but what would you know about it? Last time I checked, you still had a heartbeat."

"Becca's been able to leave," I said, ignoring her jab. "So has Timothy Barlow. You remember him, right? My next-door neighbor, the sophomore?"

Adrienne shook her head, squinting at me like I was the one who had come unhinged. "What the hell are you talking about, Ellie?"

"I did it," I said, looking away from the screen for a second, still anxious over it all. "I know how to help you get out of here. I know how to help you leave. If you really want to, that is, like you said."

"You're lying," Adrienne said immediately. "How could you possibly know how to do that?"

"I learned by accident," I said, shrugging. "Just like you learned how to do . . . what you're doing."

Adrienne stared at me hard for a long moment, assessing whether or not she could trust me now, despite the years we'd spent trusting one another. She turned Couri's head to look away from the laptop camera at some other place in the room, arms still folded against her chest defensively.

When she turned back, she said, "Okay. Tell me how you do it."

I explained what I knew, telling her what happened when I recorded Timothy Barlow and Becca. And when I was done, Adrienne looked genuinely calm as she considered everything I'd just described.

After a while, she unfolded her arms, leaned toward me through the camera lens, and said, "Being like this isn't really what I want. Not for me and not for Couri, either. So, okay. Let's do it. I'll try anything."

That's when I clicked the button on my laptop to start recording.

And Adrienne began to tell her story.

17

The Last Will and Testament of Adrienne Long

Help you understand? I'm not sure if I can do that, Ellie. There's so much on this side I don't get. At least not yet. But you know how I am. I'm always trying to learn, even if I'm not naturally good at the subject. Think about it. All those years of flute lessons just to become a *slightly* better than average player, while Couri here seemed able to pick up a bow, place it across the strings of a cello, and produce the music of angels.

Life isn't fair. Not to you. Not to me. Not to anyone. And now? It's not even fair to Couri.

I know what you're thinking. I can see it on your face. *How can you do that to her?* But calm down, Ellie, really. I'm not doing anything that bad. She's still here. It's not like she's *dead*. She's in her body, here with me. She's just, you know, been pushed to the back of the space to make room for me. And besides, she let me do this. She gave me the space initially.

And if you really want to understand why I'm doing this, here's an answer. Even though I think the answer is obvious, maybe it isn't for someone like you. For someone who hasn't died.

I want to *live,* Ellie. That's all, plain and simple. I want to be alive. Even if that means living inside someone else's body. I don't have one of those anymore. And as far as I can tell, if I don't find some other way to stick around, who I am on this side of things will die and decay the same way my remains are doing six feet under, even as we speak.

I don't know what you've seen. But here's the thing: whatever happened in Newfoundland after the outbreak, it's left some kind of . . . rift between life on earth and life in . . . whatever the next place is supposed to be. I don't even know what to call it. I don't even know how to describe it, because none of us can get there, even though we know that's where we're supposed to go to.

A gray area? How did it get that name? Well, that's just what everybody started calling it, after we were able to escape the wreckage of the school and find each other. It seemed appropriate, you know, considering wherever we walked around the perimeter of Newfoundland and its outskirts, this misty wall of gray seemed to just be there, unpassable. So I guess if I'm trying to help you understand what I've learned on this side of things, maybe that's where I should start.

⌒

The last thing I remember before I died is Rose and Becca and Noah and I working on the yearbook during free period. The principal's voice came over the speakers all of a sudden, saying there was an emergency, that tornadoes had been spotted and we needed to follow emergency procedures immediately. By then we'd all already noticed the weird color the sky had turned, this green, sour-apple sort of color. And for about five minutes before the principal rang the alarm bells, we'd been seeing tiny pieces of hail tapping against the classroom windows, collecting on the ground, glittering like pieces of broken glass out in the parking lot.

After the principal finished her message, the drill alarm started up, and we left the room to go out into the hallway, where everyone else was already gathering. Anxious murmurs filled the hall, and the voices of teachers rose above the murmurs, giving orders, giving directions. Rose, Becca, Noah, and I didn't have a teacher ordering us into any particular formation right then, since we were on our own during free period, but we'd been through enough tornado drills over the years that we automatically knew what to do. And besides, there were so many people in that hallway, we just fell in with them and listened to their teachers telling them to line up against the lockers, to kneel, to tuck our heads toward our knees and cover the tops of our heads with our hands.

I remember seeing grit on the floor, inches below my face. I remember the small dent at the bottom of the locker in front of me, and how I started to wonder who'd kicked it hard enough to make that dent and why they'd gotten so angry.

It's funny, thinking back on that now. People probably always think about strange things in the moments before they're about to die and don't even know it.

Noah was kneeling on one side of me, and on the other side of me was Ingrid Mueller. At first, everything was fine, but as the winds picked up, we could hear them howling around the building like demons trying to get in, and above the winds I could hear Ingrid starting to whimper. Noah lifted his head a little, so he could look over and try to calm her, and he kept saying things like, "It's okay, Ingrid, don't worry. We're going to be okay. Don't worry."

At first, I thought she was being overly dramatic, you know? I mean, how many tornado drills have we been through over the years? How many actual tornadoes have come and gone and never done anything to us at all? Usually, they just tear through some random track of farmland or woods and then disappear without hurting so much as a cow.

But things kept getting worse, and when dust started to sift down from the ceiling, I started to feel afraid, like Ingrid. Then there was this horrible sound of glass breaking in the classrooms behind us. I remember looking over my shoulder and, through an open doorway, saw the windows blow out, and the blinds batting and twisting in the air like they were alive. Then a sound came from above us, this awful screeching noise like metal twisting. And in the next instant, the roof came off and we were looking up at the open black sky swirling above us.

Ingrid started crying for real then, and I could feel Noah literally reach over my head to put his hand out to her, which she took hold of. All around us, people were screaming and crying. I started crying, too. Then I started praying. I started saying things I don't think I'd ever thought to say before in my life. Not ever.

How sorry I was to my parents for being such a failure.

How sorry I was to Couri for being such a bitch to her over the years, just because I was jealous.

I even went so far as to try to explain things to Couri in my head, as if she were there in the hallway right next to me. "I wasn't jealous of *you*," I whispered. "I was jealous of how *they* treated you. I'm sorry, Couri, I'm so sorry."

Then there was an explosion. It rocked everything around us, the air itself seemed to quiver, and I saw a bright white-and-yellow flash, felt a sudden heat that seemed to come at us from all sides, so unbearably hot, so unlike anything I'd ever felt before. I remember that last feeling—the burning, I mean—and I remember screams, mine and the ones from others around me, before it all ended.

Then there was only darkness and silence.

For how long that darkness and silence lasted, I can't really say. I have no sense of time during all of that. But eventually the darkness began to lift, and then light reached my eyelids, prying at them little by little, revealing a thick white fog when I finally managed to open them all the way.

Though I still couldn't see anything but the fog, I heard Ingrid sniveling beside me. And I heard Noah telling her that everything was okay, that everything was going to be all right. "I'm here with you, Ingrid," he kept saying.

And then I found the strength to open my own mouth, choking a little as I said, "So am I. I'm here, too."

"Who's that?" Ingrid asked frantically.

"It's Adrienne," I said. "Are you still next to me?"

Noah's hand brushed across my neck as he fumbled in the

fog, trying to find me. "There you are," he said, and I sighed, thinking for a moment that I'd only been knocked out during the explosion, that I was still alive.

He's okay, as far as I know. Oh, come on, Ellie, I know you're wondering. I can see it on your face. Every time I say his name, you look like my cat does when my dad yells at her for getting underfoot. I know how much you loved him, Ellie. I know. Everyone knew.

I haven't seen him for a while, though. Not since I found my way . . . into Couri. All I can say is that the last time I saw him, he was with Ingrid.

That's how it was when I woke up in that fog, too: Noah was standing with Ingrid, holding her hand so he didn't lose her, and when I spoke up, he reached down to where I'd been kneeling and found me, pulled me up with his other hand, and then the three of us stayed like that for what seemed like forever, a chain of silhouettes, until we could find our way out of the white fog.

When we finally did, it was nighttime. Stars glittered above us, winking in the black of outer space, while all around us, the world wailed with sirens and the cries of people.

We didn't know it at the time, but some of those cries were people still trapped in the rubble of the school's west wing. People who didn't die in the explosion like we did, who'd instead been pinned beneath the bricks and concrete and the pieces of roof that had fallen in. Some of them were saved, but by then the three of us already knew we were dead. That the bodies with our faces the emergency workers would pull from the wreckage wouldn't be salvageable. We'd figured it out when we tried to get the attention of a group of firefighters who couldn't hear us shouting for help just inches away from them.

Noah, Ingrid, and I eventually climbed a hillside overlooking the wreckage of Main Street to watch as the emergency crews worked to find survivors from the school. I was so jealous as I watched people loaded into ambulances, sobbing, then driven off to hospitals, where I imagined their moms and dads would meet them and hold them and cry with them and tell them how much they loved them. And I kept thinking about how, weirdly, maybe their lives would somehow be better than they were before the outbreak. Because they'd had a close call. Because now they knew what it felt like to be close to death; that it was no longer just an idea that had nothing to do with them. And because they had that new knowledge, they'd want to fix anything that might have been wrong in their relationships with the people they loved beforehand. They'd recognize how trivial their fights were, parents and kids alike, and they'd promise to never let themselves forget what it felt like in those horrible hours when they thought they'd never see each other again.

I'd never get that, I realized, as I sat on the hillside next to Noah and Ingrid, my knees pulled up to my chest, my arms wrapped around them, shivering even though it was late spring and the night air was warm around us.

Ingrid was still crying and whimpering as Noah sat beside her with his arm around her shoulder, rocking her back and forth slightly like a baby. But having just realized I would never have the chance to fix things between me and my family, that I'd never get a chance to grow up and become someone even I'd be surprised to discover if I saw her face in the mirror one day—I got angry with Ingrid, and shot her a glare.

"Stop it," I spat. "Crying isn't going to change anything, Ingrid."

At my words, though, Noah took a sharp breath and pulled back a few inches to look at me with wide eyes, and Ingrid just cried harder.

Noah got mad. He said I didn't have to be like that and that at least the three of us were together. We should be helping each other, he said, not making each other feel worse.

"But nothing's worse than this," I told him. "Is it?"

That took Noah back a little, and I felt sorry for even saying it. You know me, Ellie. Sometimes I can't help myself. The truth just flies out of this mouth like I have no control over it.

So I told him I was sorry, that he was right, and then we all looked away from each other for a while afterward, feeling bad about finding ourselves in this situation. We were just three spirits, invisible to the world, lingering on a hillside, trying not to make eye contact.

⌒

We spent those first few days wandering, trying to find other people we might know, wondering aloud occasionally about how weird it was that none of us felt hungry, that we could walk and walk without sleeping, that we made no sound wherever we stepped, even when we were in the woods, where the ground was littered with twigs and broken branches.

Newfoundland looked like a set from an apocalyptic movie. Tree upon tree toppled over long stretches of empty road. Fields where the earth had been dug into and ripped up by the tornadoes. Abandoned gas stations, abandoned grocery stores. Beyond the downtown, where the majority of the recovery efforts were focused around the school, the signs of life came mostly from birds that still sang, from squirrels that still barked at each other, from rabbits that would suddenly dart out of their hiding places, as if they could sense us approaching.

They really weren't able to sense our presence, even though stories and movies try to tell us that dogs and cats can sense ghosts because they're so much more in tune with things than human beings. Let me tell you, Ellie, dogs and cats and squirrels and bunnies may be in tune with something, but it's not with spirits.

The first time I possessed something, it was a cardinal, and I didn't even know I was doing it. I found it perched on the branch of a fallen oak tree we were sitting on while we lingered one day, unsure of where to go next, unsure if the rest of our afterlives would be this endless wandering around Newfoundland, unable to get past the gray wall surrounding this place.

The cardinal was male. I knew that from his bright red feathers. No hiding behind muddy ruddiness like the females, not him. I was taken by how close I was able to get to him, because he couldn't seem to sense us there near him. And this, I decided, was at least one benefit of being dead. You could get close to things in death that, in life, would have run or flown away from you as soon as the sound of your steps reached their ears.

I decided that I might as well take advantage of that, and crept over on my hands and knees to the branch the cardinal was perched on. No matter how close I got to him, though, he never flinched. At one point, my face was only a few inches from his, and I stared directly into his beady black eyes, which couldn't see me, watching his small body inhale and exhale, over and over. It felt like a dream, being that close to him. And the longer I watched him breathing, the closer I wanted to get. Before I even realized what I was doing, I'd taken him into my hands. It was only then that the cardinal understood something was wrong, and he squirmed, struggling to be released.

"Stop, stop," I cooed to him, trying to calm him.

But there was nothing that would make him settle again. He wriggled and squirmed, trying to get free. I don't know why, but I wouldn't let him go. I *couldn't*. I wanted that closeness, that warm body, that life he held inside.

And just like my first impulse, when I took him into my hands almost without realizing it, I leaned down now to kiss him on his beak, trying to soothe him. I closed my eyes as I held my lips against his head, and again it felt like a dream, like nothing else before that moment had been real or meaningful.

Within my hands, I felt the cardinal stop his struggle.

And when I opened my eyes again, I saw through his.

I think that cardinal lived for all of ten minutes with me inside him, taking up his bones and flesh as my own. And in those ten minutes, I flew. I flew the cardinal's body—my new body—up and into the air like a pilot, landing on a branch of a nearby pine tree, which dipped and swayed under my bird weight. And, oh, how wonderful it felt to have mass again, to be awkward, to be able to make the wiry limb of a tree bend beneath me.

Then the cardinal's heart stopped, or his brain broke, or his lungs exploded. Something. I don't know what for sure, but everything went dark, the way it did when I died in my human body, and the next thing I knew, I wasn't in the bird's body; I wasn't really anywhere. But then I regained myself and realized I was kneeling over the body of the bird beneath the pine tree, and he was as dead as dead can be.

I heard Ingrid gasp behind me. She asked what I'd just done.

I shivered and turned to look over my shoulder at her and Noah. They were looking at me and the bird with shock on their faces.

"I don't know," I said, shaking my head, stunned by what had just happened, but also excited. I already wanted to do it again.

I'd gone inside the bird without realizing it. The three of us put that together pretty quickly when I told them what I'd experienced and they told me what they'd seen happen. How one moment, I'd been gently nuzzling the bird's head, and then how I started to go fuzzy around the edges and my body seemed to dissolve into a black mist that slipped inside the bird through his beak.

Ingrid wanted to know what it was like. She seemed more curious than shaken, taking hold of my arm as she asked me how I did it and how it felt.

I had to think for only a moment before I was able to answer.

"It felt like freedom when I got closer to the sky, all blue above. It felt like being alive again."

She wanted to know if I thought I could do it again. Hearing that, Noah turned to look at her like she was crazy.

"Why would she want to do it again?" he said. It was clear he didn't like what I'd done, even though it had happened by accident.

"You heard her," Ingrid said as she twirled a daisy she'd picked from a nearby meadow in one hand. "Don't you want to feel that way, too? Not weighed down any longer? No more gray walls fencing you in?"

Noah shook his head and said he didn't know about any of it. He said none of it felt right and that we shouldn't do things like that just because we'd found out that we could.

Ingrid didn't seem to care what he said, though. She looked away from him, back to me, and said, "Come on, Adrienne. Show me."

Ingrid's first possession was a rabbit. Noah's was a snake. I know, right? In the end, he grudgingly gave in and tried it, just so he could know what it was like, and in any case, he said he hated snakes, so that helped him not feel as bad about it.

After we felt decently capable of possessing small creatures, we tried out bigger ones. Ingrid and I chose stray dogs we found wandering the back roads. We couldn't tell if they'd lost their way in the outbreak like we had, or if they'd always been on their own, out in the wild. We left their expiring bodies in a ditch, side by side, three days later.

Noah chose a cow from a farm near the ditch we left the dogs in. Of course, it was a *sick* cow, so Noah could feel like he was just putting it out of its misery if it died as a result. He spent a few days inside it, waiting to see how long he could stay, before it started to die from him using its body, then leaving to see if it would regain its strength afterward. It turns out you can keep a host alive, if you give them time to recover without you inside, burdening them. If you gave them time to be themselves again for a while.

After that, we moved on to people. Well, actually, *I* moved on to people. Ingrid and Noah just watched. It was an old woman, and she looked to be pretty much on her deathbed. To be honest, she was staying in one of the shelters your mom's been volunteering at, because she'd lost everything, every last thing, in the outbreak. She had no family, she had no home to return to. The clothes she wore were the only things she had left.

Yeah, I've seen your mom. *No,* Ellie, she hasn't seen *me.* And yes, I'll just answer the question I know you want to ask but are afraid to.

The old lady didn't die. I left her body before I caused her any lasting harm. It was hard living inside her anyway, feeling her feelings layered in with mine. She felt hopeless. Every moment was colored by her despair. I'd learned from Noah's experiment with the cow that a host didn't have to die because of us. I just needed to see if we could take possession of people, too, or if we could only do it with animals.

When I felt like I knew what I was doing, I decided it was time for me to move forward with an idea that had been forming after I first possessed the cardinal. I said goodbye to Noah and Ingrid then, so I could go home. So I could find Couri. So I could find my sister. My sweet sister, who, it turns out, didn't hate me at all, even though it felt like our parents were constantly pitting us against each other. And she said yes when I asked if she'd give me a space to keep on living. She said yes, Ellie, just like that. No hesitation. She just hugged me, and we put our foreheads together, and then we were one.

I've been making sure to leave her every now and then, so she can recover. I want to stay, after all, you know? It's not how I *want* to stay, of course. It's what I *need* to do. It's what I *have* to do, if I'm going to survive. And it hurts all the same, even though Couri's given me a place to continue living. It hurts because I've realized in all those years of hating her, I was wrong. It hurts because all of our fighting had been because of how our parents treated us, and even they didn't realize they were doing that. It hurts because we'll never get a chance to fix any of it now. That's the thing that hurts the most, really. That our chance to make things better, to make things right between us all, has been taken away from us. I'll never get a chance to become someone different, someone better, someone who wasn't consumed by bitterness, like I might have been after graduating, after being able to leave the situation to find or make a different one to live in. All their memories of me will be of who I was before that day. Before I had a chance to change.

I don't want Couri not to have that chance, either.

I'm feeling . . . weird, Ellie. Which is . . . which is . . . what's the word? Why can't I remember it?

Discombobulating?

Disconcerting?

Wait—something's happening.

Couri? Please don't hate me for this. I love you more than anything. Have I ever told you that? I'm sorry for putting you through this. But thank you. Thank you for giving me a few more days.

Ellie? Are you still there? I can't see you. Everything is blue now, blue and beautiful above me. It feels like flying again.

I'm going there. I'll see you there someday.

If, when it's your time and you have the choice to make, if you're not kept from leaving, don't linger.

18

The Last Will and Testament of Ellie Frame, cont.

It was the computer software Mom bought me last year to help me do interviews with the track team when they went to compete in nationals. I was able to video chat with them and their coach, and record it for our online newspaper. I didn't know what would happen if I switched it on to record Adrienne telling me her story—I didn't know if it would record the same way my phone did—but thankfully it worked. Not just for Couri's sake, but for Adrienne's, too. I'd never seen her so angry, or so broken. I'd never seen her so willing to do whatever she had to, no matter what the cost, to save herself from her own pain. It was worse, in some ways, than seeing Becca unable to escape her mother, even after she'd died.

Becca and Rose had been right. Adrienne wasn't herself anymore. Death had changed her. Death had turned her into someone I barely recognized. Someone desperate and clinging.

That wasn't the Adrienne I remembered. That wasn't the girl who, despite the problems she had with her parents, always had a one-liner to make any sad or tense situation humorous. One of my best memories of Adrienne was when Becca had told us why her parents had thrown her older brother out of the house. After we'd hugged her and comforted her—after Becca was feeling better, having told us the truth—Adrienne had said, "Hey, look on the bright side. At least they got rid of your competition." She'd smirked, inviting the rest of us to laugh at the reference to her own problems. And we did manage to laugh. To laugh through our tears. That was why seeing her as desperate and hurt as she was after dying shook me so completely. I realized now how much she must have been hurting when she was alive, too, but she'd kept us all at a distance from her own pain through joking about it. Adrienne's humor had always been self-deprecating, but it was never mean. Even when she complained about her mom and dad fawning over her genius little sister, she'd eventually do this thing where she'd lift her hands and arms into a position in which she pretended to play an invisible flute, and then, after putting them down, she'd say, "Sorry, but I can't play the violin for shit."

After the black mist seeped out of Couri's open mouth, collecting and re-forming into the Adrienne I remembered, Adrienne looked up and saw blue all above her finally, and rose up, leaving this world. I found my fingers hovering over the keyboard, frozen, refusing to move, no matter how much I willed them to. Eventually, they started to tremble on their own, and I was able to turn off the recorder.

On my screen, Couri slumped back in the desk chair

Adrienne had propped her up in, her head nodding to one side. I worried that I might have done something I didn't intend to. By freeing Adrienne's spirit, had I somehow hurt Couri? That's why I was shaking, really. It wasn't *just* because of the way Adrienne had changed, though that would have been enough to disturb me. It was because, in that last moment before her exit, as Couri appeared like a lifeless doll in her desk chair, hair fallen over her face, I wondered if I had killed her.

"Couri," I managed to say, but it came out as a whisper. After another moment or two, I said her name again, louder this time. "Couri," I said, "are you there? Are you okay?"

When she continued to just sit there, unmoving, mouth hanging open, I felt my breath catch in my throat.

Then suddenly a groan made its way out of her, despite her lips barely moving.

"Couri," I shouted, "wake up! You have to wake up!"

A second later, she groaned again, so I kept saying her name, trying to encourage her, trying to will some part of my own spirit into her, to give her some of my own energy, the way Adrienne had described taking Couri's space while she possessed her. I knew it wasn't possible to do that, but I was desperate for impossible things to happen.

A minute later, as I continued to plead with her, Couri slowly lifted one hand to brush the hair out of her eyes. She managed to open her eyes halfway, but she was so exhausted, that effort was all she could manage. "Ellie?" she murmured, struggling to stay conscious, her voice rough and weak, like she'd forgotten how to shape words in general. "Is that you?"

"It's me, Couri," I said. "It's Ellie."

She began to lift her head a little higher on her neck then, and blinked a few times, her strength slowly returning while she peered around her room as if it belonged to a stranger. Who was that strange woman on the poster with her legs wrapped around a cello? Who was that strange girl looking back at her when her eyes met a nearby mirror?

"Where . . . ," Couri said, pausing for a moment, wincing as she finally made herself say the name. "Where's Adrienne?"

"Gone," I said. That's all. I didn't tell her how or why right then. After a moment passed, I said, "You're just yourself now."

"Gone?" Couri said. "Are you sure?"

I could tell that she didn't really believe me. How could she, though? Why would she? For the past few weeks, the spirit of her older sister had lived inside her, had controlled her like a puppet. For the past few weeks, from what I could tell, Couri had been stuffed back into some dark closet of her own consciousness, so that Adrienne could live inside the rest of her.

"I'm sure," I told her. "Just listen and I'll explain."

I told her about everything that had happened, just as Adrienne had described it to me. I even told Couri that I wanted her to believe me when I said, "Adrienne didn't mean to hurt you." Not *really*. Not like that. Maybe Adrienne had some underlying issues when it came to Couri, but it wasn't Couri herself that had made her feel second best; in a way, Adrienne had already spent most of her life as a ghost.

As Couri sat on the other side of the screen, listening to me frantically try to explain her own sister to her, tears sprang to her eyes. Then she shook her head and said, "It's okay, Ellie. You don't have to tell me. I know all of this. She was inside me, remember?"

"I'm sorry," I said. "I didn't mean—"

"It's not your fault," Couri said. She put her hands on her face then, as if she was trying to get used to the feeling of her own flesh beneath her own fingers again. "I knew how she felt even before I let her in. Actually, that's why I let her in. I saw. I saw. I knew how they treated her. I knew how she felt about it. And after she died, I felt bad for never doing something to change things. I don't know what I could have done, really, but I felt guilty for letting it be that way, not saying anything about it."

"I understand that feeling," I said. "The guilt, I mean."

Couri nodded. And then, seemingly out of nowhere, she said, "You mean you feel guilty about him, right? About Noah. About what happened that day."

My whole body tensed, hearing her say those words. "How do you know about what happened that day?" I asked. "I mean, how do you know about our fight?"

"Because of Adrienne," Couri said. "And because of Noah, too. She was inside me the last time they talked."

⌒

At first, hearing those words, I felt something fill me up inside, like helium in a balloon, making me feel lighter, as if I might float right out of my chair. *Couri had seen him*. She'd seen him while Adrienne had possessed her. She'd heard him. It wasn't just my dad who'd seen him. Noah was *here*, lingering, like the others. And even though he wouldn't come to me, just knowing that he was here filled me with a desperate hope that I might still have a chance to say what he needed to hear, and to listen to what he needed to tell me. Everything we didn't get a chance to say before he was taken away. All of the ways I wanted to say *I'm sorry*, and all of the ways I wanted to hear him say *I love you*.

And *goodbye*. A proper goodbye, I mean. A goodbye that made me feel like I could move on to whatever might be waiting next for me, here on earth, without him.

For one brief moment, I thought everything would be easier. That Couri would know where I could find him.

But as Couri continued to talk, all of that lightness, that floaty feeling, began to fade. By the time she'd finished, I was a sagging sack of flesh and bone sitting in a desk chair, facing a laptop, the bright glare of its screen the only light in my dark room. I was hollow again. Empty. And somehow, despite that emptiness, I felt more weighed down than ever.

Because what Couri explained, in the end, was that Noah had only come to see Adrienne, after she possessed Couri, to try to talk her out of it, to try to reason with her.

"He told Adrienne she wasn't thinking clearly," Couri said. "He pleaded with her for a long time. But Adrienne didn't want to hear it. I remember her telling him not to judge her. That I'd given her the space inside me, that she hadn't taken it from me. And I remember Adrienne telling him if he'd go to you, you'd probably do the same for him."

I sat there for a long time, in shock, not knowing what to say, looking down at my hands on my desk near the keyboard, running that idea through my head on a loop. Before finding out Adrienne had taken refuge inside Couri, the idea that something like that was possible had never entered my mind. And now it had. The impossible had become possible. And even though I'd just helped Adrienne find a way out, release her from the gray area all of my friends kept describing, I started to think about doing it, too. Giving him a space to live inside me. If he'd just come to me.

I looked up from my hands and said, "Noah would never ask me to do that for him."

Couri nodded, then said, "That's actually what he told Adrienne."

"Do you know where he is?" I finally asked. "Do you know how I can find him?"

Couri shook her head. "No," she said. "He visited Adrienne here, in my room, after she came to me. They didn't talk about where he'd been. He was just trying to get her to leave me."

I was back at the edge of the hole that opened up inside me during the early days after the outbreak. There I was again, looking down into a dark and fathomless pit that seemed to go on forever, where only cold wind swirled in the emptiness, howling.

I don't know what I must have looked like then, but it must have been pretty bad. Bad enough for Couri to say, "Ellie, wait."

And I looked up, blinking, trying not to push the button to disconnect before she could tell me more things I didn't want to hear.

"Listen," Couri said, then took a deep breath afterward. "I don't know how to say any of this. And I'm afraid anything I say might be wrong. But here's the thing. I have these memories. Memories of Adrienne. No, wait. That's not it. Not exactly. Not memories of Adrienne, but what I think must be Adrienne's memories."

"What do you mean?" I said, narrowing my eyes.

"It's like," Couri said, "her memories and mine got mixed together, while she was living inside me. They're all patchwork, though, and confusing."

"Tell me more," I said, starting to back away from that hole a little.

And then Couri went on to tell me about memories she'd had that weren't hers.

A memory of Adrienne holding a flute up to her mouth during an audition for a university music program she wants to attend. Her nerves making it hard for her to catch her breath as she stands in front of the panel of professors waiting for her to start. Adrienne putting her lips to the mouthpiece, but not being able to fill it with breath. All she can think of is Couri. Couri's cello performances, Couri's acceptance to a summer music program at a school with an even better reputation than the one Adrienne's trying to get into. And then, afterward, walking out of that room to meet her parents in the hallway. Saying nothing to them, but shaking her head to let them know she'd failed.

A memory of Adrienne sitting in the bleachers during a football game, her hands folded between her knees. It's the halftime break, and instead of being down with the marching band, she's sitting between her mom and dad, who are standing up and clapping along to the music as they watch Couri march across the field. Adrienne had quit the marching band a month earlier, after the audition for the music program went so badly. Her father looks over at her mom and says how amazing Couri is, and her mom beams in agreement. Adrienne watches Couri march with the others, twirling a baton, and tears sting in her eyes while everyone around her is cheering.

"I don't want to tell you something that won't turn out to be true," Couri said, after sharing those memories. "I don't want to disappoint you any more than you are."

"Anything," I told her, "is better than nothing."

She nodded, then said, "From the bits and pieces of memory floating around inside me, my best guess for finding Noah would be to find Ingrid."

"Ingrid Mueller?" I said.

"Yeah," said Couri. "In Adrienne's memories, he was always with her. Afterward, I mean. After they died. In every memory of Adrienne's that I have, Ingrid's always right there beside him."

19

The Last Will and Testament of Ellie Frame, cont.

After Couri and I finished talking, after I disconnected the call and closed up my laptop, I spent the rest of the night tossing and turning, unable to get them off my mind. Unable to turn off my memories. Memories of Noah and Ingrid Mueller.

Ingrid Mueller turning a corner of a hallway in school, meeting my eyes. Me saying hello, her face seeming to twist in on itself in response, the shadow of a scowl. Her contempt for me so obvious.

Noah and me, the night before the outbreak. The night the fight started. We were watching television in his living room. His parents were upstairs, letting us hang out without bothering us. At some point in the evening, I saw something flash out of the corner of my eye and turned to see that a light had just come on across the road at the Mueller house. The porch light. And beneath the light stood Ingrid, hands at her sides, not moving. Just standing there, facing our direction. *Watching us,* I remember thinking. That's when I turned to Noah and said, "I don't think Ingrid Mueller likes me very much." And that's when he looked over at me, his arm, curled around my shoulders, suddenly tensing, and he told me I was imagining things, that I shouldn't even think about her. Then me pushing the issue, telling him how she acted around me at school. How, no matter what I did to be friendly, she wouldn't let me. Noah shook his head and said he couldn't believe how insecure I was. And then, after that, we just kept going back and forth, our voices ratcheting up another notch in tension each time we dismissed each other's feelings.

Until I stood up, grabbed my things, and stormed out.

And then the continuation of the argument the next day in the school parking lot. That was the memory I'd been playing on a loop ever since. The memory I was trapped in: the two of us saying horrible, petty things to each other. Not knowing what would happen later that day. Not knowing I'd never see him again. Not knowing we could never say, *I'm sorry.*

I cried enough that night, turning those memories over and over in my head, until finally, out of sheer exhaustion, I fell asleep. The next day, when I woke and went downstairs, I found my mom waiting for me at the breakfast nook table. A cup of coffee steamed in front of her, and she'd already set out another one on the opposite side of the table for me. Between the two mugs, in the center of the table, she'd propped up a large mailing envelope against the cups of sugar and cream. And as I sat down to lean in closer, I saw that it was addressed to me.

"What's this?" I asked, wrinkling my nose a little, an instinctive tic I had whenever something unexpected came my direction, postal surprises or otherwise.

"I don't know," Mom said, shrugging but wrinkling her nose a little at it, too, as if she wanted to affirm my instincts when it comes to surprises. "It's for you. The return address is from a town in New York called Salamanca. Do you know anyone who lives there?"

I blinked and looked off to the side, trying to think if I did, but eventually I turned back to Mom and said, "No. I don't think so."

Then we both sat in silence, staring down at the envelope like its contents might be highly dangerous. White powder from terrorists. A magic spell that might call down another disaster to wreak havoc on us, like the tornadoes. We'd had too many recent surprises that had turned out to be horrific. So we sat there and didn't move, not wanting to disturb the world any further with some kind of butterfly effect, just by opening that envelope.

"Well?" Mom said after a while, not very enthusiastic. "Are you going to open it, or do you want me to?"

I didn't say anything. But I reached out and picked up the envelope, then brought it closer to look at the fine, looping cursive the sender had used to write my name and address. After a moment, I finally unsealed it and shook out the contents.

Pictures—photos, to be exact—slipped out, one after

another, onto the table in front of me. Photos *I'd* taken. Photos of people from school. The basketball team after they made it to regionals. The principal shaking hands with a novelist who grew up in Newfoundland, who'd come to speak to us about his career. The concert choir performing a routine in the auditorium: the girls' dresses twirling as they spun, the guys in the midst of reaching out to grab their dancing partners' hands.

And photos of Noah. Photos of Becca and Rose. Photos of Adrienne. A picture of them all at a basketball game, sitting in the bleachers, chanting a fight song. Another from a soccer match, where I'd caught Noah in action, bouncing the ball off his head, his hair flying midair, with beads of sweat rolling off it. A photo of Becca and Rose and Adrienne laughing at a table in the all-night diner in Cortland, where we sometimes went after seeing a late movie on the weekend. Selfies of me and Noah, my outstretched arm holding the camera up in front of us as he kissed my cheek, me beaming as his lips pressed against my skin.

And then, last to fall out, a folded piece of paper that turned out to be a letter, handwritten in the same looping cursive as on the envelope, from a woman named Margery Addison, who lived in Salamanca, New York, about 175 miles away from Newfoundland.

To Miss Ellie Frame,

It is with great pleasure that I write this letter. The other day, I was working in my garden when I came across a tattered envelope containing these lovely photographs. I think you must be the photographer, as there was a receipt from the place where they were printed along with them, with your name listed for pickup. I'm not someone who knows all the ins and outs of the internet, but my granddaughter has helped me locate you, based on the information on that store receipt. I'm confident that you're the correct person, as she also found your high school newspaper online, where you're credited with many of the photos. If we're incorrect in our conclusions, would you please be so kind as to send these photos back to me, so we can try to find the correct Ellie Frame once again? And if we are correct in our internet sleuthing, could you please write to confirm that you received these? The photos are beautiful. Such young and happy faces. I said to myself as soon as I saw them, someone will be missing these faces right now, and that's why I hope to know if they have found themselves back in the right hands.

I don't know how they ended up in my garden, nor how long they've been there waiting for me to find them, but my granddaughter says she believes they were carried here on the wind. I've read about the horrible storms that came through your town recently, and so we have no other way to explain it. If this is the case, I hope you and yours are safe and well.

With warm regards,
Margery Addison

One of the letters in Margery's name—the *n* in Addison—suddenly blurred, and I realized I was crying. A tear had fallen onto the page and turned her ink into a messy blue spiral.

"What is it, honey?" Mom said, and I looked up, shook my head, unable to say anything right away. My throat was tight and seemed to close tighter with every passing second. I shook my head again, felt more tears spring hot to my eyes, and handed her the letter.

By the time my mom finished reading it for herself, she was wiping tears away from her face, too. "Ellie," she said, looking across the table at me. "What a gift this is. What a beautiful gift this woman has given you."

I blinked and clenched my teeth, not feeling the same way as Mom just then. The last time I'd seen those photos, they'd been in my locker at school. They must have been carried away by the tornadoes, like Margery and her granddaughter imagined. Sent in their original envelope like a flying carpet on high winds, only to land in the garden of an old woman nearly two hundred miles away. And all I could think about as I looked at them now was how horrible things must have been for them—for Noah. For my friends. For everyone there that day, even the people who were safe in the east wing. If the door of my locker had been ripped off, allowing this envelope of photos to be torn out of the building, along with the concrete and bricks and metal and glass and all of the other materials I'd heard Becca and Rose and Adrienne describe being sucked out around them, what had *they* gone through? How afraid must they have been? And then how terrifying it must have been to wake up and still find yourself there, in this world, but at the same time *not there* and with no way of leaving, of moving on from this place, even though they felt compelled to?

They'd told me their stories, but they spared me so many horrific details, even in death, trying to be good friends to me. The one who'd come closest to giving me graphic details had been Adrienne, but even now I realized that in her desperation over what happened, she must have still held some things back. Things she might have said but didn't. Things that might have disturbed me even more than what she did tell me.

"Ellie?" Mom said. "Honey? Are you okay?"

And even though I knew how to keep my sobs stuffed down inside me like a pro by then, I couldn't stop the tears. I just kept shaking my head in answer to her question, my tears falling hot and fast. I kept my mouth set firm, though, so that the howl from that hollow place inside me—that gone away place—couldn't escape.

Mom got up and came over to sit in the chair beside me. She put her arms around me, pulled me to her, held me tight, her chin resting on top of my head. And because she held me so tight, I felt like I could let go of those sobs I'd been holding in. Soon she was rocking me back and forth, saying, "Oh, sweetie. Oh, my poor girl, it's going to be okay. I promise you. Just let it out. Don't keep any of this inside you."

I couldn't admit it to her, not right then, but I wanted to correct her. I wanted to say, *Nothing. There's nothing inside me. It's all been taken from me now. It's all gone away. I'm nothing. I'm no one without them.*

When it was finally over, when I'd released all of my tears in a slow but orderly fashion, as if I were a professional releaser of body-convulsing howls, I lay still in her arms for a long while, breathing in her scent, wishing I were a little kid again, before I knew how awful the world could be. Before I knew how horrible it would be to lose the people you love more than anything.

Afterward, Mom took the photos and letter, and put them back into the envelope, saying, "I think I'm going to hold on to these for you for a while, unless you want to keep them with you. I can write to Margery for you, too, if you want."

"No," I said, wiping the last film of tears from my face, shaking my head. "I can keep them. I want to. I need to. And I'll write Margery, too. You're right. What she did was really nice. I just wasn't prepared for it, that's all."

"That's understandable," Mom said, holding the envelope out to me. I took it and set it on my lap, looking down at it before looking back up at Mom and thinking about how beautiful she was, about how strong she was, about how she was my best friend. Not just now, either, after I'd lost all of my friends, but before anything horrible had happened. I don't think I had ever recognized that, to be honest. I don't think I'd understood how fierce her love for me was until a nightmare descended on us, snapping us out of the illusion that life would go on as it always had. And right then I was grateful that, despite everyone I'd lost, she was still here with me.

I got up and hugged her, as tight as she'd held me, and kissed her cheek before I let go.

"What's all this for?" she said, laughing a little.

"Because you're wonderful," I said. "That's all. Thank you. For everything."

Then I plucked my car keys from the rack on the wall behind her, and headed out the side door.

I drove aimlessly at first, just circling around old roads I knew by heart. I still knew where they went to, of course. But after the outbreak, some roads had been closed off, the detours making everything feel unfamiliar. Some were completely unrecognizable. Roads that had once been lined with ancient maples and silver oaks were now lined with freshly turned soil, and where the fallen trees had been removed, the earth had been tamped down afterward. Roads where gray-green stunted stalks of corn littered the fields on either side, when instead they should have reached to several feet tall—waving their fronds at passersby—this late into spring. Baseball diamonds, where dugouts and backstops had been leveled, lay empty and silent as I drove by. I thought of how, in summers past, it seemed I could never drive by a baseball field without hearing the crack of a bat or the gruff voice of an umpire.

I'd never been interested in baseball, to be honest. *It's the most boring sport in the world,* I would have answered if anyone asked. But as I drove past those fields, I wished so hard to see people filling them, hurling and hitting balls, no matter how boring I may have found the game.

Eventually, I found myself driving toward Noah's house. In

the back of my mind, I knew I'd been headed there from the start, even though I didn't want to admit it. I'd been avoiding the place for over a month. At first, because I couldn't bear to see his parents, their faces weighed down with a grief even larger than my own. And then, after going to his funeral and learning that his parents were going to leave Newfoundland to stay with his mother's sister and put themselves back together, away from this place, I'd stayed away out of respect and out of fear of Mrs. Mueller seeing me from across the road and calling the police on me for breaking and entering. Because, technically, that's what I'd be doing if I went there.

But a few minutes later, the Cadys' house came into view, and then I was turning into their driveway, parking in the turnaround area by the garage, which sat behind the house a little, hoping my car wouldn't be visible to anyone driving past, or to Mrs. Mueller. When I got out, I immediately looked up at the second-story back window, the one directly above the kitchen. That window was in Noah's bedroom. I'd been up there a few times in the last few months, but only briefly. His parents didn't like leaving us alone in there; they were old-fashioned like that, so the door always had to be open, and occasionally one of them would make an excuse to come upstairs to use the bathroom, even though there was one downstairs, just so they could pass by and look in on us, like patrol officers. My parents weren't much different. That's why Noah and I would go to the lighthouse, at least in decent weather, to be alone.

I stared at his window for a while, hoping that if I looked long and hard enough, the curtains would suddenly pull back to reveal his face behind the glass. But no, nothing like that happened, no matter how much I willed it to, so I headed for the back door.

I knew where the Cadys hid their spare house key: in the flowerpot next to their back doorstep. I'd seen Noah sift through the potting soil once before, when I'd driven him home from school because his car broke down and he'd forgotten to bring his keys with him in the morning. And I found the key still there, the metal cold in my fingers as they curled around it.

I slipped the key into the lock and turned the knob of the back door, letting myself into the house, where the only thing I could hear was the sound of their old grandfather clock—handed down from Mrs. Cady's mother—ticking in the hallway. I hesitated for just one moment, telling myself I shouldn't be in there, that what I was doing was wrong, that I should leave. But in the end, if I could find him here, in the place that had been his home all his life, doing something wrong would be worth it.

So I moved further into the house, taking light steps, as if I might wake someone. I walked past the entry to the kitchen, where the prep island with the granite countertop sat empty, except for a blue glass vase of withered funeral flowers that Mrs. Cady must have forgotten to throw out before she and Mr. Cady left town. Then past the grandfather clock I went, brushing my fingers across the glass panel of its door briefly, until I came to the living room, where I stopped and stared at the couch where Noah and I had sat and argued the night before the outbreak.

Don't even think about her, Ellie.

That's all in your imagination.

You are so insecure.

His words still stung a little, but now not for the same reasons they did when he'd said them. Now they stung because they might be among the last words I'd ever hear from him, if I couldn't find him.

I turned away from the couch and went upstairs, letting myself into his room, the first door on the left, which squealed a little as I swung it open. And then my mouth fell open as I stood in the doorway, looking into a room where the bed was unmade, the comforter hanging down the side of it, the pillows in disarray. A room where three pairs of shoes, some for soccer and others for everyday use, were still out on the floor, instead of being packed away in the closet. And the closet door itself left halfway open, revealing the arms of shirts and sweaters lined up under the glare of the light above them. A glass sat on the nightstand next to his bed, with a shadow of whatever Noah had been drinking still left on it. All of it, everything, left how it had been over a month ago, on the morning he'd left for school, where we'd argue in the parking lot. On the day when he and all of my closest friends would die while I was safe in the lighthouse, watching it all happen, hypnotized.

I gasped for breath, as if someone had hit me in the stomach, as if all the air had been sucked out of me while I remembered moments from the day my friends and so many people I'd known for my entire life were taken away. The room seemed to spin around me then, slowly at first, but moving faster with each passing second. My heart climbed into my throat, beating hard, pulsing over and over, and I began to whisper, "Please, please, please. Oh God, please. Why won't he come to me. I miss you so much. I need you so badly. Please, Noah. Please."

And then, before I nearly passed out from vertigo, I saw him. Right there. Right in front of me.

He blinked into view, as if by magic or teleportation, wearing his soccer jersey—the one my dad had seen him wearing as he walked into the woods behind our house nearly a month ago, haunting us, haunting me without me knowing it—and when I nearly retched at the sight of him, putting my hand to my mouth, he came over and put one hand on my shoulder, the other on my waist, steadying me, looking into my eyes before saying, "Ellie, stop this. You need to stop this right now."

I could *feel* him. I could feel his touch. The pressure of his hands on my body. Just like when he was alive. Just like I'd felt Becca's weight dip into the bed beside me. *I managed to do it,* I thought. I'd managed to call him to me.

"I'm sorry," I said, "for forcing you to come here. But I need you. I need to say things to you."

I didn't get the chance to do that, though. Not really. Because as soon as I opened my mouth to say those things, he disappeared, leaving nothing but open air right in front of me.

I fell to my knees, gasping for breath, thinking I might pass out, realizing that my desire to find him had made me delusional. I was seeing things, imagining things, I told myself.

But I made myself get up a moment later, and soon I was frantically running from room to room, swinging doors open, calling his name, hoping I was wrong, that what I'd seen was truly him and not my mind playing tricks on me.

But wherever I looked, he wasn't there.

When I went back down to the living room, I stopped in front of the picture window to peer out at the house across the road, where the grass had started to grow high again without anyone around to cut it.

There was only one thing I could do now, much as I didn't want to. If Noah wouldn't come to me. If he wouldn't let me see him.

I would have to visit Ingrid Mueller's mother.

20

Calliope Mueller—Dealing with Ghosts

"The mind and spirit have a way of giving us everything we need," Dr. Arroyo said as she stretched out her hand, palm up and open, and waited for me to respond.

It was a test, I knew immediately, the way psychologists and therapists are always testing to see "where people are" with whatever troubles them. I went through all that after my husband, August, died nearly a decade ago. An outstretched hand, though, an offering of intimacy, that's a different test from any of the ones the therapists I saw back then put to me. I knew what it was, and looked down, considering her hand carefully, to show that I was at least someone she wouldn't need to "track" for however long she'd be in Newfoundland. She could rest easy about me, if I said and did the right things, despite having lost the last remaining member of my family. A daughter this time, instead of my husband.

I put my hand in Dr. Arroyo's and let her gently squeeze. "Thank you, Dr. Arroyo," I said, and immediately she shook her head.

"Eva," she said, smiling. "Please call me Eva."

"Eva," I said, testing the name in a way I thought would sound polite, soft, and hesitant. "Thank you, Eva."

"Do you believe what I've just told you, Callie?" Dr. Arroyo asked. "Do you feel what I say is true inside you?"

I looked around the room, a plain, white-walled makeshift office in what had previously been a vacant downtown storefront, and thought about how that room and its starkness, holding only the bare essentials of a desk and several chairs, were how I truly felt inside.

I nodded anyway, and continued to lie.

"I do," I said, and she offered a fast, supportive smile. "I've been through all this before," I said. "I know what hurdles to expect in the long run. I know what I'll have to do to move on from this. From losing Ingrid."

"You are such a strong person," Dr. Arroyo said, eyes slightly widened, shaking her head slowly. "Many people here haven't had to deal with this kind of damage in their lives, like you have. Where your bones were once broken, now they are strong. I sense that you really do know what you have to do to get through this. But tell me. Isn't it harder, losing a child?"

She was smarter than the therapists I saw after August died. That much I could tell right off. They'd been easier to lie to. Maybe because they were men, and they'd assumed losing a husband was the ultimate devastation a woman could face in her lifetime. They'd coddled me, they'd given me prescriptions

231

for a variety of anxiety pills. They'd looked on as I spoke of my grief with such sympathy, the same way the rest of Newfoundland had responded, with an overflow of support. I was always grateful for that support, but I do wish I hadn't had to lie in order to receive it. I wish I hadn't had to lie about how grief-stricken I was after August died, because in reality, losing him had been a relief.

It's more difficult losing a child, like Dr. Arroyo suggested. She understood that, she said, being a mother herself. She had a family she'd left behind in Columbus in order to tend to the troubled souls of Newfoundland as a trauma specialist. When I asked if she had any pictures, she showed me several on her phone. She had two girls of her own. Dark hair like hers, tidy pigtails, pinkish-brown skin, bright smiles, and an attractive husband who, she'd told me earlier, taught history at Ohio State.

"I'll be honest," I said, even though that was another lie. "It's definitely harder to lose a child. It was terrible to lose my husband, it was. But losing Ingrid . . . Well, even though I know how to work through this doesn't mean it's going to be easy."

"It's hard to say goodbye to a child," Dr. Arroyo said, nodding, releasing my hand to lean back in her chair. "It's the worst thing in the world."

"Especially when that child was the only good thing you've had in your life for nearly a decade," I added. I met her eyes so she could tell I was clear-sighted about everything, so she could see I wasn't another small-town sort of person who didn't understand the gravity of her own situation.

"I think, Callie," she said, "that someone like you could

possibly be of great use to others as Newfoundland tries to heal itself."

"Me?" I said, pulling back a little, narrowing my eyes. This was a test I didn't immediately know how to pass. "How? I haven't been useful to anyone in a long, long time."

"You could show others how to deal with their grief. You already know the path forward. Others, you may have heard, are having a much more difficult time."

"You mean the ghosts," I said, and waited to see how she'd respond to that.

After a long pause, Dr. Arroyo nodded, her lips pursed. "The ghosts," she said, as if we were on the same team, sharing a secret. "Yes. Many are claiming to see the dead lately."

"But I don't know anything about dealing with ghosts," I told her.

"No," said Dr. Arroyo. "Because you've learned to manage the trauma of your loss in other ways. Other people don't have those skill sets in place. Your friends and neighbors have had such a large hole ripped in the fabric of their reality that the ghosts they're seeing are nothing more than delusions born of grief."

I pursed my lips and nodded now, too, to show that we were on the same page. "That's definitely sad," I said, blinking hard, as if I were trying to push away simmering tears. "It's real sad. It's sadder than anything I experienced after August's death, I have to admit. But it's also understandable."

"Consider it, Callie," Dr. Arroyo said, before she started to wrap up our session a few minutes later. "If you think you might want to help out in the near future, come see me again, and I'll take you to some of the community workshops I'm planning to hold."

———

I left her office the same way I'd come to it: bitter, angry, clear-eyed to the point that I couldn't concoct a delusion even if I'd wanted to believe in something unbelievable. Just down the street, though, lay the ruins of the high school, where one wing had been reduced to blackened rubble. And just down the street in the opposite direction were the remains of the town hall, now mostly a razed space—like a construction zone—with fencing put up around it. And here and there, down side streets, a few abandoned vehicles still littered the sidewalks, waiting to be hauled away. The only businesses in town that seemed to be doing well after the tornadoes came through were the two funeral homes that, over the last month or so, had become far too regular gathering places.

There was nothing in the world I could look at and lie to myself about, even if I could lie easily to other people. Everything in this place was ruined. Everything this place was had either been torn up or lifted up and flown away. There were no delusions my mind could invent to deny the reality of that.

Despite not having been downtown in several years, I walked through those ruins like it was something I did every day. It was a show for some of the Newfoundlanders whose paths I crossed, I'm sure. The county road crews as they attempted to clear up and to repair what remained, a few of the local business owners who had come out to set up shop again and were now forlornly waiting to see how long it would take for customers to return. I hadn't been seen beyond my own property lines in a long, long time at that point. Even when it came to things like parent-teacher conferences, I'd phone the school to talk to Ingrid's teachers instead of meeting them face to face. They all understood. They all let me make these kinds of arrangements after my husband was killed. And though it had been nearly a decade since that occurred, they still left me alone like I wanted.

It took me just over an hour to walk the three miles home, but it was uphill, and there were no sidewalks once I left the downtown square, and there were still places where the road crews were clearing debris or cutting up fallen trees. Whenever I came across a work site, I headed into the woods on either side of the road to avoid them, and returned only after I'd moved far enough past them, hidden within the shadows of the trees.

I'd only gone downtown because of the email, and then the phone call, that had come from Dr. Arroyo's assistant. She was trying to see as many residents as possible individually, so she could "address our needs as a community." I didn't know what to expect from a therapist sent in by the state, but I decided to get the session over with, or else one day there'd be a knock at my door, and when I answered, she'd be on the other side, wanting me to invite her in for a cup of tea or coffee. Maybe just a glass of water, if she was the type who didn't want caffeine to sully her health. She seemed like that type.

That was never going to happen. My home is my sanctuary. I don't let anyone in unless I have to. For years, it had been only

235

Ingrid and me, other than the occasional postal delivery or when Noah Cady came over to fix things—even when I knew how to make the repairs—because having him around made Ingrid happy. If she hadn't had those times to interact with him without feeling the eyes of everyone in school watching, she'd probably have become even more sullen than she already was. And that would have been too much for either of us to bear for very long, let me tell you.

It was a cross for Ingrid, really, living in the way I demanded: solitary, removed from the kind of normal, daily life others led. And by *normal,* they meant marriage; children; attending school concerts; taking pictures with sons and daughters in their rented tuxes and the fancy dresses they purchased from the discount dress store over in Sharon, Pennsylvania, as Newfoundland tradition demanded; then watching their kids drive off to homecoming or prom before going back inside after all the photo-taking was over, to sit in the living room and reminisce about their own lost youth.

That wasn't the sort of thing I'd ever wanted. But like a lot of girls in Newfoundland, I made mistakes in life before I knew those mistakes were there to be made. I'd started dating August Mueller during my senior year of high school, and despite being valedictorian, with grades higher than Mount Everest, I ended up following my mother's advice when I found myself in a "predicament" (her word), and her advice had been for me to drop out after completing only one year of college so that I could have the child I carried.

I don't regret having Ingrid, but I do regret marrying August. There wasn't anything wrong with the man, but I realized early in our marriage that I didn't love him. We were too different. I read novels, dug into history books as if they held the car chases and explosions of blockbuster movies, and I painted with watercolors, which my mother had taught me how to do. August fixed cars for people around town, right in the old barn behind our house, hunted any animal in any season that wasn't illegal, collected firearms, and fell asleep watching sports after drinking five or six beers. Don't believe anyone who tells you that opposites attract. That's a *true* delusion. Opposites repel. I learned that in a psychology course, right before marriage and motherhood took me out of the world of ideas and returned me to Newfoundland, the land of consequences for bad decisions. It was only after August was gone that I decided it was time to give myself something I wanted again. And that was a life lived away from other people.

So when I finally arrived at the foot of my gravel drive after my session with Dr. Arroyo and saw an unfamiliar car there and someone standing in front of my home, I stopped, trying to make out who it was who planned to disturb me right after I'd gone out of my way to alleviate the concerns of the state-appointed shrink. And when I finally recognized the person, it wasn't anyone I'd have ever thought I'd see waiting at the foot of my front porch.

It was Ellie Frame, the girl who had stolen the boy my daughter had loved for years. I'd only seen the girl in person a few times, before August died, when she was just a child and I still went out into the world. And, of course, in the school yearbooks Ingrid brought home over the years. I'd seen her at the memorial for Noah Cady, where the girl was obviously shocked by my presence, not that any Newfoundlanders weren't surprised to see me. The only things I really knew about Ellie Frame were that her mother was a local real estate agent, her father worked for the power company, and that Noah Cady changed how he did his hair and came around to visit Ingrid and me less after he started dating her.

"Hello, there," I said as I walked up the drive and met her at the foot of the porch steps. I gave what I hoped was a somewhat friendly smile, but cocked my head to the side to show how I thought her appearance here was curious. "Can I help you?"

"Mrs. Mueller," she said, with a manner that approached Dr. Arroyo's level of professionalism. *Oh, dear girl,* I thought, *you'll either get far with that attitude, or else you'll dig yourself an early grave.* "You don't know me. At least I don't think you do. My name is Ellie Frame. I was in your daughter's class." Then the girl abruptly stopped her self-introduction to blink over and over, as if she'd forgotten what she'd planned on saying next.

"I'm familiar with your name," I said, nodding, but offered no details as to how or why I knew it. "Is there something I can do for you, Miss Frame?" I thought she'd like being addressed that way, since she was in the business of being so serious.

The girl's face fell after I said that. It broke like a dam. Tears poured out of her almost instantaneously, and she quickly brought her hands to her face to wipe them away.

"I'm sorry," she said a few moments later, after she'd collected herself. "I'm so sorry, Mrs. Mueller. I didn't mean to come here just to cry in front of you."

"Well, even if you did," I said, "that's okay. But why don't we at least go up on the porch in the shade?"

She smiled briefly and nodded, perhaps grateful that I hadn't turned out to be the strange and abrasive solitary sort or the sad widow type, which I imagined were the only two roles people had cast me in over the years. "Thanks," she said, and followed me up the creaking planks of the stairs, onto the creaking planks of the porch, to sit across from me in one of the two cane chairs I kept out there for me and Ingrid.

"Now," I said, once we were settled in, "I imagine this has something to do with what's happened recently." The girl's eyes went wide after I said that, surprised like she thought I'd just read her mind. Poor thing. Her emotions were painted all over her face, and she hadn't yet learned a way to hide them. "With the storms and all," I added, to see her reaction, which was to furrow her brows in disappointment. I knew that she hadn't wanted me to mean the storms. She'd wanted me to mean the ghosts.

"It is," she eventually managed to say. "I mean, sort of. I mean, yes, it's about what's happened recently. But not just the storms." She stopped then and pulled her bottom lip between her teeth, while through her clear blue eyes I watched the gears of her mind move and creak. How to open this conversation? That was what she was trying to figure out. It was a great difficulty to her, I could see, especially since we were essentially strangers. And probably even more difficult because—if I knew Ingrid and how transparent her feelings could be—this girl probably knew Ingrid had been jealous and brokenhearted over her having taken Noah Cady away.

"What else is it about, then?" I asked, giving her an opening, already knowing her answer.

"The ghosts," she said, and her voice came out as thin as a whisper.

"The ghosts," I said, and cocked my head to the side again, pursing my lips in the way Dr. Arroyo used to show her concerned skepticism. "Ah, yes, the ghosts people claim to be seeing."

Ellie Frame narrowed her eyes a little at that. "You mean . . ." She paused for a second before continuing. "You mean you haven't seen anything like that?"

"Call me Callie," I said, imitating Dr. Arroyo again, whose familiar approach to people was something I figured would probably work with a girl like Ellie Frame, a girl too open—too vulnerable—for her own good. "And no, I haven't seen any ghosts. At least not yet. Why? Have you?"

The girl leaned back in her chair and sighed, though I couldn't tell if it was a sigh of relief to hear that, or a sigh of frustration, like she'd wished I had. She looked down at her hands, which she'd folded in her lap, nervously twining her fingers together. When she looked back up, she pushed a piece of her corn-silk hair away from her face and said, "I have. I've seen some."

Here we go, I thought. *We're getting to the crux of what the girl had come for.*

"Who?" I asked. "How many?"

"A few," she said, suddenly pulling into herself a little. "Friends of mine," she added. "Friends who were in the wing of the school that collapsed that day."

I closed my eyes and shook my head slowly. "I'm so sorry for that, Ellie," I said. "It's a lot to take in all at once, I know."

And after a long pause, during which the girl's lips moved a little, trying to get the words out, she said, "And, from what they've told me, Ingrid was with them."

I opened my eyes wider when my daughter's name left the girl's mouth. It set me off, hearing her say Ingrid's name, even though I knew we'd eventually have to talk about her.

"Yes," I said. "I know that. Ingrid was in that wing of the school, too, I'm sorry to say."

"No," the girl said, shaking her head briefly, her mouth still parted slightly in this way that spelled out just how much she didn't want to admit what she said next. Which was: "Mrs. Mueller. I mean, Callie. My friends. The friends I've seen recently. The ghosts of my friends, that is. They said Ingrid had been with them. Not just during the collapse, but afterward. Still here. Still alive, sort of. Just . . ."

"Dead at the same time?" I offered, to put the girl out of her anxious misery.

Then she finally closed her fool mouth and nodded.

I took a deep breath and felt my heartbeat quicken, even though I'd known this was what the girl had come for. "So these friends of yours—their ghosts, that is—have told you they've seen Ingrid as well?" I managed to say. I just repeated what the girl had already told me, to keep myself in check, to try to remain neutral.

The girl only swallowed a lump in her throat and nodded.

Then I sat back and looked away from her to stare at my front lawn, which was overgrown with weeds and dandelions now that Noah Cady wasn't around to mow it for me. All those puffs of white seeds, the former heads of bright yellow petals having fallen into the weeds. Mr. Cady had come over once to mow it for me after Noah's funeral, as if he was taking over the duties his son had so generously performed over the years, but then, soon after, he and his wife had left to visit her sister in Arizona. He'd said he wanted to get her out of Newfoundland for a while. Otherwise she wouldn't stop thinking about Noah. I could understand, and said as much.

As I stared at that weedy, dandelion-ridden lawn, I chewed on my bottom lip like what the girl had said truly worried me. Then, eventually and with an amount of seriousness to match her own, I turned back to her. "I'm afraid I haven't seen her, Ellie," I said, shaking my head slowly, adding a second later, "for which I am very grateful. And I'm sorry that you've had to witness things of that nature. Grief is a powerful force, it is. But tell me. Why is it that you want to find Ingrid? Were you friends with my daughter?"

The girl opened up once again like a book, tears spilling fast and hot, no filter to keep them back from people who might try to take advantage of her feelings, and said, "Because I can't find Noah. He was my boyfriend. You probably know that already. And I need to see him. I need to tell him something. He's out there, too, I know. Others have said as much. But he's . . . he's avoiding me, I think. And I think he's with Ingrid. And I was hoping that, if I could speak to Ingrid, she might know how to find him. They were good friends, after all."

This girl, I thought. *I've had enough of her.* How could she sit there and cry for a dead boyfriend whose ghost wouldn't come to her, when she sat in front of a woman who'd lost a daughter in the same way? How could she be so worried over her own feelings, when her former boyfriend and my daughter were dead? Who cared if they were spending their time together in whatever afterlife they might have had after dying? If this was how selfish the girl was in general, it's no wonder she took Noah away from Ingrid without giving her a second thought.

I kept myself together, though. "Ellie," I said, leaning forward in my chair toward her, putting a hand on one of her knees. "Honey, I think you're going through something real awful right now, I do. But I don't think there are any ghosts out there, to be honest. Not real ones. Only the ones people are seeing because all of this is too hard for everyone to handle right now."

"You don't believe what everyone's saying, then?" the girl asked, seeming shocked that I didn't.

"No," I said. "I don't. Not in that way. I do believe they're seeing things, but it's most likely products of their own imaginations." I remembered reading Henry James and Edith Wharton in my first year of college, and how ghosts in those books were just memories that had taken on lives of their own, haunting the protagonists of the stories in a way that was even sadder, because the truth of the matter was that no real ghosts existed. Just memories. Huge memories. Huge memories of the people they'd lost and couldn't or didn't want to forget.

"I'm sorry," she said quickly, and stood up, flustered, embarrassed. "I'm sorry for coming here and for bothering you, Mrs. Mueller. I'm so sorry."

I stood now, too. "No, no, Ellie, you're fine. No need to be sorry. Please. It's okay, dear. You thought I might have answers for you. And I wish I did. I really do."

She frowned and bit her lower lip again, then said, "Thanks for talking to me. I do appreciate it."

She stepped down from my porch a moment later, and when she was halfway down the drive, opening her car door, she stopped to look over her shoulder and gave me a sad little wave. I waved back, a sad little wave like hers, for good measure.

It was the only thing to do, really. To be warm to someone else in such a tragic situation, even to the girl who had brought nothing but heartache to my daughter in the months before the outbreak.

I went into the house only after the Frame girl had disappeared down the road, and locked the door behind me. And before I could even turn around to face the front room, with its dust-covered furniture and the piles of unopened mail, I heard the floor creak behind me. And then her voice softly pushed its way into the air of this world.

"Is she gone, Mother?" Ingrid asked from behind me.

And I turned to face her, my poor dead daughter, standing in the kitchen doorway, her mousy brown hair framing her face, wearing that awful old dress I'd picked out at the Goodwill store on her birthday, the grayish one with tiny blue flowers decorating it. The cashier, I remember, had lifted that dress up to examine it before entering the price into the register, and had said that those flowers matched Ingrid's eyes. I'd smiled to be nice, and stroked Ingrid's hair once, not pointing out the fact that Ingrid's eyes were gray, not blue.

I nodded to Ingrid now, my poor dead baby girl, whose face was paler than the moon, whose eyes were like two black holes leading to another universe, and said, "It's okay, baby. She's gone. It's just us now. It's just you and me."

She sighed then, relieved the girl had given up and gone away.

"But you're going to have to do something about her," I warned her. "She's getting close, and I don't think she's going to stop looking for him."

21

The Last Will and Testament of Ellie Frame, cont.

At home, after I shut the front door, I paused in the foyer for a moment, my hand still wrapped around the knob, and stared down at the pattern in the braided rug Mom had thrown over the tiled entry. I don't know what stopped me like that, in that particular place, but for some reason I couldn't pull my eyes away from the rug. I was noticing each thread of color in the rug and each tile visible around the fringe—as if I were seeing these things for the first time ever.

Maybe it all looked unfamiliar because I'd hit a dead end. Maybe it was because every path I chose, every step I took, only managed to get me nowhere. Because now, after I talked to Mrs. Mueller, there wasn't anywhere left for me to go. It was all gone away now, everything I once thought I knew, it was all gone away from me.

Except my house, this little bubble that seemed to be the only thing in my life that hadn't changed in the last month. The place I'd hidden myself away in for weeks on end, not wanting to face what lay outside it. That ruined world. This, at least—what I had in front of me—had remained mostly unchanged, a safe haven I could rely on. I let out a small laugh just then, thinking back to how, only a few months ago, I'd taken so much for granted, including this place and the hard-to-keep promises a home holds out to people: constant shelter and a small world in which the people you love will always surround you.

All easily taken away in the passing of a day.

"What's so funny?" Dad called from the living room, and I turned to peek around the corner, finding him sitting on the couch, wearing a Pittsburgh Pirates jersey and gray sweatpants, his steady uniform for days off, when he made no plans to do anything but lounge. He held the TV remote in one hand and muted it as he waited for my answer.

"Nothing, really," I said, shrugging.

Dad lifted one side of his mouth, giving me a half smile of disbelief.

"Okay," I said, trying harder for a satisfying answer. "Life? Life is funny, I guess."

"Funny *good*," he asked, "or funny *bad*?"

"Both," I said, nodding in a defeated sort of acceptance.

"I hear you," he said, sighing. Then he patted the couch cushion beside him. "Want to talk about it? I've been working so much lately, I feel like I don't get to see you anymore."

I went over and sat down, leaned my head against his shoulder, my arm against his arm. We didn't actually talk for a while. We just stared out the picture window, at the abundance of bright sunlight, the watercolor-blue sky, and the clouds that coasted over Newfoundland like phantom ships. It was so damned beautiful. It was so damned beautiful, in fact, that I couldn't believe what Becca and the others had told me: that a gray area was domed over us, like some kind of strange, spectral weather phenomenon, keeping the dead from moving past it, keeping the living clinging to their dead.

"I don't know," Dad said, after we'd sat like that for a while.

"You don't know about what?" I asked.

"I don't know if life is funny *good* anymore," he said.

I pushed my arm harder against his, took his hand in mine, and said, "I know what you mean. I think I've laughed all of once or twice in the past month, and both times I laughed mainly out of panic."

⌒

Across the Ohio-Pennsylvania border, the Pirates were scheduled to play that day. And when the game came on a little while later, Dad snapped out of his sad spell and unmuted the TV. I had the weirdest feeling, seeing him get excited about something as normal as a baseball game, and I watched him watch the game for a little while, just to see him so happy about something so ordinary. Eventually, I got up and left, still hearing the crack of bats and the sportscasters commenting on plays behind me as I went up to my room, where I threw myself on my bed and stared at the ceiling, wondering what I could possibly do next. Wondering how I might still find Noah.

The dead end I'd arrived at? I couldn't accept it.

As I stared up at the ceiling, my eyes tracing the perimeter where it met the walls, I tried to go over everything from my conversation with Mrs. Mueller. *Call me Callie,* she'd said. *And no, I haven't seen any ghosts. At least not yet.* And how, to almost any question I asked her, she'd just answer me with a question of her own.

It occurred to me now as I lay there tracing and retracing the perimeter, recalling the visit with a more analytical eye, that while she'd been nice to me—while she'd gone out of her way to make me feel at ease—she'd also seemed cold. Too eager to shut down my questions, as if she was hiding something. And one thing I know about politeness from living in a small town is that it's often just a cover for not-so-polite inclinations. What Mrs. Mueller had wanted, I realized too late, was to get rid of me as quickly as possible.

Which made me wonder about what she really did know and who she might have actually seen in the wake of the outbreak. And why she'd want to hide what she knew from me.

My phone buzzed beside me then, breaking me out of my thoughts. It was Mom. She was at the shelter and was texting to say she'd be home a few hours later. *I'll pick up something easy for us to eat on my way back.*

By *easy,* she most likely meant pizza. Nothing she had to make herself. Every day she worked at the shelter was a day she'd come home exhausted, sometimes looking as if she was on the verge of tears from subjecting herself to a constant view of tragedy. People who had lost their homes in the outbreak. People who had lost a spouse, a parent, a child, a friend. People who had lost everything except for their heartbeats and the breath that still filled their chests. I'd begun to suspect that, for Mom, volunteering must equate to some kind of penance for having survived the outbreak, and for having lost so little in the process of surviving. And even though she said she'd cut back on her hours, I think she may have actually signed up for more than usual.

I could cook for us, I texted back, even though I knew I was exhausted in a different way from Mom. Exhausted from my own thoughts. Exhausted from not finding what I kept looking for. I'd seen something at the Cady house, but I knew it wasn't Noah so much as my mind melting down momentarily. *You don't have to do everything,* I texted Mom. *Just tell me what you'd like, and I'll go to the store.*

Oh, honey, she replied a minute later. *You've got enough going on.*

I did have enough going on, most of which I didn't tell her about so that she could keep her own grip on things. Someone in our family shouldn't have to deal with ghosts, I figured. She could deal with the living, while I dealt with the dead as best as possible.

If you don't suggest anything, I'll just come up with my own idea.

Okay, Mom said, giving up. *Lasagna?*

You got it, I wrote back, sending her a heart emoji with the message. Then I pulled myself off my bed to ask Dad if I could pick up anything for him while I was out.

"A candy bar," he said, not looking up from the game on the television.

"I'm on it," I said, saluting like a soldier, even though he didn't see me.

⌒

Twenty minutes later, as I went through the store's automatic front doors, I passed one of those two-way mirrors where someone on the other side can see customers coming and going, even though the customers can't see them. Mom said the manager's office was on the other side, and I'd always joked about the grocery store being Big Brother, sometimes making funny faces at whoever might be watching me as I came and went. This time, though, when I looked into that mirror, I almost didn't recognize myself. My skin was paler than I'd ever seen before, probably from shutting myself away from the world so much over the past month, and the skin under my eyes looked almost purple. Not sleeping much was taking a toll on me, as well as seeing too many things I shouldn't even be able to see.

I walked the aisles with the fluorescent glare of the overhead lights making me feel even paler, bloodless. And I must have looked like a zombie to anyone else who saw me, too, because as I stopped and stared at the endless rows of pasta for a time that was probably longer than normal, a stock boy asked if I needed help.

"Finding something, I mean," he said, looking at me with a kind, questioning face.

And I snapped out of my spell only then, realizing that I'd forgotten what I'd come to buy, even though it was right in front of me.

"I think . . . ," I said, trying to collect my thoughts. "I think I need to buy lasagna noodles."

He nodded, but looked slightly weirded out by how much thought I'd been giving lasagna noodles. Then he leaned a little in front of me to choose a box off the shelf. Handing it over to me, he said, "This is the kind my mom always buys. I think they're pretty good, at least."

We shared an awkward moment when I said, "Thank you," and he said, "No problem," and as he walked away, I said, "Thank you again," making him look back over his shoulder with that same weirded-out, worried-for-me look on his face, as if he thought I might not be able to navigate the rest of my shopping trip without him.

I wandered away in zombie-like fashion, gathering up the rest of the things I needed, then went to the cash register and nearly forgot to pick out a candy bar for Dad until the cashier had swept all of my stuff over the sensor and started bagging it. "Oh, wait," I said, rising to break the surface of awareness again. Quickly, I scanned the candy bins on both sides of me, then settled on a chocolate bar filled with caramel, one of Dad's favorites, and asked the cashier to ring that up, too.

Outside, I carried my bags back to my car with the same sort of detachment I'd gone about gathering ingredients in the store. My mind was elsewhere, obviously. My mind couldn't see anything in front of me because it was looking backward, into the past, into that time and place before the outbreak. And if my mind wasn't focusing on the past, it was obsessing over the strange things that had occurred ever since the outbreak. My mind felt almost like a separate part of me at that point, as if that other me I'd seen in the chair at Noah's memorial service really existed, taking up half my thoughts the way Adrienne had pushed herself into Couri.

After I finished loading the back seat with the grocery bags, I loaded myself into the driver's seat, as if my body was just another thing to be lifted and moved. I turned the key in the ignition, and told myself I really needed to snap out of this, because I still had to stay aware long enough to make the drive home. Then I inhaled deeply as I pulled out of the parking lot, shaking my head every now and then to see if I could rattle myself back into this time and place, into this here and now.

And that happened, though not from any head shaking. Something else rattled me, rattled me so much that I truly woke back into full awareness.

As I was cresting a hill just a few miles from home, I saw the Newfoundland Lighthouse in the distance. And though the sun was going down behind me, making the sky into a field of lavender, I swore I saw the lantern room light up.

I slammed on the brakes and sat there, stopped in the middle of the road, my thoughts racing to ridiculous conclusions in the space of seconds—immediately thinking it was Noah, that he was there, *of course* he was there, that he was trying to send me a message—until the lantern room went dark in the next instant, and all of those thoughts crashed with it.

I waited for a few more minutes, telling myself what I'd seen was just another symptom of being exhausted, but also wishing it had been real. And when I saw a car approaching in the rearview mirror, I gave up and continued driving.

After I got home, I immediately began making the lasagna. Boiling water, cooking the noodles the stock boy at the grocery store had picked out for me, layering the pan with the noodles, the cheese, the sauce, then sitting down, with my legs folded under me, in front of the oven to watch it bake through the window, as if cheese and red sauce bubbling over pasta were an amazing occurrence.

But despite having all of that to distract me, the lighthouse still filled my thoughts, the lantern room beaming its light in my direction, over and over, calling me to come to it.

When eventually the timer I'd set dinged, I was able to push the lighthouse signal out of my mind long enough to take the lasagna out of the oven. And soon after that, thankfully, Mom came home to find me slicing a knife through the cheese and noodles when she came in the back door.

"Look at you," she said. "I won't even have time to sit down, you're so ready."

I looked over my shoulder and gave her the smile I knew would make her happy. "Salad is in the fridge, keeping cool," I said.

Mom stood in the kitchen entrance, smiling back at first; then quickly that smile faded, and she started to shake her head and frown.

"What's wrong?" I asked.

"Oh, nothing," she said. "Nothing at all. It's just good to see you up and about again, doing things like you used to. But it makes me a little sad, too, because it reminds me that you're going to go away to school in another month or so."

We hadn't talked about my going to Pitt in the fall since the outbreak happened, but clearly now that I'd done the grocery shopping and made a meal for everyone, Mom was starting to hold out hope that I'd have myself together enough to make the leap out of the disaster Newfoundland had become and move on to what she constantly referred to as "better things." I shrugged, as if I wasn't so sure, not wanting to give her more hope than I thought realistic. Because the truth was, I still couldn't see further than a few hours in front of me, let alone weeks or months or years. And I wasn't sure if I could buy into the idea of "better things" any longer.

"Well, we'll see," I said, and her face shifted, eyes widening a little in concern. "I mean, I don't know. I might want to stick around here for a while. Maybe take some of the first-year classes at the community college in Warren or something. Then, just, you know, maybe I'll see how I feel."

"If you're worried about leaving your dad and me alone, Ellie," she said, "you shouldn't be. We can take care of ourselves. And it'll give us an excuse to get out of town to come visit you."

I laughed lightly, moving to the fridge to take out the salad bowl, then put it on the table. "I'm glad to hear I don't have to worry about you guys," I said.

What I didn't say was how it was really me, not them, who I wasn't sure about. Newfoundland, after all, was a gray area. And though I wasn't one of the dead enclosed within it, I still felt as if I couldn't move beyond that wall of fog and gray skies my friends had described to me, either.

Dad came into the room just then, so Mom and I put away our conversation. "Dinner's ready," I said, and then she and Dad sat at the table to let me serve them.

The meal was good, and when we finished, I made them both go do whatever else they wanted, insisting that I'd clear the dishes. Once the dishes were in the dishwasher and it hummed with hot water, I went into the living room and found myself—even to my own surprise—telling them that I had plans to meet Couri Long at the diner in Cortland, where her sister and I used to go with Rose and Becca on weekends after seeing a late movie at the mall.

"I did what Dr. Arroyo suggested last time we saw her," I said as they looked at me, clearly surprised to hear this. "You know, about building bridges back to others around me. I talked with her on the phone the other night. I think it was good for both of us to be able to talk about Adrienne."

Mom's mouth opened, and I could tell she wanted to question me. But I knew she wouldn't. As someone who went out of her way to help others all the time, I knew she'd understand what I'd wanted to do.

Dad just said, "That sounds like a good start, Ellie." Then

he got up and came over to give me a kiss on the top of my head.

"Well," Mom said, tilting her head to one side, seeming to struggle a little about it. She could sense the lie, I knew, and I started to worry.

"I won't be out late," I said, trying to keep one step ahead of her, to make things seem normal.

"Okay," she said finally. "I know you're exhausted, that's all. Just be careful driving."

And that was it.

"I'll be careful," I said. "I promise."

"Love you, Ellie," Mom said from where she sat on the couch, still looking a bit skeptical.

And before I left, I leaned down to give her a quick hug and a kiss goodbye.

22

The Last Will and Testament of Ellie Frame, cont.

The sun had long slipped below the horizon by the time I left the house, draping everything in a cloak of shadows. Many of the streetlights at busier intersections had been replaced by then, but even before the outbreak, the rural roads most of us lived on were tunnels of darkness at nightfall, and headlights failed to illuminate much of the road unless you switched on the high beams. I didn't have far to go, though. Within ten minutes, I was turning into the gravel drive that led up to the parking area that surrounded the lighthouse.

The gravel crunched beneath my car's wheels, and right then it was the most hurtful sound in the world to me. Because it was *familiar,* because it was the sound I always heard when Noah and I went to the lighthouse to be alone.

When the lighthouse came into view, I looked up at the stony tower and shivered as silence rushed into the car like water filling the empty spaces of a sinking ship. The lantern was lit, just as I'd seen it flicker to life momentarily several hours before. He was up there, I thought. He had to be. Only Noah would light that lantern room to call me to him.

I didn't bother driving all the way up to the parking lot itself. Maybe because I wanted to leave my car there as an obstacle to anyone else who saw the lighthouse beaming from afar and decided to investigate. My mind whirred with the high winds of tornadoes, and my feelings had all been sucked up and out of my body. I was operating without knowing why I did anything at that point.

After I got out of the car, I stood looking at the lighthouse on the hill, remembering the day of the outbreak and being inside the lantern room—being stupid, being immature, hiding from Noah after we'd fought about a girl he innocently paid attention to. A girl he'd been friends with since they were little. A girl whose dad had died in a hunting accident years ago. A girl without real friends, who needed someone besides her mother to care about her. And as I stood looking up at those lantern-room windows, my self-hatred rose once again to the levels it had reached in the early days after the outbreak. There were so many things I could call myself right then. Horrible things.

I'd been lucky, everyone had told me afterward, not to have been at school that day. Not to have been there, crouched in the hallways, with my boyfriend and best friends alongside me. I didn't feel lucky, though. Not even close. I just felt like I'd unknowingly cheated death. And because they'd all died without me, surviving didn't feel very much like good fortune so much as a curse.

I took my steps up the gravel driveway slowly but steadily, willing myself to put one foot down and then the other. And eventually, after what seemed like an eternity—the way running stretches out in your dreams and nightmares—I made it to the tower, where the lantern light made an amber-colored flicker in the window above me, a rectangle of warmth set against the gray stone of the lighthouse and the black sky behind it. Goose bumps rose on my arms, but I rubbed them away, reminding myself that I was finally going to see Noah. To really see him.

The lighthouse door's hinges squealed as they always had, followed by the familiar rattle of the old bolt settling into the slot of the door frame as I closed it behind me. Then came the familiar scent of dust and the glint of a spider's web growing in a nearby corner. Then the soft echoes of my steps as I climbed the staircase to the lantern room, the place I'd been hiding when the tornadoes descended on Newfoundland. The room where I'd watched three twisters race back and forth across the downtown area, mowing down or ripping up building after building, as well as the lives that breathed within them.

At the doorway to the lantern room, I stopped and put my hand to my chest, felt my heart beating hard inside my rib cage, so hard, it seemed like it might explode. I took a deep breath, then another. *This is what you wanted,* I told myself. *Don't mess it up now that he's here, waiting for you.*

I took two more steps up after that, and passed through the stone archway into the lantern room.

"Hi, Ellie."

These were the first words I heard, but I didn't recognize

the voice that spoke them. I looked around the room, at the stone walls flickering with shadows thrown by the lantern fire, and at first, I couldn't see anyone there with me.

A moment later, though, a figure stepped out from behind the lantern pillar. A figure who still wore an old blue-flowered gray dress, belted at the waist, which she'd worn the last time I saw her. A figure with uneven hair, which might have looked cool on some girls, but looked only sad on Ingrid Mueller, since we all knew she cut her own hair. She grinned, her teeth flickering in the lamplight, and said, "Aren't you going to say hi back? I know that was something that always annoyed the hell out of you when I didn't say hi to you at school. At least that's what Noah told me."

"Ingrid," I said, unsure of what else I could or even should say.

"Not who you were expecting," Ingrid said, smirking just a little. "I know. But Noah was busy today, so I decided to come see you instead."

"I don't understand," I said, shaking my head, feeling like I might pass out from the surprise.

"You wouldn't," Ingrid said, laughing, short and sharp, with a gleeful sound I'd never heard her make before, not while she was living. "You were always pretty dumb, Ellie. Or maybe you were just good at pretending to be pretty dumb whenever it suited you."

"Listen," I said, although I wasn't sure what I had to say. She'd tricked me into coming here. Things I'd been thinking about all day, things that had been mysteries to me hours ago, all came into a sudden, crisp clarity for me. What I'd sensed

Mrs. Mueller lying about, but couldn't put my finger on at the time, was that she'd seen her daughter's ghost, despite telling me otherwise; that she knew where to find her, had possibly even been hiding her somewhere in that rambling shack they lived in. She probably also knew where Noah was, even though she told me she didn't.

"Listen," I said again, still unsure where I was going to take this conversation.

"No, *you* listen, Ellie," Ingrid said, stepping toward me with a raised finger. "It's my time to talk. It's *my* time to tell you all of the things I always wanted to say to you back when I was alive, back when you didn't give me the time of day, except *after* you started dating Noah."

"I'm listening," I said, my voice even. I wanted to back up a few steps, to spin around and run down the stairwell. But I kept still, remembering how quickly Becca had appeared to me in her room, seemingly out of thin air. Remembering how Timothy Barlow would appear on the back deck of his house and how he would disappear just as suddenly. I wouldn't be able to run from Ingrid. She'd be able to appear wherever I ran to next. So I needed to buy as much time as I could, hoping I might be able to either reason with her or figure out some other plan.

"Good," Ingrid said. "I'm glad that I have your attention. Maybe after I'm done here, I'll go back to your house and type up an article and post it on the school news site, a sad yet inspiring eulogy for Ingrid Mueller."

I felt my eyes narrowing as I tried to understand what she was saying. "What are you talking about?" I asked.

"What I'm talking about," Ingrid said, "is what I plan to

do after I'm *you*. I'm talking about how I'll use your body as my own."

Ingrid folded her thin arms under her chest, and her face changed from anger back to that smirk of self-satisfaction she'd flashed a few minutes before, and it was then that I realized why Noah had not come to see me all this time. Why he wouldn't come even when I tried to call him to me. I remembered what Becca and Rose had said about Ingrid, how she seemed different in death from how she had been in life. And I remembered Adrienne talking about the animals she and Ingrid had possessed, how much delight they took in it. Noah, I realized now, had simply wanted to keep them away from me.

"Ingrid," I said calmly, "you don't want to do that."

"Don't tell me what I want and don't want," Ingrid said, her gray eyes flashing in the amber light of the lantern.

"I mean, you don't need me," I said. "The gray area here, it's going to lift one day soon. It's just a matter of time. Rose is certain of it."

Ingrid laughed and rolled her eyes. "Rose Sano," she said, almost hissing Rose's last name. "The girl who's been too scared to leave her house since she died."

"With good reason, obviously," I said, losing a bit of patience. Ingrid could say whatever she wanted about me, but not one of my friends.

"She's just afraid," Ingrid said. "Afraid of learning how to live on this side of things."

"She doesn't need to live on that side of things," I said. "She's waiting until she can leave on her own."

Ingrid shook her head like I was the most ignorant person

in the world. It was strange to feel so judged by her, a girl almost everyone in Newfoundland had looked at with the same sort of pity she was now applying to me. "Rose better hope she's right," Ingrid said. "Me, though? I'd rather stick to the things I've figured out since dying."

"There are other ways," I said, trying to get her to be reasonable. "If you'd let me, I think I can help you. There's something I've figured out how to do, too—"

Ingrid scoffed before I could finish what I wanted to say. "What do you know about anything?" she said. "You're not on this side of things. You may have talked to a few of us, Ellie Frame, but that doesn't make you an expert on being dead."

"No," I said, shaking my head sadly, realizing she wasn't going to see reason. "It doesn't." And she was right. Nothing I'd gleaned from my discussions with the dead could amount to anything my friends had experienced. Nothing.

Ingrid looked satisfied, however, now that I'd agreed that my knowledge of things fell short. And she must have felt like she'd won that battle, because soon she unfolded her arms from her chest and took on a less aggressive stance, letting her shoulders fall a little, releasing her hands from the fists she'd held them in.

"Instead of you telling me what you think you know," she said now, "let me tell you what I know. What I know to be true. What I knew to be true even before I died that day."

"Okay," I said. "Tell me." I wanted to hear what she had to say, actually. I'd wanted to hear what she had to say for the past few months, really. She just wouldn't let me become friends with her.

"You messed up," Ingrid said, sounding like a parent trying to scold me.

"I know," I said, nodding, even though no reason for my mess-up had been given.

"Do you?" Ingrid said. "Do you really know? I don't think so. I mean, the day we all died, you were safe somewhere else. Why? Because you'd had a fight with Noah. A fight with Noah about *me,* of all people, Ellie. I was surprised to find out later that you apparently saw me as some kind of competition."

She smiled then, clearly satisfied that she'd been able to tell me all of that.

"It's true," I told her. "I saw you as competition. I didn't want to. I didn't mean to. I just . . . I just didn't understand Noah's relationship with you."

"I still don't think you understand," Ingrid said, taking a few steps across the room to come closer to me, her anger flaring again.

"What . . . ," I said. "What do you mean?"

"You weren't there for him, Ellie," she said. "I was. I was always there for him. To be an ear when he needed someone to listen to his problems. To tell him how well he played after his soccer matches. I was at them, too. I know you never saw me. I tried to stay out of your way. Sometimes it's better to let someone like Noah realize the person who really cares about him was always there, right in front of him, after he came to his senses about the person who never really cared about him that deeply."

"Ingrid," I said, almost in a whisper. My hands were shaking, and my eyes pricked with hot tears. She was saying aloud

265

everything I'd feared was the truth for the past month, after the outbreak, and maybe even before the outbreak, when I'd pushed Noah to talk about his relationship to Ingrid. It made me uncomfortable, seeing him take care of someone else in a way that I wanted to be taken care of, even if I didn't need to be taken care of the way Ingrid did.

I was stupid, though. I wasn't able to see through my own insecurities.

"What?" Ingrid said. "Nothing to say now that the truth has all been laid out in front of you?"

"That's not the only truth," I said, shaking my head, refusing to let her make her version the only part of the story. It wasn't just her story, after all. It was mine, too. It was all of ours.

"What else, then," Ingrid said, "would explain why Noah hasn't come to you since he died?" She made a horrid face, a shaming face, raising her brows and grinning, as if she were a cat and I a mouse pinned in a corner.

"He loved me, too," I said. "I know that. If he didn't, we wouldn't have argued in the first place. If he hadn't cared about me, he would have ignored me when I complained about not understanding his relationship to you. He didn't, though."

"You can tell yourself whatever you need to hear, Ellie," Ingrid said, taking yet another few steps across the room toward me. "But I know the truth. You pushed at him. The last thing you did before he died was start a stupid argument. And what did he do while we were all kneeling in the school hallway? He stayed with *me*. He comforted *me*. He protected *me*, and he's done as much since it all ended. He hasn't come to you, even though you've been looking for him. Oh, you seem surprised to hear I know about that. Well, I know because Noah himself told me."

I could barely breathe at that point, listening to the heat of her words as she hurled them at me. Every single thing I worried about, every insecure thought, confirmed. And I stood there, feeling my legs start to weaken, the room beginning to spin around me. *Run,* I told myself, even though I knew I might only make it to the bottom of the steps, and by then Ingrid would most likely be waiting for me on the other side of the door, waiting to tell me more horrible things.

I buckled in the end, and fell to my knees, wishing I hadn't been so stupid to come here, wishing I hadn't convinced myself that Noah was the one trying to reach out to me, when it was clear all this time that he'd been avoiding me.

Noah, I thought as I knelt on that old stone floor and began to cry. *It was supposed to be you. Where are you? Where are you?*

"I'm here, Ellie," he said, and I looked up to find him standing on the other side of the room, under the arch of the entrance I'd come through. I gasped for breath, as if I were just then breaking the surface of water, taking in air.

"Noah," I said, "you finally heard me."

He didn't reply to me at first, but instead looked at Ingrid and said, "You need to stop this. You need to stop this right now, Ingrid."

Ingrid crossed the room toward Noah, leaving me crumpled on the floor, defeated by everything she'd said. Yet as she moved closer to him, I began to feel stronger. Strong enough to lift myself back to my feet. Strong enough to stay quiet as Noah and Ingrid began to talk.

"Noah," she said, just that, as if his name alone were a plea.

Noah looked past Ingrid's shoulder to meet my eyes, and I mouthed the words *thank you,* not wanting to attract her attention again.

Ingrid must have noticed him staring past her, though, because her hands, which had been dangling helplessly at her sides while she was facing Noah, clenched into fists once again. "Why?" she said. "Why her? What is it about her, Noah? Why can't you see that the person who loves you more than anyone, the person who *knows* you better than anyone, is standing right here in front of you?"

"Ingrid," Noah said, gently holding his hands out, as if offering them to her to hold. "We've been through all of this already. You know I love Ellie. I love you, too. But things are different, now more than ever. You and me? We're going to continue being together. It's Ellie I have to say goodbye to now. You know that. Please don't make this any harder."

Hearing Noah say all of that, I felt tears slip from my eyes, and I wiped them away as quickly as they came. They were hot against my skin, but a smile kept weakly breaking through the tensed muscles of my face. He'd said the exact thing I'd been needing to hear him say, this last month.

Ingrid, though, clearly didn't want to hear any of this. She raised her fists into the air and punched down at Noah's outstretched hands, pushing him away at first, before she finally turned and seemed to almost deflate a little as she walked toward the window on the opposite side of the lantern room. In profile, she looked hunched over, as if in a split second she'd aged into an elderly woman.

"You keep saying that, Noah," Ingrid said. "But I don't understand how things can be easier. Not after everything we've been through. Not after everything you've done for me. I remember the first time you came over to my house with your mom right after my dad died. Your mom had made a roast chicken with all of these vegetables. I can still see them, still smell that meal. My mom hadn't cooked in days. She and my dad had never been what anyone would call a close couple, but after he was killed, she just shut down. Stopped everything. She wasn't even taking care of herself like a normal person. Your mom could tell because she took my mom's hand and led her back to the bathroom, drew a hot bath for her. You told me not to worry. That everything was going to be okay. You asked me where everything was, and you set the table and served up the food on your own, while I stood there watching. You've always taken care of me, Noah. You've always been the person who loved me more than anyone."

"Ingrid," Noah said. "I'm still here, aren't I? I still care about you. I'm still your friend. None of that has changed."

"I want to keep all of those memories," Ingrid said, looking down at her feet, seeming distraught, as if the memories she kept talking about were spread out around her and might be swept away at any moment. "They're all I have of you. They're all I had of you after you chose Ellie. Memories of how kind you are to me. They bring me warmth even now, in this god-forsaken place we're stuck in. Don't take them from me. Don't tell me not to remember."

"Ingrid," Noah said softly. He looked at me then, sadly, as if he was about to give up reasoning with her.

That's when I said, "You don't have to give up anything, Ingrid. You don't have to stop remembering. If you'll listen to me, just for a minute, I can explain."

Ingrid slowly turned her head toward me, and although she was wearing a faded scowl on her face, she gave me a quick and solitary nod to go on.

So I told her. I told her what I'd discovered by accident. The thing that let me help Becca and Adrienne leave this world, the way I knew Ingrid must want to leave as well. "It's all too much," I told Ingrid, "from what the others have said. The grief of your families and friends holding you here. I don't know what it really is, the gray area they've all mentioned. I only know I've been able to get them past it."

Ingrid looked skeptical, frowning a little as I went on. But eventually, she asked, "How? How do you do it?"

And I told her about the last wills and testaments, the ones the others had let me witness and record for them. I told her about how my friends had lifted up right in front of me and were able to leave this place the way they'd wanted to from the beginning.

"If you do it, Ingrid," Noah said, "I'll be right behind you. I'll do it, too."

Ingrid sighed, looked away, first down at the stone floor, then out the lighthouse window, as if she wasn't sure she really wanted to give up everything she knew, even if she did feel some vague compulsion to depart this world.

Eventually, though, she turned back to look first at Noah, then at me. "How does it work?" she asked. "I mean, if I were to do it, that is. How does it work? What would I have to do?"

"Tell me a story," I said. "Or tell Noah. Tell whoever you want to hear something real from your life. Something meaningful, something you wish someone else knew. Something you want to live on after you've left."

"That's easy enough," Ingrid said, casting her eyes down at the floor again briefly. When she looked up, she pushed a few strands of hair away from her brow and sighed, then said, "If you'll do it, too, Noah, I guess it's okay. Are you ready?"

I took my phone out, switched the camera on, then held it up, listening to her talk until eventually I saw her appear on my screen.

⌒

"Remember that time you took me to dinner at Giancola's, Noah? It was where everyone going to homecoming that year was eating beforehand. You knew my mom would never be able to buy a dress for me, and it's not like I had a date anyhow. So you just said, 'Homecomings and proms are stupid,' trying to make me feel better about not going. But you never asked anyone to go with you, either. You said, 'Hey, Ingrid, why don't we just go to Giancola's anyway?' And when I said I didn't have anything nice to wear, you said, '*Anything* you wear is nice. Don't let that stop you.' So I found a dress in my mom's closet, this old dress from the nineties that I'd never seen her wear. It was crushed green velvet, with these straps crisscrossing the open back. I'm taller than my mom, so it wasn't a perfect fit, but it was the best thing I'd ever seen in person, so I wore it. When my mom saw me come into the living room wearing it, she gasped and actually smiled—you know how she hardly ever smiles—and she said, 'Ingrid, *baby*!' in this way that made me feel like, for the first time since my dad was killed, she'd finally seen me, recognized me, and loved what she saw. That was probably the best day of my life. That moment when putting on a dress was like a magic spell that could make your mother see you and love you in a way that she hadn't been able to do before. Or like a spell that could make the boy you wanted to notice you fall for you in the way you wanted."

"Ingrid . . . ," Noah began.

I shook my head at him, though, and he stopped, understanding.

And Ingrid kept telling her story.

"The meal at Giancola's was decadent, compared to what Mom and I usually ate. You said you'd been saving up money, and to order whatever I liked. I didn't know what half the stuff on the menu was, so I just went with the spaghetti and meatballs to stay safe. I remember you laughed and said, 'Really? You don't want to try something different?' So I asked you to choose for me, and you ordered that dish of little pastas shaped like purses, and inside were four different kinds of cheese and pieces of pear. I'd never thought of fruit being inside of pasta, but it was the second-best thing I'd ever eaten in my life. The first was that roast chicken and vegetables your mother brought over after my dad died. Nothing will ever beat that one.

"That night, I thought I'd walked through a portal into a magical world where suddenly I'd become the person I'd always wanted to be. The person you'd want to be with. But no. It was a short-lived fantasy. Those books and movies where stuff like that happens should probably be banned, because they only set people up for disappointment. Because the magic was only for that one night, and even then, when you took me home, there was no good-night kiss on my front porch, even though I was hoping there would be. I watched you go into your house afterward, and a few minutes later, I saw your silhouette through the window shade as you took off your shirt, and then a moment later the light went off again. I realized then that nothing from that evening was going to keep you up all night, thinking about me. Thinking about us, the possibility of us."

Ingrid turned away from the lantern-room window to look at Noah with a sad smile. "I don't blame you. You were just trying to be good to me. In the end, I don't blame anyone for anything, really. For how alone I've felt. For any of my sadness. I just wish—"

Ingrid made a funny face then, and she put her hands on her arms, patting and squeezing them a little, almost as if she was checking to see if they were still there. If *she* was still there. "Something's happening," she said, a little breathless, smiling, but unsure. "Noah? Is it happening to you? Do you feel it, too?"

And then, a moment later, before Noah could say anything, Ingrid Mueller's soul drifted up into view.

I let the video on my camera continue to run, even after Ingrid disappeared, leaving behind only dust motes spiraling through a shaft of amber lantern light where she'd been standing. I was still crying, had never really stopped, but this time the tears weren't coming for the same reason they did when I heard Noah say he loved me. These tears were for Ingrid Mueller. Not for that girl who'd seemed to hate me, the one who'd confirmed all of the fears I'd had since Noah had died. These tears were for the girl who'd just shown me how sad and fragile and beautiful she'd been in life, even though only a handful of people had ever seen her for who she was, for who she could have been, if given the chance. She'd been closed up all her life, like a door that's always been locked, no one ever coming or going from it, so that even as people walk by, they forget that it's there to be opened.

I was crying for her. I was crying for that girl.

"Is that how you've been doing it, Ellie?" Noah asked in a hushed tone, and I looked away from my phone to face him where he stood beneath the arch of the entrance. I nodded, then turned the recorder off.

Then it was just the two of us in there, looking across the expanse of smooth gray stones we used to sit curled up on, my head on his shoulder, watching through the lighthouse windows as the stars blinked to life in the night sky over Newfoundland.

"How . . . ," he said, pausing for a moment. "How does it work?"

I shook my head, bit my bottom lip for a second, then said, "I don't know for sure. But it has something to do with telling stories. With telling your truth to someone who can bear witness. Someone who can hear it. Someone who can see you."

He crossed the room, and we sat on the floor, like old times. He put his arm around my back, his head nestling in the crook between my neck and shoulder. I put my arms around him then, too, and squeezed as tight as I could, breathing against him.

"You've been listening to others tell their stories for a while," he said. "Why don't you tell me something about yourself?"

I squeezed him tighter for a second, then pulled back a little to put my hand in his hair, just to feel it run through my fingers once more, and nodded.

I told him about how it had all started, just days after the outbreak had torn apart our town, the west wing of the school destroyed when the gas tanker exploded, the tornadoes leveling neighborhoods and cutting down woods until they were no more than fields of broken sticks. I told him how I'd seen the ghost of my neighbor Timothy Barlow, playing his saxophone on the back deck, even though he'd been killed in the school collapse. I told him how I'd initially tried to record Timothy so I could prove I wasn't insane, if I had to, to someone like my mom and dad or to Dr. Arroyo. Or, even, to myself. But when Timothy's soul drifted up, flying free, I realized something else was happening. That I'd accidentally stumbled upon a way for the souls trapped in the gray area to escape and go to wherever it is they felt compelled to go to.

When I was done telling him about how I'd done that for Timothy and Becca and Adrienne, when I was done telling him about how Rose and her family had their own plans and were following Japanese traditions, Noah said, "So things haven't changed all that much, really."

And I looked up into his face, ran the fingertips of one hand across his cheek, and said, "What do you mean?"

"You're still watching us," he said. "You're still listening to us, even though you didn't have to be there with us."

An involuntary sob rose in my throat when I heard those words, but Noah pulled me against him, said, "I know what you're thinking about. And I want you to know, I'm glad. I'm glad that you weren't there. I'm so happy we had that argument, and that I was stupid and blew off your worries. I'm so happy you were strong enough and mad enough to leave and not come back to school that day. The only thing I'm really sorry about is that I hurt you like that when I didn't mean to."

I still cried through everything he said to me right then, but I kept holding on to him, as tight as possible, wishing I could make him live again.

And when he was done saying what he had to say, I thanked him for it, pulled away to wipe the tears from my face, and began to apologize in the same way, telling him how awful I felt and how stupid I was, and how much I loved him, and how, on some days, it was hard to even see my own face in a mirror, to lean in close and see my own breath appear on its surface. I told him how I wished I'd been there with them. I told him how I wished he would have come to me sooner than this, and he explained that he hadn't because he'd wanted me to be able to move on, not to be caught up in what had happened, not to live in a past I couldn't fix.

After a while, I looked down at our laps, where Noah held my hands in his, softly running his thumbs over my knuckles. When I looked up again, he said, "Would you do it for me, too? What you've done for the others?"

I felt my face tighten, my jaw clenching so hard, my skin pulled against my bones and started to hurt. Fresh tears came, but I managed to let only one fall before I wiped it away. I bit my bottom lip, sighing, then nodded before I said, "If that's what you want. But I don't want you to go away. Not now. Not after I've finally found you."

"I found *you*," he said, giving me a slight grin.

"Thank you for that," I said, leaning my forehead against his for a moment before looking up to kiss him.

"My pleasure," he said, after we broke away from each other.

For a while after that, we rocked a little, back and forth, hugging, as I said, "Thank you, thank you," over and over, into the crook of his neck and shoulder, trying not to cry any longer. "I love you," we both said, over and over, until we'd said it so many times, we both understood and believed what the other one said was the truth.

And when we were quiet again, my chin still hanging over his shoulder, I whispered, "Okay, then. Let's hear it. Tell me your story."

23

The Last Will and Testament of Noah Cady

One of my first memories is being a little kid, maybe three years old—four at most—and lying on my back on the floor in our living room, looking up at the ceiling. It has this decorative imprint in the plaster that looks like swirls and waves cresting. There are sparkles in it, too, which made it even more interesting to me, because depending on the time of day and on whether I tilted my head a little to the left or to the right, different sparkles would appear, flashing like stars above me. I think it might have been the first time that I had an actual, conscious memory. Like, you know, *really* conscious. No longer a baby with nothing but a split-second memory.

It's one of the few memories I have from being that little, and it always makes me happy to recall it, because I can inhabit the memory so vividly that I can actually feel the texture and thickness of the carpet beneath me, and I can smell the cookies my mom's baking, and I can hear my dad tapping at his laptop behind me, where he's sitting in a recliner. Whenever I've been sad or mad about something, I've called up that memory, so I can live inside it again, and it always makes me smile.

The first time I recalled this memory, I was feeling pretty low. I was thirteen and I cost the soccer team a trip to the finals because of a crap shot I took, trying to show off. It didn't even come close to the goal because the kick went so wild. I had no control. After that, the other team got the ball and basically kept it from us until the clock ran out.

Afterward, I spent the next few days feeling like an idiot because I hadn't thought about what I was doing. I'd just acted impulsively, which you have to do sometimes in sports, sure, but in my case if I hadn't been so eager to be a hero, we might have actually got a goal in and tied things up. But I didn't think, and as far as I was concerned, not going to the finals was entirely my fault. And even though the coaches told me not to feel that way, I did.

That is, until about the third or fourth day of telling myself how stupid and selfish I was. I was lying on the couch in the living room, watching a baseball game on the TV. I wasn't paying attention to the game, though. Instead, I was looking up at the ceiling, not really thinking about anything other than what a crappy teammate I'd been, replaying that lousy shot over and over. Then suddenly a shaft of sunlight came in through the front window at just the right angle, and a section of those sparkles in the ceiling plaster glinted. And suddenly I was transported back to that moment when I was three or four, lying on the carpet, smelling cookies, hearing my dad tapping on his laptop behind me.

Before I knew it, I was smiling. And when I realized how hard I was smiling, I thought, *Remember this. Remember to remember this moment.*

I got down off the couch and onto the floor after that, and let myself sink into the memory even further. And when I got up a little while later, I didn't feel bad about losing the game. Not even for a minute.

Since then I've used the same trick any number of times. When I'm down, when I'm angry, when I don't know what to do about some problem and my thoughts just keep running around inside my head like some cat and mouse chasing each other. When I didn't know what to do about you being mad about my friendship with Ingrid, which I admit I didn't handle very well, but only because I didn't know how to handle it at all. And when I didn't know what to do during the outbreak, while we were kneeling in the hallway, and the ceiling tore back and all I could see was something large and dark swirling above me, but definitely not stars. And then later, too, when I woke up like this. Dead, but not dead. Somehow living, but somehow not alive, either.

But that trick didn't do me much good after a certain point. Maybe I'd used it too often, or maybe I used it too much in too short a space of time after I died. Because I've felt more alone and more afraid every day, for myself but also for you, not wanting you to stop living. I've hated to see how alone you've been, despite having your parents to lean on. It's gotten so that even that memory trick isn't enough to make me feel better about anything.

Instead, I've started to think of something else to make me feel better. And that's you. You and me. The two of us, together. I've started to think back to the first time we came here to the lighthouse last October, and how you told me the story your mom told you when you were a little girl. The one about the guy Ephraim Key, who founded Newfoundland, and how he built this lighthouse for the woman he married, because she was from a shipping family in New England and wasn't used to living so far away from the ocean. So he built this lighthouse for her, in the hopes that seeing something that reminded her of where she'd come from would make it easier for her to feel at home in this place.

I've started to think of that night when you told me that story while I held you in my arms. You'd lit the lantern, even though I worried it would attract someone's attention and we'd get caught. "We aren't doing anything wrong," you said, and we weren't. And no one ever did come to see who was up in the lighthouse, even if they noticed that the lantern had been lit.

That's the memory that's gotten me through life after dying. And that's the memory I want you to think of when you think of me. After I finish this story and we look at each other for the last time, at least for a long time. Please don't ever forget that night, that story, every detail of it, because if you can recall it the way I can, Ellie, it should make you happy. And as long as you're remembering it, we can be together whenever you want to. If you keep it alive inside you.

If you remember to remember.

I love you, Ellie. I wish things hadn't happened the way they did. But they did. Don't blame yourself for anything any longer. Don't ever think that you should have been there with me, or with any of us. I want you to live, and I want you to live happily.

I love you, Ellie. So much. Please don't cry. Now you know this isn't really the end.

It's a new beginning.

24

The Last Will and Testament of Ellie Frame

A new beginning.

After he was gone—when the last moment came and Noah began to shimmer as his soul drifted up into view, then flew away in the next instant—it didn't feel much like a new beginning. But I'd nodded and promised when he asked me to think of it that way. For him. So that he could feel at peace about leaving. And despite the weight of longing for him pressing down on me even harder, I promised that I'd think of it that way for myself. I couldn't hold up that much grief forever without crumbling completely. I knew that much, even then.

For a while after, I sat under the lighthouse window with my back against the wall, listening to my own breath go in and out of my body. I sat there and thought about him, thought about them all. I thought about Becca. About Rose. About Adrienne. I thought about Timothy Barlow and poor Ingrid

Mueller. Along with all of the others whose lives were taken away the day of the outbreak. I wanted to gather them all up somehow, not just to carry inside me—though I will do that, like Noah said to do—but to carry them inside something more permanent. Something that will serve me well after years have gone by, like I know they eventually will, and when my memory begins to fail me. I didn't want to misremember any of them at some point, the way my mom and dad will sometimes argue about someone they knew back when they were in high school, disagreeing on how something happened, or who was there. I didn't want my mind to change details in the face of what seems to be the inevitable amnesia that happens over time to all of us. I didn't want to make up anything about them. I just wanted to preserve them in their clearest light, however possible.

I looked down at my phone and realized that I at least had that. That I at least had their stories. I had their voices, their last frowns and smiles. I had their last words.

After a while, I pulled myself up, dusted my pants off, and decided to leave the lantern room. I opened the old door on its squealing hinges, and outside I found a dark expanse of sky, filled with stars. I imagined Noah's ceiling from his childhood, the glitter imprinted in the plaster design, and I kissed my hand and lifted it up for him.

⌒

At home, I found Mom and Dad curled up together on the couch. Mom was asleep against Dad's side, and he lifted a finger to his lips, grinning. I smiled back and nodded, then slipped upstairs to my room, not wanting to wake Mom, not wanting to have to talk to her about my made-up meeting with Couri. There would be time enough for that in the morning over breakfast, when I knew she'd have at least ten questions about it.

I spent the next hour or so in bed, staring up at my ceiling, which didn't have any decorative plaster whirls or sparkles the way the ceilings in Noah's house did. It was plain and flat and white, and when I looked at it, I wished there was something more to it that could distract me. To distract me from the sounds of my own existence. My breath as I sighed, suddenly there for a moment, audible. The hard beats of my heart as they pressed against my chest.

But in the end, maybe not having anything to distract me made me notice something else. Something that I was immediately grateful for. That hole at the center of my body, where for weeks on end I'd only heard the sound of emptiness—that gone away place—didn't feel so big, so deep or wide, as it once did. It had closed up a little. And for the first time in a long time, I fell asleep without crying into my pillow. I was able to sleep through the night, too, until the next morning, when I woke and began to make good on my promise to Noah.

⁓

The first thing I did was to tell my parents something they'd been hoping to hear from me for a while now. They'd been skirting the issue, not wanting to push me, just wanting me to want things for myself again. So they were happy and relieved when I told them that I needed to start getting things together if I was going to move into a dorm room in Pittsburgh in just a few weeks. It was probably the only way to get Mom to cut down on her volunteer hours, which is what she said she'd do immediately, so she could divert the time to help me get ready.

In the later weeks, I wrote to Margery Addison in Salamanca, New York, to tell her that I was in fact the Ellie Frame she'd been looking for, and to thank her for going so far out of her way to return the photos I'd taken of my friends. I told her their names, and I told her something I treasured about each one of them, and I told her that they were all gone now. I told her having their photos back, particularly this set, where I'd tried to capture each of them in a moment of happiness without their realizing I was taking their picture, meant more to me now because I'd never see them again, except in my memory. I told her she'd given me something beyond value in her act of kindness.

Then I printed that letter out and took it to the post office in Cortland, since the one in Newfoundland was still being rebuilt, and sent it out before driving back to Newfoundland to pay a visit to the Sano farm.

I found Mr. and Mrs. Sano drinking glasses of iced tea on their front porch when I pulled into their drive. Mrs. Sano gave me a wave as I got out of my car, and as I came up the steps to join them on the porch, Mr. Sano said, "We've been wondering if we might see you sometime soon, Ellie."

"Why's that?" I asked.

And Mrs. Sano said, "Because Rose is gone now, sweetie.

She's safe now. She was able to leave. And she wanted us to make sure you knew that."

I sniffed and forced the tears that sprang to my eyes to stay there, put my hands on my cheeks while I looked up at the porch ceiling for a moment, then looked back down and told them, "That's a relief. Thank you. I didn't know how I might even begin to ask you about her."

"We know, Ellie," Mr. Sano said, smiling sadly. "Rose told us you'd been over to see her."

They invited me to stay, and gave me tea and told me of how Rose was certain that the gray area all of the dead had spoken of was starting to fade. "Like mist or fog," Mrs. Sano said, quoting Rose, "burning off the fields in the morning."

We talked about Rose for a while, remembering her, and as the sun reached its noontime peak above us, I said, "I'll leave you to your chores now." Because I knew from all the times I'd stayed overnight at the Sano house for the past ten years that noon was when Mr. Sano would begin to see to the various tasks he had to do each day on their farm.

They kept me from leaving for only a moment, while Mrs. Sano went inside the house and returned with a bottle of the rose-scented perfume Rose's grandmother would send her each year from Japan for her birthday. "I can't," I told them, but they laughed and assured me that there were others. That Rose could never get through one bottle, it seemed, before her grandmother sent another.

Back in my car, I spritzed the perfume and inhaled, and saw Rose so clearly in my mind's eye that it felt as if she were sitting right there next to me, ready to pick up Becca and Adrienne so we could drive over to Niles to see a movie or go to Cortland to get coffee at the all-night diner.

I didn't go back to Becca's house, because I'd had my chance to say goodbye to her. But I did email her mother the video of her last will and testament, which she'd asked me to show her parents. And I did text Couri to tell her that, even though I'd be leaving to start college in a few weeks, she should feel free to call or text me if she ever needed to talk. About Adrienne or about anything at all. She texted back and said she hoped I meant it, because she would, and that hopefully in a few years I'd know Pittsburgh well, because she wanted to go to Carnegie Mellon after she graduated.

I drove out to Noah's house, too. His parents were still gone, though, still visiting family in Arizona, trying to grieve away from the place that would only remind them of their son on a daily basis. I just sat in their drive for a while, looking up at the front of the house before getting out to walk around to the back, where I stared up at the window that was Noah's bedroom. I made myself remember the first time he and I went to the lighthouse and the story I'd told him that night about why it had been built in the first place. The story my mom had told me about the way I'd know someone loved me, back when I was a little girl.

And when I got into my car afterward, he was right: I was smiling a little. Just like he said I'd be.

When I backed out to leave, I saw Mrs. Mueller across the road, sitting on her front porch, and I waved to her through my window. I waited for a moment afterward, and eventually her silhouette raised one hand into the air above her.

This is the hardest story I've ever had to tell. Not because I don't have anything to say, though. And not because I don't have anything of value to leave behind. It's the hardest story I've ever had to tell because *I'm* the one who had, at least at first, been left behind, and now I'm the one leaving everything else behind—my town, my family, the past seventeen years of my life—all so that I can move on and into a future where I'll start making the next part of my life. This is the hardest story I've ever had to tell because I've never had to do anything like that before, and I'd be lying if I didn't say that leaving everything I've ever known is a little bit scary.

But I can't stay here, either. I can't let what's gone away remain an empty space inside me. I need to fill it with new places, with new people, with new love, if possible, and with new life. And I'll do that. I'll do that even as I carry everything I can from my past—all of my lost loved ones—along with me into whatever future it is I'm moving into.

And someday, when my soul drifts up into view, I know they will all be there to greet me, and all of us will be together again.

Until then, I'll remember.

I'll remember to remember.

AUTHOR'S NOTE

I was ten years old in 1985 when an outbreak of over forty tornadoes swept across Ohio, Pennsylvania, New York, and Ontario, Canada, over a nine-hour period. Many of the tornadoes produced that day registered as F4, and one in particular registered as F5, on the Fujita scale. An F5 is a rare type of tornadic storm, the damage from which is characterized as "incredible" on the Fujita scale, and aptly referred to as "the finger of God" in the 1996 film *Twister*. In all, the May 31, 1985, tornadoes killed ninety people, injured more than a thousand, and resulted in over a billion dollars in damage to the communities they tore through. The outbreak is still considered by the National Weather Service to be one of the most significant tornado events of all time in the United States.

I grew up in Trumbull County, Ohio, where the largest and fiercest of the tornadoes appeared that day in the greater Youngstown area, stretching more than three hundred feet across and moving relentlessly at speeds of fifty miles per hour, staying on the ground for forty-seven miles. The towns within its reach were left looking as if a giant had trampled through, leveling a shopping plaza, collapsing the roof of a roller rink, which, only an hour later, would have been full of kids and teenagers, destroying all of the homes in many neighborhoods, picking up three thirty-foot-tall petroleum storage tanks that weighed 75,000 pounds each, crumpling them like paper cups and hurling them across the street. A steel-framed trucking plant was demolished and partially swept away. Cars were piled up along the roads, and some were left in fields where they'd been dropped. The National Weather Service described the area as looking like a "bombed-out battlefield."

My father was a supervisor at the Trumbull County engineer's office at the time, and in the days that followed the storms, my family barely saw him. He and his colleagues, along with the National Guard, were working constantly to clear the streets in the county. Once they were clear, though, he returned and took my mother and brothers and me on a guided tour of the devastation. I had never seen the world I lived in so disordered and ruined. One of my eeriest memories is passing through a town where the tornado had pulled the headstones and statuary right out of the earth in a cemetery and deposited them throughout a nearby neighborhood. I remember seeing the statue of an angel whose wings had been broken off when it landed on the sidewalk.

People in this area still talk about that tornado, about that day and the days that followed. Everyone has a story, either from their own experience or one that they've been told by older relatives or friends. It was an event that touched everyone in some way, and it remains a part of our shared history.

Memories of tragedies and disasters on this level can eventually fade, though, especially for those of us who were kids at the time. The outbreak of my childhood was something that I've always remembered, but recalled with less frequency over the three decades since it occurred. It wasn't until 2011, when another natural disaster struck—the tsunami that wiped out a large swath of the Pacific coast of Japan, where I'd once lived for two years teaching English—that I began to dwell again on the tornadoes of 1985.

Though I'd returned home in 2006, I still had people I loved in Japan five years later, including former students and colleagues who continued to live and teach there after I'd left. In the days and weeks after the tsunami hit, I had a difficult time reaching most of them. Frantic for information, I spent a lot of time on the Internet, trying to learn whatever I could, hoping that none of them had been affected, worrying as the death toll rose into the thousands that this might be an outsized hope, and grieving for strangers as images of that ravaged coastline began to appear.

For a long time, I kept track of the aftermath of the tsunami and the efforts taking place to reconstruct the lives of so many people who had lost everything. And over the months and years that followed, some of the most fascinating stories were reports of those ruined communities being haunted by those who died in the tsunami. People claimed to hear their dead loved ones communicating with them as disembodied voices. Others claimed to see their ghosts. Cases of possession by dead family members began to appear. In 2014, the writer Richard Lloyd Parry reported extensively on this phenomenon in the *London Review of Books,* and has recently published a book about it called *Ghosts of the Tsunami.*

These stories of the communities that suffered so much and lost so many at the hands of a natural disaster that they began to be haunted would not leave my mind. And the images of the ruined towns stirred my memories of the 1985 tornadoes in my own hometown, bringing similar images to the surface, similar stories of people here who had lost someone in that storm. It was this collision of memories that compelled me to write *The Gone Away Place.*

In this new world where we're experiencing more frequent extreme weather events due to a changing climate, and natural disasters continually threaten, it seems we should brace ourselves for more challenging times, not just as individuals but also as communities, both local and global. We will need one another to recover and to grieve all that we have lost and may still lose. It is my hope that this book might serve to make others experiencing tragedies of this kind feel less alone as they find their way forward in their own stories.

ACKNOWLEDGMENTS

Thank you to my agent, Barry Goldblatt, for all that he does to keep me telling stories, and to my editor, Melanie Nolan, for pushing me to go further and for keeping me honest. Thanks, too, to my mom and dad, for recounting their stories from the May 31, 1985, tornado outbreak and for finding old photos when I asked for them.